The Cruel Game

The Cruel Game

*THE INSIDE STORY
OF SNOOKER*

JEAN RAFFERTY

Photographs by Mary Rafferty

Elm Tree Books · London

With love for our mother and father,
Molly and Peter Rafferty

First published in Great Britain 1983
by Elm Tree Books/Hamish Hamilton Ltd
Garden House 57-59 Long Acre London WC2E 9JZ

Copyright © 1983 by Jean and Mary Rafferty

British Library Cataloguing in Publication Data

Rafferty, Jean
  The cruel game.
  1. Snooker
  I. Title
  794.7'35'0922   GV900.S6
  ISBN 0-241-10950-7
  ISBN 0-241-10951-5 Pbk

Filmset by Pioneer
Printed and bound in Great Britain by
R. J. Acford Ltd, Chichester

Contents

Acknowledgements

The author would personally like to thank Val Williams, Norman Cattanach, John Sandilands, E. G. Jones, and Jan Harkins.

We would both like to thank the snooker press, who have all been most generous, in particular Ted Corbett, Clive Everton and Janice Hale.

We would also like to thank the snooker sponsors who gave us their hospitality, in particular Embassy, Pontins holiday camps and Lang's Whisky. The chapter on the Lang's Supreme Scottish Masters refers only to its inaugural year, 1981. By 1982 it had become a fine tournament which hopefully will be part of the snooker calendar for a long time to come.

Finally we would like to thank all the players, managers and snooker people who gave us their co-operation and Rockney, Towerbell Records for permission to reproduce lyrics from 'Ain't No Pleasin' You'.

Whitewash

The last of the summer sunshine is hitting the Romiley Forum car park. Willie Thorne hobbles across it on crutches, both legs in plaster from a go-karting accident he had during the holidays. It's only mid-September, yet the 1981 snooker season is starting already. It gets earlier and earlier, barely time to fit in the holiday in Majorca before the new season is on you. The previous season has hardly ended when some new tournament begins, some new sponsor jumps in, eagerly brandishing thousands of pounds in prize money and anxious to secure a slice of the magically mushrooming spectacle that is modern snooker.

Ten years ago the pros would hardly have got their cues out of the cases by now. There were only four then — Ray Reardon, John Spencer, John Pulman and Rex Williams. Alex Higgins had still to play his first major professional tournament. That was in the spring of 1972, one of a series of round robin tournaments sponsored by Park Drive, the tobacco people. Apart from their events there was only the World Championship.

Now in 1981 the calendar is crammed with snooker events. For the first event of the season, the Jameson International, there are thirty-one players trying just to qualify, as well as another twenty-one in the main draw. There is prize money of £66,500 and a case of the sponsor's admirable product — Irish whiskey — on offer every day for the highest break. And the cream on top of the coffee is an astounding jackpot of £100,000 — set up by a series of judicious wagers on the part of the promoters — for the first player to achieve a maximum 147 break after the quarters. It's better than Spot the Ball. It's better than winning Wimbledon. It's snooker eighties style.

And the man most likely to take the title, hit the jackpot, is Steve Davis, who has compressed a career of Borg-like dominance into one single year, one dream year. From November 1980 till now he has won five major titles including the World Championship. Only in one, the Benson and Hedges Masters at Wembley, has he tasted defeat — at the unexpected hands of South African Perrie Mans in the first round. Even Joe Davis, up till now the greatest player in the history of snooker, never enjoyed a year like this, never tested himself in the cockfight atmosphere of the modern game with the TV cameras trained to record his every twitch, and single points worth more than just points, worth thousands of pounds.

One image is left of the 1980—81 season — Steve Davis holding up the winner's trophy, flashlights exploding all around him like champagne, gleaming silver cups flashing bright as fireworks under the television lights, Steve Davis winning and winning and winning. A year or so ago the other players thought of themselves as winners. They had nice houses and fancy cars. They no longer had to work down coal mines or in factories or selling insurance to earn a living — winners all. But now that Steve Davis has won everything they are all losers. The image of him holding up his trophy in triumph has been burned into the brain of every other snooker player in the country. It follows them, haunts them, torments them. Some it has almost destroyed.

Cliff Thorburn checks into his hotel in Stockport at midnight. He has driven up from Surrey in the pale blue Daimler Sovereign that is the trophy of his own wins. The 1980 World Champion is worried. He knows if his opponent is playing well and he plays the way he's been doing recently the chances of his winning are pretty slim. He tries to relax, has some coffee with a few friends. A bottle of the sponsor's product is opened up but Cliff has only one drink before going to bed.

His preliminary match the following day against Graham Miles is watched by barely a hundred people in the Romiley Forum, a modern civic entertainments centre out in the polite, posh suburbs of Stockport. It's standard civic entertainments centre design, pine strips and brick walls and a little stage that at present is banked up with seats for the spectators. There are lots of old ladies and gentlemen in the audience, pensioners who would come in of an afternoon whether it was a nice film or a game of bingo or snooker as it is today. It was packed out the night Higgins played his preliminary match here but apart from that the attendance has been pretty sparse.

Thorburn's opponent, Graham Miles, is a man once regarded by the public as the best player in the game because he won 'Pot Black' two years in a row. The players knew better though, as he has reached only a few major finals in his career — the World Championships in 1974 and the Benson and Hedges Masters in 1976 — and won none of them. He has the distinction of being one of the few players in the world

10

whose cue action starts up around his ears, but he is fluent and unpredictable and capable on his day of upsetting the best. He shambles round the table with the air of a man wearing carpet slippers, his shirt rumpled, his waistcoat riding up at the back. No matter how expensive or recent his suit he always looks as if he is pottering about in his gardening clothes.

Cliff Thorburn by contrast has the elegance of an Edwardian gentleman dressed for the theatre, the seducer's moustache and air of ruthlessness of a man inspecting the chorus line for his next mistress, or deciding which method of removal to choose for his last one. The hard attritional nature of his play, the granite-like patience he brings to wearing down his opponents, made him, till Steve Davis came on the scene, one of the most feared men in the game. But 1980, when he won the World title, was ripped out of his hands by Davis who crowned the year by crushing him in the World semis in 1981 when he had seemed to be in control of the match. The young Londoner went on to win the title. For Cliff Thorburn that image, the cold young face, the shiny cup above the head, was the last thing he took away from his year as World Champion.

Because of the vagaries of the governing body's seeding system (the World Professional Billiards and Snooker Association) Cliff is seeded number one in this tournament, but no-one expects him to win it. He doesn't. By the interval Graham Miles is already four frames up, needing only one more to win. In the rest room they're saying Thorburn has just had terrible luck. He's too good a player to go out without winning a frame. The quality of silence as they play out the last frame is intense. It always is when Thorburn plays, so oppressive is his concentration. He stares at every ball for minutes at a time as if looking at some curious and undefined object he has never seen before and which presents its own peculiar set of problems.

The problem he now has to face is that he has been whitewashed, that he has played in a match without one single frame to testify that he was there. The whitewash is the dread of every professional player, because it puts all his skills at nought, says that the expertise he places his life and his income on is worth nothing. The players don't mind if they only win one or two frames because then people can say they had an off day, but to lose without taking a single frame is to be so off that you might not have bothered turning up.

Despite the misery of his defeat Cliff Thorburn, ever gracious, agrees to play a couple of exhibition frames. During the actual match the Canadian has played with the accuracy of a man trying to shoot a moving target in the dark. Now that the pressure is off and he has nothing to lose because he has lost everything, he makes a fantastic pot. The very back of his neck looks relieved as he rises to study the next shot. Down he gets to the table again when someone in the audience suddenly shouts out, 'Why didn't you play like that before?' The ex-champion freezes. His voice is harsh with the effort of controlling the fury contained in it as he asks the man why doesn't *he* take a walk. The adjective he chooses appears to be impolite. He tries to start again but then just turns and walks away. 'I'm sorry. That's enough for me.'

The voices babble out from the crowd. 'He didn't like being whitewashed. That was what it was.'

'They want to take that man's name and not let him in again.'

'Gone down in my estimation Thorburn, he has.'

Graham Miles stops the audience before they leave. 'I know Cliff hasn't been playing his best but he's been under a lot of pressure and I think you should understand that.'

Pressure, the pressure of that image of Steve Davis always there with him, eating into the perfectly preserved facade of coolness and control that is Cliff Thorburn's public personality. The last time he made such an unguarded outburst on the snooker table was during that momentous semi-final against Davis in the 1981 World Championships. After the afternoon session it had seemed as if Davis was crushed, his flawless technique ground into the dust by Thorburn's relentless play. In the evening he had come bouncing miraculously back, confidence so high that on the final frame of the session he had gone to shake hands with Thorburn before the final pink was potted. The story is well known. The Canadian had no chance of taking the frame at that stage but, outraged by Davis's breach of snooker etiquette, had ignored his outstretched hand, mimicked his habit of sipping water and gone to the table again before conceding the frame. Later in the corridor he had been heard to call Davis an arrogant bastard.

The challenge he threw out so ferociously in that corridor at one o'clock in the morning — 'I'll see you tomorrow' — rebounded on him the following day as Davis took six frames in a row and his place in the final. It had gone on rebounding inside him. Cliff Thorburn was a loser before he ever became a winner. He was known as a man who had lost often from winning positions, a man who couldn't quite stand up to the real white-hot blowtorch pressure of major championships. He had finally taken the title, taken the final step into the winner's

Steve Davis winning and winning and winning . . .

Whitewash for Dennis Taylor — the helpless hopeless position of a spectator

enclosure, only to find that he had to get used to the losing all over again.

Losing is not something Steve Davis has learned about yet. As the Jameson's Whiskey tournament moves into its televised stage at the Assembly Rooms in Derby, he moves inexorably towards the final. Not even Perrie Mans, the tough South African who bounced him out of the Benson and Hedges in his dream year, can topple him, though it is a tight tense sticky match. Of all the top players Mans seems the one who unsettles him most, partly because Perrie's not afraid of him. And why should he be when he's been champion of his own country for seventeen years?

He's not like the rest of them, there for every tournament, watching Steve Davis win everything. Over the past year the main suspense in snooker has been not whether Davis will get to the final but whom he will meet there. The supporting cast are all here as usual, all except Cliff Thorburn. There's Dennis Taylor, the man who's always coming second, with a curly perm and without some surplus weight. There's Terry Griffiths talking and singing to himself as usual. There's the Hurricane coming down to breakfast in his hotel with a pint of beer on one side of the plate and a cup of tea on the other. In the end it is he who gives the Invincible his hardest match. He doesn't win though Davis is tired after flying to Jersey and back for an exhibition in between matches. Not too tired, though, to clinch the deciding frame with a break of ninety-five. Always in the past year when he has been in his tightest situations he has managed to pull out something special. He comes from Plumstead in South London but he has the survival instinct and cool brain of a jungle warfare expert, hacking through the undergrowth trying to drag him down, and coolly despatching the crocodiles trying to snap him up.

He meets Dennis Taylor in the final, a man whose wit can be relied on in a crisis though his snooker is more doubtful. Dennis has become known as the eternal runner-up in snooker, beaten in the final of the Canadian Open, of 'Pot Black' twice, and most memorably in the 1979 World Championships when Terry Griffiths took the title at his first attempt. He is, though, a fine player with a wide range of shots, a shrewd tactician whose only limitation perhaps is his orthodoxy. He is certainly not a pushover.

Snooker is one of the cruellest games in that you can be playing well but never get a chance to show it. It's not like golf where you cover the same course as your opponent, or tennis where you battle it out for

14

each single point. In snooker once a player is on the table he can control the game as long as his skill, luck and nerve will allow. His opponent is reduced to the helpless hopeless position of spectator.

Steve Davis is the master of such shut-outs, having steam-rollered even such great players as Terry Griffiths without the loss of a frame. His snooker this afternoon in the bright clinical light of the Assembly Rooms is as near flawless as any human activity can be. Patiently, as methodically as a butcher slicing up a carcass into sections, he dismembers Dennis Taylor's game. Eight frames of perfect deadly snooker. Eight-nil. One frame left to play in the evening session and Steve Davis claims it almost as a right. Whitewash for Dennis Taylor. Consternation for the promoters, with a packed crowd expecting to be there for the evening.

As is customary in snooker when a match finishes earlier than expected, the players are called upon to give an exhibition. It is hard to imagine the participants in any other sport agreeing to such a practice, and impossible to imagine any other sport's officials having the temerity to suggest, 'I'm sorry, Mr Coe. Will you run that race against Mr Ovett again please?' It's like saying to a player that the great competitive struggle he has just been engaged in was all right for starters but does he have any other tricks please?

Snooker players are no less aggressive and no less serious than other sportsmen, but they are very concerned about the image of their game, and deeply grateful to the sponsors who have provided them with the kind of lifestyle they could only fantasise about ten years ago. Even now that they are in a different tax bracket from their fans most of them would think that the cost of an evening session ticket should cover more than one frame of snooker.

All the same it's an inhuman request to make of any sportsman, that having been humiliated for the entertainment of the public he is now expected to make them laugh as well. Dennis Taylor has just suffered defeat by an embarrassing nine frames to nil. He has confirmed many people's opinion of him as lacking in 'bottle', the ability to perform under pressure which distinguishes the winners from the losers. But his performance tonight is as brave and gracious as any champion's display on the table. For forty minutes he makes people laugh, entertains them with trick shots and eases the awkwardness of the situation with his dry self-deprecating wit.

Steve Davis sits slouched in his chair cold-faced. There is not a flicker of expression on his face as the affable Irishman redeems the humiliation of defeat and turns the evening into a triumph of character. 'Do you think you can get it in?' shouts someone in the crowd. Dennis is studying the table intently. He doesn't even look up. 'Well I could if the pockets were as big as your mouth,' he says amiably and pots a red. 'Is he a big fellow?' he asks, to much laughter from the crowd. Steve Davis's head is bent. He has a box of matches in his hand and he keeps taking the matches out and lighting them, and dropping them before they burn his fingers.

He has had the most complete victory any sportsman could wish for. He has crushed his opponent completely and yet it is the other man the people will be talking about as they go home, his jokes they will be laughing about, his humour they will remember. Already they will have forgotten the play of the champion, as cold and brilliant and sharp-edged as an industrial diamond, grinding its way through the hardest substances in the world.

Barry Hearn

Just Another Flash Lad from Dagenham?

Romford High Street on a grey ordinary afternoon. It could be anywhere, has all the characteristics of just about every town centre in Britain — the pedestrian precinct, the chain stores, the Macdonalds hamburger place, the shops that always have hundreds of acrylic jumpers in the windows because no-one ever thinks it's worth paying £2.99 to take them out. Just off the High Street is the Lucania snooker hall, unremarkable, with its big room filled with tables and the staircase up to it painted in that drab green they have in schools and hospitals and even less agreeable institutions.

This is the snooker home of Steve Davis, the champion as remarkable

Barry Hearn in his Romford office — there
are images of Steve everywhere

as his setting is unremarkable. Where Hurricane Higgins, with his well-publicised extravagances of character brought the game into the seventies, Steve Davis has spearheaded snooker's rise as a game for the eighties. He has helped bring it from the obscurity of halls like this one and dingy working men's clubs into leisure centres and civic halls and on to the television screen. He has won every title there is to win and more money than any snooker player before him, and is probably Britain's best known sportsman apart from Kevin Keegan. He has had his picture on the front of every daily newspaper, he has written his autobiography at the age of twenty-four and every week he reveals his innermost thoughts and feelings — or those which can be consigned to print — in his column for the *Daily Star*. There is more information available about him probably even than there is about Kev, and yet when you start talking about him you end up talking about his manager Barry Hearn.

Barry sits in his vast office that looks as if it was designed to impress all the people that walk in there. It's all chic brown shaggy carpet and cork tiles and the desk is right in the corner with a vast expanse of floor to cover before you get to it. There are images of Steve everywhere though they all come down to the same picture in the end — Steve Davis as winner, holding one trophy after another up above his head. Barry leans his elbows on the desk as he conducts a conversation on the telephone. 'No,' he says. 'Steve's current rate is two grand a night,' and, 'Yes,' he says, 'he'd do it for one and a half but that's already a cheap rate.' He gives an amused shrug at the presumably apoplectic person on the other end of the line. Well, he has to make sure the boy earns a pound or two, he says, and sure, we want to be big in Yarmouth.

He fills a very special place in Steve Davis's life. It's almost as if he's the public Steve Davis, the one Steve's too shy or too reserved to act out himself. Where Steve has to be seen as cool, unemotional, monastic in his dedication, Barry is loud, extravagant, ebullient, galvanising others with the electricity of his own enthusiasm. Where Steve is restrained, correct in his demeanour, Barry is flash and brash. Where Steve is cautious, Barry is a gambler, an adventurer, a swaggering, marauding, ruthless business man who's built up an empire just for the fun of it. You can't speak to Steve Davis unless through him, and he usually charges for the privilege — and that's the way Steve likes it. Barry is his minder, protecting him from the encroachments of the outside world, even inspiring him with a faith in his own ability that Steve did not at first have.

'When he first came over here,' recalls Barry in his East Ender's twangy voice, 'there's no way I thought he was a champion. I just thought he was trying his nuts off. He didn't say a word to me for two years. He didn't say a word to anybody. He was a mess. His jumper was always too short and his shirt was always coming out at the back. I can't believe him now. I saw him on the television the other day and said, "That's never Steve." They just used to verbal him to death up there.'

Up there is up the green-painted stairs in the billiard hall above. This is where Romford's greatest characters are to be found. Steve Davis's supporters are more than just emotional back up. They're a travelling road show. The stars are Mizzle and Robbo, who're up here this afternoon. Mizzle is the referee who knows everybody and is known to everybody for his circumlocutionary 'Good Old Days' form of speech. He's a romantic, dewy-eyed about snooker, Steve Davis, and Romford itself. Robbo is sharper, a mover who likes to go with the action. When Steve is at a big tournament he's usually to be found behind the Davis goods stall, flogging the posters and books to the public — if he's not down getting his money on the three-thirty at Doncaster.

Mizzle and Robbo say that there's always been snooker in Romford. Millicent Martin's grandfather started it off with a billiard hall called the Regal and the singer's dad used to take her in there to watch when she was a child. Once one of the Romford men issued a challenge to the great Joe Davis. People knew about it everywhere — Ilford, Leytonstone, Romford. There was only a little shed down there for Romford station then but you knew everybody in the area. Today there might be a big plane crash somewhere and you wouldn't worry about it, but in those days news was news.

The market used to be full of gamblers and villains years ago, and the billiard hall attracted these kind of people. 'This is why Romford always brought out good players,' says Robbo. 'All the gamblers came here. When Barry came along he had different ideas.' It was Barry who made the smaller hall here into a match room. There were five tables in here before. Now there are red leather banquettes round the room and a green fringed lamp above the match table.

Mizzle says he can remember when Steve first came to Romford. He'd been to Neasden with the Essex junior champion and had heard all about this new boy running around London, name of Steve Davis. Mizzle asked Bill Davis, Stevie's dad, if he'd like his son to come along and play Vic Harris. Robbo says that Vicky was beating all the professionals at that time so he really brought Steve's game along. 'At Preston when Steve won his first major championship,' says Mizzle, with a catch in his throat, 'he played the best snooker he'll play in his life in front of one thousand people. I said then, "Everything that I was searching for in my love and dedication for snooker happened down there."'

The warmth and humour of the Romford crowd are unexpected in view of the hard ruthless image Steve Davis has on the snooker table, but these are the people he feels at home with. The things that the Romford crowd value — guts, flair, willingness to have a go — underpin that seemingly cold, cautious game of Steve Davis's. His decorous demeanour in any case never prevented him from going along with the brash build-up that Barry Hearn gave him when he first came to prominence. After Steve won his first major title, the Coral UK, Barry was already telling journalists they couldn't talk to him unless they paid a nice fat fee. 'Steve's going to be the best player in the world,' he said. 'What does he need that for?'

Barry built up Steve's reputation to a level of Ali-like proportions within the game. In doing so he alienated the rest of the players to such an extent that many of them came to resent him. 'Barry used to tell him the overall things he should be saying,' says Terry Griffiths. 'He put things in the papers like, "All the other players don't like me because I've got perfect technique." When he came on first of all and beat me in the World Championships he'd come out of nowhere as far as the public was concerned. He was leading me seven-one and he said things on television like, "Oh I knew I was going to be seven-one up. I shouldn't really have lost that last frame," instead of saying — and it doesn't matter if you believe what you're bloody saying — instead of saying, "Oh Christ, I never expected to be in this position because Terry is the World Champion. If I could just have won the first session I'd be happy." If he'd said that then he'd have made a lot of friends. But he lost a hell of a lot of friends, especially within the game, because people didn't understand. He never said anything about me. It was all about himself, and that's a bad mistake in the public eye.

'A lot of it was Barry. He was putting the psychological side into the game. Barry was trying to get to the other players all the time. You could see that. He did it very well, Barry did. Steve could never do that. He's not that type of person. But he did it through Barry and it worked well for him.'

Barry Hearn, of course, is a very convenient person for Steve Davis to have around. He drives a hard business bargain without Steve appearing to be avaricious. He can fend off the press without Steve appearing to be uncooperative. He does all the ruthless things that Steve Davis can't do without tarnishing his public image. In return Steve reserves his ruthlessness for the snooker table, and in the process earns them both a fortune.

In the beginning their partnership was merely a financial one, not the close bond of friendship, almost brotherhood it became later. 'Everything I did with Steve in the early days was purely out of business,' says Barry. 'Thinking what do I need? I was looking at things saying, "Well OK, if it's helpful for me we'll do it and if it's not we won't." There's no way anyone ponces off me, even Steve. Especially Steve. Because if he was going to be good then he'd got to learn to do it the right way. No-one gives you anything for nothing in this life. He loved it when he got the car.' (Barry sent him round all his clubs in it.) 'Now he says, "Remember that poxy old car?" But he never takes liberties with me.

'I've never done it for the money. I want to see Steve Davis become so wealthy as to be a joke. Not for any other reason other than it's a game. It feeds my ego. I love to think of him being worth millions and I'm the one that's done it. I don't want the money. I'm a wealthy man in my own right.'

Life as a game. Barry Hearn's office even has fruit machines in it and Barry himself is just about incapable of watching a snooker match without taking a bet. If his companions won't take him on he'll turn to people sitting in the seats next to him and offer them odds. Like all gamblers and games players he likes to win and will go to considerable lengths to do so, although the game is more important to him than the winning. He wouldn't stop playing if he lost.

He is uninhibited in his approach, though, and as a result not the most popular man in snooker. 'I suppose there's quite a few people probably don't — you know — like me. But I'm not in the business to be liked. I like it if my people like me. I look after them. But I'm not in it to go into Parliament. I don't want to get votes. In a way it's a compliment to me every time someone goes on about how ruthless I am. People joke about Mr Earn, but I'm representing *my* players and my job is to see they get their rewards. There's no value in me being Mr Nice Guy, because all I'd be doing is hurting the people I should be protecting. Their job is to perform on the table, to give me the weapons to fire. I don't care what time they phone me up day or night as long as the boys are earning. With me they're always earning.

'But what is the difference between earning four hundred thousand and five hundred thousand? It's just a game.'

It may sound like a fairly ferocious game, but then Barry Hearn's sense of fun springs from an aggressive exuberant nature. The result is a gaiety, a gallantry that have informed the whole Davis voyage to stardom. 'I like adventurous things,' he says. 'I like being first in things.' He enjoys putting his considerable energies into new things all the time, which no doubt contributes to the continuing tattiness of several of the Lucania halls. Barry is more interested in the super snooker centre he's building in a shopping mall in Peterborough. And he likes the sort of contracts he's getting for Steve now. They've taken snooker to new highs where money is concerned.

Like the best of those working in any field of activity, he is creative in his work. It just so happens that his work is making money. 'That's what I'm good at,' he says. 'I'm a specialist at making money. I'm not good at anything else. I can't bang a nail in the wall. I am actually the most useless person but I have got a knack of making money.'

He started off as just another flash lad from Dagenham, smart enough to be taken on at twenty-one as a chartered accountant by one of the biggest firms in the country. After two years he was already a manager but he reckoned he'd never become an actual partner if he'd stayed there two *hundred* and two years. He wore white suits, didn't he? The company were as perplexed by him as he was bored with their too-straight world.

He moved on then — his career has always embodied the principle of upward mobility. He became finance director for an investment company which wanted to diversify. That led him into new worlds, the exciting world of fashion and the heady feeling of flying first class, walking into the best hotels in the world. He was twenty-five and he came from Dagenham and here he was operating in New York and Los Angeles and Tokyo. Fashion, he found, was a really good way to lose a quarter of a million pounds. But there were other worlds to try too — share dealing and property and print design. And snooker.

When he first started negotiating for the Lucania chain he had never been in a snooker hall in his life before. There were several clubs in and around Dagenham, his patch, but he had walked past them without ever seeing them, without realising they existed. And yet, he says, 'The moment I walked into a snooker club for the first time I just felt that

that was where I should be. It was incredible. I'd never played and I'd never known they were there, but I walked in and the atmosphere just seemed to hit me. I've always been a fairly physical person and I liked the aggressive dog eat dog thing.'

At that point snooker was just one of a whole clutch of business activities, but one day in 1975, Barry Hearn found himself going up the North Circular for the umpteenth time and wondering what on earth he was doing there. He'd been working eighteen-hour days and he felt dreadful. It was a moment of decision for him. He pulled into a side road and just sat there and thought. He realised that he had become a snooker person and decided he'd buy Romford and turn it into a match room and billiard hall combined. He was whistling when he set off on his way home. People remarked on how cheerful he looked the next morning as he headed down to South London and his factories. When he got there he blew a whistle and sacked all his workers.

'I decided then, I'm not going to ever do anything that I don't want,' he says. 'I knew very basic things about how to motivate and control people. When that got outside my control I got murdered financially. So, nothing that doesn't involve people. And no more stocks and shares. I could do my money in the Middle East and it would be nothing to do with me.'

Watching him with people at Romford it is obvious just how important personal contact is to him. Several times during the afternoon he hands out wads of notes to people who're doing jobs for him. He clearly trusts them for he isn't even sure how much he's given to one of them. These are his people, and he'll do anything for his own. 'I'm not a non-committed person,' he says. 'I have to be one hundred percent in things. When I was working in fashion I thought I was producing the *best* clothes. With Steve I said, "This boy's going to be the World Champion." My wife said, "You can't really believe it," but I just said, "I've *got* to believe it."'

No doubt for that reason, he hates the phrase Mr Ten Percent. 'I only started charging Steve after he won the World Championship. I took ten per cent last time, which is a joke at this level. He's full time twenty-four hours a day. I want to influence their entire life like Mark McCormack with Arnold Palmer.' He has, his critics say, influenced Steve Davis too much, filling his schedule with supermarket openings, exhibitions, challenge matches, personal appearances. Even a day out turns into a televised event with him. Steve Davis in his hands is no longer just a snooker player. He's a sports personality. Barry Hearn looks blank when the question is put to him, does Steve Davis need more leisure time than he has now. He shrugs. 'Your whole life's pressure. Steve's good as gold to manage. If I saw that he was in Cheltenham, opening stores, say, there's no way he won't go on the telly picking horses. I just give him a schedule the week before and he goes out and does it all.' He looks puzzled. 'What else would he do anyway?'

And so the game goes on. He thinks the money in snooker is unbelievable and that the Hearn-Davis partnership has hardly even started yet. Tony Meo has signed a contract with them now and, strangely, he'd like to take Terry Griffiths on though he doesn't usually get much fun out of taking over an established success. He reckons Terry isn't making nearly as much as he could from the game, because he's such a nice guy. Too nice. Terry sold the UK poster rights to his ads for Welsh Bitter for two and a half grand, with six shows thrown in for good measure. Barry says you don't do poster rights for less than ten grand. Terry should have got £15,000 on that deal. 'People will always take advantage of you. They don't owe you any loyalty and you don't owe them any.'

He makes the game he's playing sound a dirty one, one you need stomach for, just as you do to be a champion snooker player. Barry thinks that you can't make champions. To get to that level they've got to be born to do it, he says, and you wonder if the same is true of champion money makers. If he lacks Steve Davis's dedication Barry Hearn has a relish for what he's doing that makes up for it. He sips tea out of his mug with 'Boss' on the side. He says he and Steve were doing down to Bideford in Devon last week and they passed this forest. Now forests are big in accountancy circles because they cut down your tax liability. He doesn't spend his money and Steve doesn't spend his. So when he suggested Steve buy a forest the answer was, 'I'll buy a forest if you buy a forest.' They've ended up with two forests.

The Worst Tournament in the World

It's the first actual tournament the Friends of Maccabi have organised and they want to get it right, but they're learners at the game and in the end they get everything wrong. Lang's Supreme Scottish Snooker Masters turns out to be the Worst Tournament in the World — for this year at least.

There have of course been various contenders for the title, most notably a pro-am in Malta six months before, where play ground to a halt on at least one occasion, when Cliff Thorburn queried the scorekeeping. That tournament at least attracted big crowds, which is not to be the case in Glasgow. The advertising campaign beforehand is, to say the least, low key, and the few newspaper advertisements that *do* appear omit the price of tickets, vital information in a working class city. By holding the tournament mid-week too, the Friends of Maccabi manage to miss that most lucrative source of revenue, the weekend crowd. Glasgow may have a high unemployment rate but there are a few people there who still have jobs and can't legitimately class watching snooker on a Wednesday afternoon as part of their duties.

The Friends of Maccabi are running the tournament for a worthy cause though, so much must be forgiven. They are a Jewish charity and are trying to raise money for their youth work. They already have a gymnasium, two squash courts, a judo hall, table tennis match room, and social centre with banqueting suite in Glasgow, but they would like to be able to provide even bigger and better facilities for young people.

This is not actually their first venture into snooker. Several months previously they have arranged a Steve Davis—Alex Higgins challenge match, where a capacity crowd of nearly 3,000 people filled the Kelvin Hall Arena and responded with such extravagant Glaswegian fervour that Steve Davis said it felt like a football crowd. The atmosphere was fantastic. Out of this world. That success misleads the Friends into using the same venue for the Lang's tournament. It's a disastrous decision. In that huge hall, with seats for 2,750, little crowds of a couple of hundred people sit strung out like lonely birds on a telegraph wire. Only for the final do the crowds top 1,000.

The Kelvin Hall is one of those places where sooner or later they get every form of entertainment devised by man. They've had Frank Sinatra singing there and Jim Watt fighting and even Jim Watt singing. Not Frankie himself can rival Jim's rendition of 'Flower of Scotland'. But most of all the Kelvin Hall has always been known as the home of the circus, with international acts from all over the world congregating there every Christmas — clowns tumbling in in baggy trousers and red noses through the very entrance where the svelte snooker players are now being introduced, lions and elephants roaring in the menagerie outside. And above the very seats where the snooker spectators are sitting stretches the high wire, the man solitary, very lonely, inching his way up such a very thin wire, with no safety net beneath to catch him should he fall.

And that after all is what the audience this week will come to see, what modern sport is all about — the man on the high wire, taking risks for us, laying himself open to the discovery that his best may not be good enough. It's danger and daring of a type our fragile egos could not withstand, and why else is Alex Higgins still the biggest draw in snooker? The Hurricane is here for this tournament, one of seven invitees for the eight-man draw — the last is to be settled with a qualifying match — along with Steve Davis, Doug Mountjoy, Cliff Thorburn, Kirk Stevens, Ray Reardon, and the Hurricane's natural successor, Jimmy White.

Jimmy White is the sort of person who never had a choice, who would have played snooker wherever it was played, in whatever conditions. Perhaps he would even have been better suited to the early days of the modern game, when snooker was played in the half-light and not in the full glare of publicity as it is today, when players trooped round the country to grotty little clubs, not all of whose members could be numbered among the respectable citizens in their communities. Jimmy White has had his image laundered to match his surname. His teeth have been straightened, his hair curled, his face robbed of its cheeky grin and photographed by the Earl of Lichfield. He is the hottest property in the game, World Amateur Champion at nineteen and now the one player who looks as if he has the potential to challenge the Invincible, Steve Davis. And yet if he should reach the final this week he might not be able to play.

26

He is due in court on Friday afternoon charged with taking part in looting during the recent Brixton riots. Jimmy's first story is that he and his girlfriend come out of the pub and well, he's a bit pissed, like. The crowds have been rioting and there's this shop window smashed so he jumps in and starts dancing about in the window with his girlfriend's handbag, just mucking about. That's when the coppers nab him and take him in for stealing ladies' handbags. If he is found guilty the press speculate there's a chance he'll be sent down as the average sentence for rioters is turning out to be three or four months.

Ah well, Friday is another day. There's snooker to play first, which is what Jimmy likes best. That green table, the big lamp above marking out his territory, the rush of the balls, that's when he feels real. He and Ray Reardon, his first round opponent, are alike in that. They both move round the table as if claiming possession of it, never so physically at ease as when they are playing snooker. Such grace, such fluidity. You could almost be deceived into thinking that that was all there was, that there was no struggle for supremacy being fought out here by the old and the young. The young inevitably wins, leaving the older man disgusted at his own weakness. He doesn't want to carry on playing, says Ray Reardon, if he's going to play so badly. It's embarrassing. He's seriously thinking of retiring, he says.

The great onslaught by youth ends there. Kirk Stevens, the other young and supposedly coming player in the tournament, distinguishes himself only by his dress. For his match against Cliff Thorburn he turns up in tight black leather trousers that cling to his plump little thighs, a white waistcoat and white training shoes that he clearly feels he has to live up to by sprinting round the table at an even faster rate than usual. With his blond hair and bland good looks he is like nothing so much as a member of Bucks Fizz. Any minute you expect him to burst into a rendition of some banal pop song. 'Making Your Mind Up', as he ponders his next shot. Cliff Thorburn, in a sombre dark suit, beats him five-one.

Jimmy must carry the banner of youth on alone, which he does in style by beating the not-altogether-decrepit Steve Davis in the semi-final. This is the first time Steve has been beaten in a major tournament in almost a year, though in the event, Jimmy White's success seems less momentous that it might have been, as the tournament is being televised only in Scotland and not nationwide. Still, it's an exciting result for the snooker world to ponder, even if Jimmy's main worry is whether he can actually be there for the final or not. Six months later he and his girlfriend, now his wife Maureen, are to be cleared of the charge of theft. In the meantime, while Jimmy's solicitor is arranging to speak in court for him so that he can take his place in the final, Cliff Thorburn and Alex Higgins are fighting it out for the other place. Cliff, the mild-mannered 1980 World Champion, is generally regarded as one of the most gracious men in the game, but even he has been known to express irritation at the Hurricane.

His match with the Hurricane proceeds to the noise of beer cans popping open, crisp packets rustling, beer cans being knocked over. A drunk woman in the audience creates so much disturbance with her heckling of Cliff Thorburn that she has to be removed by the police. Cliff looks sternly at the Hurricane. 'Is she with you?' The Hurricane is outraged. 'I don't bring pissed women to tournaments,' he says in dignified tones.

More than anything Glasgow audiences love virtuosity, the showmen, dazzling displays of skill and nerve, and they are more vocal than the polite southern audiences in expressing their appreciation. Where in the normal audience you get shouts of 'Come on Alex,' in Glasgow they roar it. Cliff Thorburn's more recondite skills meet with a less vocal response though he is holding his own on the table, playing the tight cerebral snooker that once earned him the tribute from Barry Hearn of being the second hardest man in the game. 'Steve's the hardest,' said Barry. 'He's so hard he brings tears to your eyes.'

The match is at two frames all when the Hurricane starts querying the score. Now the scoreboards at the Kelvin Hall are of a type that constitutes an optical obstacle course. Telescopes and calculators would be required to decipher and then compute the score accurately from them and neither commodity is made available to the players. The Hurricane isn't sure what the score should be but he knows he's losing out somehow and demands that Cliff start the frame over again. Cliff, who is on the point of winning it, has no intention of doing so, particularly as he has been tailoring his play to what the scoreboard tells him he requires.

In a normal tournament any mistake in the score would be checked against the written cards of the score keepers, but this is the Worst Tournament in the World and no-one is writing the score down. No-one even knows if it's been recorded by the TV cameras. The Hurricane wants the officials changed but the Friends of Maccabi can't do that as they don't know whether the officials are right or wrong. And they can't start the frame again as they don't know whether the officials are right or wrong. To the accompaniment of helpless looks from them, confusion from the audience, and fury from the Hurricane, Cliff Thorburn closes out the frame to take a three-two lead.

It is no ordinary three-two lead. He comes back after the interval with a huge psychological advantage over an opponent still fretting about the scorekeeping and the officials and the organisers and Glasgow. The Hurricane has no energy left over to devote to snooker and rapidly loses the next two frames to let Cliff Thorburn into his first final in this country since winning the World Championship the year before last.

Later Cliff is having a quiet drink in the North British Hotel with a group of players round him when the Hurricane bursts in. 'I was right,' he says. 'The video shows I was right.' Someone asks him has he seen the video and he says he hasn't but a man came up to him in the interval and told him he hadn't been given four points he'd won for a foul early on in the frame. The video showed he was in the right. He wonders if the BBC would let him see the video.

Cliff Thorburn sips his drink with ferocious precision. He refuses to entertain either the notion that he withdraw from the final or that he support Higgins' protests. The Hurricane stares at him unblinkingly. 'Well, if you want to win so badly,' he says, and wanders away.

He drifts from group to group, a lonely figure. Finally he ends up standing beside the journalists Janice Hale and Ted Corbett. He has a tour of challenge matches with Steve Davis coming up in Scotland soon and he says he's not going to do it if conditions are like this. It wouldn't be worth it.

He's lost a lot of prize money on this match. It was a different game after the fight. There's no way he could have lost if *he'd* been ahead three-two at the interval.

His face is as pale as if the blood had all been drained out of him by the dispute. He says at least *he's* not a cheat. That's the secret he has up his sleeve, that he plays fair. He can sleep easy in his bed at nights, he says, though this is rumoured to be exceptional. He's standing up and being counted all the time. Snooker's his life but no-one hears him. They leave him sitting there like little boy lost. He didn't have anybody to turn to tonight. Ray wouldn't help. In Malta, says the Hurricane, Ray Reardon came up and told him he'd let down the pros by letting an amateur win £2,000. If a man beats him on the table, says the Hurricane, he's welcome to the money. Vic Harris told him tonight he was right but then says he's got a wife and three kids to support. 'I've got my

Kirk Stevens in his tight black leather trousers

The victor Jimmy White, surrounded by the sponsor's product

baby bird at home,' says the Hurricane, peering through misty eyes at Janice, who is clearly his confidante among the press corps.

'The rest of them kill to win,' he tells her earnestly, though his voice trails away as he muses that Reardon and Pulman and them can't win any more anyway. 'I'll fight to the death any time but I just gave up tonight,' and he looks bereft. Janice says kindly that there's no use crying over spilt milk but the Hurricane says he's too manly to cry. 'I did have a little cry in Derby,' he concedes. 'But it wasn't because I lost. You know that.' As Janice nods in agreement he tells her that none of the rest of them have got any courage. Janice clearly thinks that this statement does not coincide with the reality. 'Some people just think of other things than snooker,' she remarks diplomatically. 'No, it's courage and honesty,' he says, stalking proudly off into the night.

Much later, at three o'clock in the morning, he phones Cliff Thorburn in his hotel bedroom and says that he hopes Cliff's little boy doesn't turn out like his father.

It is the beginning of a nightmare for Cliff Thorburn. He leads four-three after the afternoon session with Jimmy White but the evening's entertainment is provided by the spectacle of his slow torture. There are actually 1,000 people here, for not even the Friends of Maccabi can dissipate the publicity generated by a televised dispute between two of the world's top players. But if the spectators are expecting conflict tonight they are to be disappointed. Nerveless perhaps because, as some observers say, he is brainless, Jimmy White picks off one frame after another to take his first major professional title without allowing his opponent another frame.

He's beaten three World Champions on the way but still hasn't the confidence to make a speech when he's presented with his silver tankard and his Lang's whisky and his cheque for £8,000. The promoters try to get Cliff Thorburn to make a speech instead but the urbane Canadian won't speak unless the victor does. Finally Jimmy is persuaded to come to the microphone. In that gravelly Cockney voice he delivers his oration. 'I'd like,' he says haltingly, 'to thank Lang's Whisky for a lovely evening,' and he clutches his cheque like a child taking home a present from a party.

Lang's Whisky, according to the Friends of Maccabi, are well pleased with the tournament. The Friends are not quite so pleased, though the tournament is now guaranteed for a further two years. This year Lang's have paid a third of the expenses. Next year they'll pay ninety percent, and the year after that the Friends might start to make a profit. Who knows, perhaps they'll know the problems so well next year that they'll run the Best Tournament in the World.

Tony Meo

'The Spic' Signs with Hearn

'What do you think that bastard's done?' The gravelly voice and elegant use of the English language are Jimmy White's. The man at the other end of the telephone is his manager, Geoff Lomas of Sportsworld, the company who gave Jimmy a new set of teeth before he'd even signed a contract.

'Who?' asks Geoff, not unreasonably. Jimmy's voice is impatient. 'The Spic,' he says. 'He's signed with Hearn.'

Jimmy's use of the English language is about as accurate as it is graceful. 'The Spic' — the word usually applied to people of Hispanic origin — is Jimmy's pet name for the half-Italian Tony Meo. Jimmy and Tony are very close friends. They lived down the road from each other in Tooting when they were growing up, and both went to the same school, the Ernest Bevin Comprehensive — though not often. At the age of fourteen Tony discovered the delights of Zan's billiard hall and introduced Jimmy to them too. They both decided they preferred to get their education from this extra-curricular activity rather than from the pages of textbooks.

Tony's dad had died the year before and his mum didn't know what he was up to. He had been a star table tennis player at his local youth club till someone told him to take up snooker, but he soon found he had even more of a flair for this new game. 'All I wanted to do was to be the best player in the club and I achieved that within a few months.'

Jimmy, hardly big enough to see over the table at first, was a prodigy

32

Tony Meo

too, and the two had very soon begun to make a name for themselves. A man called Bob Davis came from the other side of London to see them and from then on they became money players. Bob Davis drove them to all sorts of places, backing them for money and eventually getting them exhibitions in working men's clubs. They grew up together in the snooker halls of London.

'At one stage we were always billed together,' remembers Tony. 'Whoever was mentioned the other would be too. It was exciting but when you're playing money matches you've got nothing to lose except your money. With the big tournaments it's pressure. You're out to do well. In my first year as a pro I played well but I got beat a couple of times when I shouldn't have. Most players learn the hard way and I think I have done. You can't go straight in and win, though it does happen.'

It's happened, of course, with Jimmy White, the new Lang's Supreme Scottish Masters' champion. Jimmy, more flashily brilliant, has always been that bit more in the limelight than Tony, but it was Tony who was first to make a century break, eighteen months after he started the game, when he was fifteen-and-a-half. He is still the youngest ever player to have made a 147 maximum break, when he was seventeen years and five months and he probably knows the number of days as well. He is very aggrieved that it isn't in the *Guinness Book of Records*.

Still there is no rivalry between him and Jimmy and they've always done everything together, which is why Jimmy thinks it's too bad of Tony to go and sign with anyone other than his managers, Sportsworld. Geoff Lomas is a little puzzled. He spoke to Tony the week before Jimmy came to an agreement with the company. 'Look Tony,' he said, 'the time isn't ripe yet. We'll sign Jimmy up. Give us two or three weeks. But we can't do them both together because the contracts have been drawn up with Jimmy and all the publicity's ready. You'll get lost in Jimmy's publicity, Tony.'

There's nothing he can do about it now but Geoff has a word with Tony anyway, just to find out what went wrong. Jimmy and Tony had both been under contract by then to a well-known snooker character called Henry West. Sportsworld had to buy out Jimmy's contract. According to Geoff Lomas, Tony didn't like being left alone to the tender mercies of Mr West. 'Henry West,' opines Geoff solemnly, 'was a very hard taskmaster.' This is the only printable opinion he offers on Mr West's character and behaviour. 'And Tony felt so insecure when Jimmy left that he had to go somewhere. He either couldn't wait three weeks or else he didn't believe what I was saying. I don't know.'

Tony doesn't seem to realise that he's done anything wrong. In fact he's grateful to Barry Hearn. 'Lots of players have asked to be managed by him. But he said I was the only one he would have taken. It's very nice of him to take me on. He did say to me, "If you ever want to come I'll manage you because I've known you a long time." With Steve doing so well it's someone to follow. I've had a few battles with Steve in younger days and Barry knew me then. We always got on well even then. I think he's always liked me. I'm quick and I smack them in. I'm the aggressive type,' he says with his sweet, almost shy smile.

The wild side of his nature ceased to be a reportable fact several years ago, though he still loves to gamble. He's even given up disco dancing now — he once won a prize for it. Soft, always plumper than he wants to be, he is a person who enjoys the good things of life and even as a child had as many of them as his mother, who owned a restaurant, could afford. 'I was spoiled,' he says with a grin. He in his turn has an open, generous nature — he even claps when his opponents are introduced, and he has no inhibitions about praising other people, a trait not always evident in competitive sportsmen. Of Barry Hearn, the man they all love to hate, he says, 'He gives you confidence. He says, You just go out there, and I feel better. It's something you can't explain. He just says, Try your best. He doesn't put any pressure on you. You just do it, don't you?'

Barry Hearn sits behind his desk in Romford and smiles with satisfaction. Hidden in one of its drawers is the Meo cheque book. Tony's tastes come stamped all over with the famous Gucci initials and Barry is determined that Tony will hang on to at least some of the fortune he is going to help him earn this year. 'There's no turn-on for me to get someone who's already there. Like Alex, for instance,' he says. 'But Tony. I can make something of him. That turns me on. Tony Meo this year will earn what Ray Reardon earned in his last year as World Champion.'

Geoff Lomas is cynical. 'Tony'll do quite well,' he concedes. 'But he'll always play second fiddle to Steve Davis.'

Team Spirit

Man against man. Snooker is a duel fought on green baize, not greensward, with cues instead of swords. In this arena of combat you are alone, no second to mop your brow, just *your* skills, *your* nerve to win you victory or defeat. And being alone you must empty your mind of all but the task before you. Pressure from outside would be intolerable.

It's all intolerable. Here at the Hexagon Theatre in Reading, where the State Express World Team Classic is under way, the stars of the game are lungeing at shots with all the finesse of Desperate Dan, missing pots that even Dan could make. Pressure, there's just too many pressures. There's the other members of the team to worry about, and whether your performance is as good as theirs, and whether you're bringing enough points to the team, and there's the awesome burden of playing for your country.

It's like playing Russian roulette for your country. The matches are played over the best of just three frames, which is like asking steeplechasers to line up in the sprints. Usually the big stars play over at least nine frames, often more, though the newer professionals, not long out of the amateur ranks, are more accustomed to short matches. All these new professionals, hard after the big stars, big fish, but in a tank full of piranhas.

It seems as if there's an ocean full of them. There are six national teams here, with a new snooker country in the Republic of Ireland — Wales, England, Canada, Australia, and Northern Ireland are the others. An Australian team has been brought over at a cost to the tournament of over £5,000 but the fiction has been abandoned this year that the best players from outside the main countries could be crammed conveniently into one team and labelled The Rest of the World. This time the Rest of the World must be presumed not to exist, or at least not to contain any snooker players of note.

The lads from the Republic of Ireland are delighted at their good

36

fortune in being invited. This is the first major televised tournament for Eugene Hughes and Dessie Sheehan, whose eyes are not closed to the benefits that might accrue to them from being seen on the telly. They stick close to their captain Patsy Fagan, who knows what it's all about, having once been a world top tenner. He is only thirty-two but is something of a legend to Eugene Hughes, whose family lived ten doors down from his in Dun Laoghaire. Eugene says he grew up on Patsy Fagan. 'You see someone like Patsy and he's from the exact same background as yours and you think, if he can do it, if I put a lot of hard work into it, maybe I could do it as well.' And of course Eugene has the opportunity to do it on BBC Television, which Patsy never really had in his heyday.

Still, he has been seen often enough since on the BBC to be a well-known player. Last year he played in this tournament too but as part of an all-Irish team with Alex Higgins and Dennis Taylor. 'Team' may be somewhat inaccurate as a description of a conglomeration containing both Mr Higgins *and* Mr Taylor. In any individual sport it would be difficult to throw top players together and say, 'Be a team.' With Higgins and Taylor it is impossible especially this year when Higgins feels his status threatened.

It's not just that they don't like each other — though they don't. They have probably learned to tolerate each other better than they used to, but personal pride is involved and neither is prepared to concede to the other the ascendancy which would be implied by the title 'captain'. There *should* be no argument. Dennis is the national champion and is also higher in the world rankings than the Hurricane. But when he won the title in 1980 he refused to allow the Hurricane the chance to win it back the following year, challenging Patsy Fagan instead. It sounds unfair but has its precedent in the Hurricane's own behaviour as champion. The world rankings are calculated with such little regard for the synchronisation of achievement and reward that they must be seen as creative rather than informative. Besides, the Hurricane has lost so many places through being penalised for Hurricane-like behaviour that he is hardly even *on* the list any more.

The argument is inevitable. When the Hurricane breezes in Dennis is busy practising. Funny how the Hurricane is always said to breeze everywhere, but then he really can't just walk quietly into a room like everybody else. He plunges into the explication of the various reasons why he should be Northern Ireland's number one, not the least being that if a match should come to a play-off between the number one and

England's Steve Davis, he considers himself better equipped than is Dennis Taylor to vanquish the Invincible. The tolerant Dennis is prepared to dismiss the Hurricane's attitude as being 'just a bit childish,' but he won't back down, so the Hurricane immediately changes the subject. His eye lights on Dennis's playing partner. 'Who the hell's this?' he asks, studying nineteen-year-old Tommy Murphy, the third member of his own team.

This, it may safely be said, is the nadir of Northern Irish team spirit, which is henceforth carefully nurtured by the ingenious tactic of having the team all stay at different hotels. The Hurricane abandons all attempts to impress with his leadership qualities and says of the captaincy question that he personally thinks it's by the way anyway. He abandons too his current posture of having a personality that can be contained within the limits of the team and confesses that team competition has no greater pressures for him than individual. 'I just try to go out and pot the fellow off the table,' he says. 'It's not as if it was the Olympics or the World Cup or something, with the importance of having a whole nation behind you. Maybe that would make a difference.'

Dennis Taylor takes it all more personally. Last year he was found crying in the dressing room because he felt he'd let his team down by losing his crucial match in the semi-final. 'When you're playing on your own it doesn't matter so much,' he says. 'But when you're in a team you're under far more pressure because you're worried about letting the other two team members down.' Taking his responsibilities seriously he has had a little chat with Tommy Murphy, who has been a professional for only five months and has just recently moved to this country from his home in Newtonards near Belfast. Tommy's job prior to becoming a snooker professional was almost as much a matter of life and death. He was a coffin maker and says it was good fun but that he had to give it up because he was being driven crazy by the thought that he might have to shave the occupants of the coffins. Quite why he should think that would ever be an integral part of coffin manufacture is uncertain, but he clearly is a man to be put off by only the most extreme of pressures. Dennis tells him he'll miss easy shots at first and he's not to worry but Tommy Murphy isn't worried. In fact he surprises himself with just how unworried he is. 'I thought I'd be shaking at first,' he says. 'But I hardly even noticed the TV cameras,' though the TV cameras notice *him*, picking up a wide range of facial

Tommy Murphy isn't worried . . .

contortions which record more realistically than he himself does the extent of his nerves.

He is given sound advice by both members of his team. Not wanting to make the younger player nervous and put him off the Hurricane tells him, 'Look babe, just go out and enjoy yourself.' Tommy Murphy is an unknown quantity to the Hurricane, who thinks that *as* an unknown quantity he's doing all right. Tommy is doing better than all right. He is generally regarded as having done well for himself this week and is much praised for the soundness of his cue action though the impetuosity of his safety play makes the Hurricane look like the Bjorn Borg of the green baize. Tommy takes frames off most of the players he meets and even beats a top star, the Australian Eddie Charlton. The story is in the papers the following day. Tommy is a star for a day, or at least the star of the hour.

The star of the following hour is the Republic's Eugene Hughes, who beats the Canadian number one, Cliff Thorburn. Eugene is not exactly what you'd call a star back home but he is one of the best known Irish players and has been making a good living for himself over the past two years playing exhibitions all over the country. Eugene has been a pro for less than a year though he applied several times before that and was turned down. 'They hurt my mother and father when they did that,' he says. 'And they hurt me.'

Eugene, it will be inferred, is a self-dramatist of a superior order. He sees life in dramatic terms and believes utterly in the various scenarios his agile brain concocts. He is all glowing skin and bright eyes, with a zest for life that comes at least partly from his constant delight in making up reality as he goes along. Eugene sees the State Express as his big break and takes positive steps to ensure that his brief moment of stardom stretches out as long as possible. He likes the limelight and wants to stay in it.

The Irish team accordingly arrange themselves some publicity. They'll go to the local health club for a training session, they decide. Now snooker is not actually a sport. It's a game, one where a playful or inventive mind can negate physical differences, not one where you can pound your opponent into submission with your power. Physical fitness must be desirable but it's not necessary. Golf is the pros' favourite game mainly because the open air is such a novelty to them. Eugene has chosen a publicity stunt unique in the annals of the game.

Patsy Fagan, his captain, being assured already of his own small portion of snooker immortality, stays in his bed, but Dessie Sheehan,

Eugene Hughes in his
dressing room at the
Hexagon, Reading

Dessie Sheehan in the training
session at the local health centre

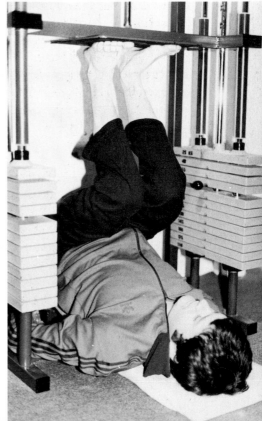

the Irish number three, creeps warily along to the Mall Health Club. Dessie, like Eugene, has been a professional for less than a year and is still working full time as a clerk with Radio Telefis Eireann to support his family. His first big tournament is turning out rather differently than he expected. Dessie is pale and slight, with the sort of build that Charles Atlas would love to get his hands on. He looks as if he has been brought up without the benefit of sunlight, on a diet of chips and not too many of them. As the staff welcome the team to the club Dessie looks uneasily at the tank of fish in the waiting room, there presumably to calm the clients' nerves. But the fish are big and black and menacing and patrol the tank like California traffic cops and he looks as if his fears are not allayed.

The gym itself is not reassuring. Ranged round the walls are various machines that look like medieval torture instruments. They are clearly designed for the dual purpose of punishment and ridicule and Dessie looks prepared to give up his closest secrets without a struggle. Eugene has done some weight training in the past and acquits himself well on the machines. He can do all the physical jerks too, in spite of his total inability to go forward in concert with the rest of the group and backward when they go back. Dessie looks defeated. His arms feel like logs, he says. When he actually plays snooker later he fails to take a frame off his opponent, Canada's Big Bill Werbeniuk, who has trained by the more conventional method of consuming his daily dozen pints of lager.

Big Bill has a hereditary nervous disease which makes his arm shake when he's playing snooker and which can only be combatted by a large intake of lager. As it is considered to be a necessary aid to his professional life the lager is tax-deductible. It also puts Big Bill into the unenviable position of having to play snooker while under the influence of large amounts of lager, a task he manages with some distinction.

As his teammates are ex-World Champion Cliff Thorburn and rising star Kirk Stevens the Canadian team must be considered one of the strongest in the competition. They reached the final last year though this year are two games down to the Republic of Ireland team before they realise what's happening and fight back. The irrepressible Eugene Hughes puts his one-frame victory over Canadian captain Cliff Thorburn down to determination. 'It's a very very funny game, snooker,' he muses. 'Once people are determined they can do anything. I went in against Cliff with him quoted three to one on to beat me, but

42

I felt determined to win. Of course he's still a better player than me but that doesn't mean I'm going to go in and lie down.'

Eugene is possessed of determination greater than the average, a most dramatic amount of determination in fact. 'At the start I was never ever good at snooker but I had a terrible determination about me,' he says and nods wisely as if agreeing with what the speaker's just said. 'A fierce determination about me. Fierce determination. And I'm going to be someone in snooker, so I am. I'm going to fight tooth and nail all the way. As the years go on I hope to climb up the ladder and reach the top. I certainly won't settle for being number four or five or ten or twenty. As long as I'm alive and no-one kills me, that is.'

Eugene's concern about his personal safety may just be a pious fear of offending the Almighty by presuming too much, but reality is rapidly catching up with the Hughes projection of it. Over in the Butts Centre just opposite the Hexagon, the Bomb Squad are at this moment removing a device from the Belfast Linen Shop. Belfast Linen has been established in Cambridge for over fifty years with no connection whatsoever with its eponymous city, and the bomb turns out to be a hoax, but just for a moment the razor edge of mortality slices into snooker's enclosed world.

It is only for a moment. The Hexagon staff find someone's briefcase outside the BBC sound box and immediately rush round sealing entrances and peering suspiciously into people's eyes, but the press display classic journalistic insouciance in the face of potential news, and speculate idly on whether the Bomb Squad came by helicopter or up the M1. They never write about bomb scares anyway because there are so many — nine during last year's World Championships alone.

In any case the most explosive substance to come out of Northern Ireland is the Hurricane and he makes better copy. He watches part of the Republic's evening session against Canada on the closed circuit television but decides it is better sport to tease Big Bill Werbeniuk. Big Bill, lager in one hand and girlfriend on the other, is avidly following Kirk Stevens' progress against Dessie Sheehan and is unwilling to concede that there is even a possibility of his team-mate losing. The Hurricane pretends to inside knowledge about Dessie's marvellously smooth cue action, his brilliant snooker brain and his infallibility on certain types of shots that seem to predominate in this match. He is of the opinion that Mr Sheehan will bury Mr Stevens, or Wonder White, as he christens the young Canadian. Big Bill eyes the Hurricane in awe. 'Jesus,' he says. 'You really get me hot and I never get hot,' a statement which seems to gratify the Hurricane. Wonder White's winning score of two frames to none doesn't please him quite so much. 'You can just see all the Paddies in Dublin being sick into their Guinness,' he says, before he wanders off to watch the football.

Canada win without his support but cannot repeat the feat the following day and go out in their semi-final against England. Eugene and the Republic must look to the future now that their chance for fame and fortune has slipped out of their grasp. The eternal optimist is not downhearted. Eugene's fertile mind has already seized on a stunt of breathtaking audacity to bring him to public attention. This, if he can pull it off, will be of much more benefit to him than physical jerks or even than winning a measly snooker tournament. Eugene proposes himself as the first ever snooker player to pose nude for the *Playgirl* centrefold. Kevin Keegan has turned down an offer to bare his all on behalf of football and Eugene considers that *Playgirl* might like a sporting substitute.

'I'm terrible serious about this,' he says, with an intensity of seriousness that amounts to the dramatic. He says that the snooker authorities think he's crazy anyway and that his family back in Dun Laoghaire will just think it's a laugh. His sister will be disgusted and his mother's a bit religious, as most people in Ireland are, but his father will be delighted, just delighted. What a snooker player needs, he's decided, is an image. There's Kirk Stevens wore a white suit on the telly and everyone knows who he is though he's hardly won a game since. 'You've got to have terrible neck in this game,' says Eugene, with the air of a man who has just illuminated a dark corner of human experience. He considers himself to be a man with the requisite amount of neck. He has such a very terrible amount of neck he'd even go on Parkinson with a bow tie and his cue and nothing else.

As Eugene is composing his master-plan for personal advancement the Hurricane is engaged on an equally creative enterprise on behalf of his team. Northern Ireland are playing Wales in the semi-finals and he has devised a new break-off designed to flummox his opponent Doug Mountjoy. It is actually designed to flummox Steve Davis, the press decide, seeing in it the latest Higgins scheme for vanquishing the Invincible. As the break-off consists of nicking the cue ball just in behind the reds without disturbing anything on the table, so that the players only need to glance the cue ball lightly off the back red, it is unlikely the Invincible would ever get a game, much less be vanquished in it. Wales' Greatest Supporter, Keith Robinson, freelancing for

44

Cardiff's *South Wales Echo,* partly at his own expense, watches the players hitting the cue ball back and forth behind the reds and says he done that down the Coronation Club in Barry once and they said it wasn't a proper game.

The Hurricane looks gleeful. This little piece of mischief has made up for the afternoon session when he just lost to Terry Griffiths after forcing him to a play-off on the black. Tommy Murphy predictably has lost his two matches but both the Hurricane and Dennis Taylor beat Mountjoy, so if Dennis can beat the out of form Ray Reardon in their match and then the play-off, Northern Ireland will be through. The Hurricane zooms off into the night immediately after he wins, telling people he'll see them the next day for the final.

Terry Griffiths waits for the result of the match, watching the closed circuit television with a look of acute anxiety. He reckons it's worse watching than it is actually playing. 'Everybody's nervous,' he says. 'The only one that's not more nervous than normal is Alex and that's because he's a bundle of nerves all the time.' As Dennis Taylor wins both frames in his match against Ray Reardon and prepares to play off for the match Terry looks back to last year and Dennis's dressing room distress. 'This time,' ponders Terry, 'he could turn it all round. He'll be their hero,' he says, adding that you wouldn't catch him crying. He notes that it's not what he wants if Northern Ireland win, but it's what everybody else wants.

Not quite everybody. Wales' Greatest Supporter refuses even to contemplate defeat. He crouches alertly in front of the TV screen with his clipboard. Ray Reardon, he instructs the room, is going to win. As Dennis Taylor has a history of losing big finals and Ray Reardon is a six times World Champion there are those there who agree with him, despite Ray Reardon's present poor form. Keith speculates aloud that if you sent those two players into a closed room and said that only one was to come out alive, that one would be Ray Reardon.

Ray Reardon does. Dennis self-destructs by making a mistake early on in the frame and Reardon makes a fifty-one break to lay the basis for winning the tiebreak and the match. Wales are through to the final for the third year in a row, much to the delight of Mr Robinson, who brings in a red pottery dragon with Wales is Wonderful on it to celebrate.

England must soldier on without such external aid though they do have an even more valuable asset than the grotesque dragon in Steve Davis. Over the week the England team of the Invincible, David

Taylor, and John Spencer has become steadily more like a team, due in great part to the youthful enthusiasm of Steve Davis, who snaps his fingers in the air and whoops when the English players win. Against Wales he is impeccably invincible, beating both Doug Mountjoy and Ray Reardon in two straight frames. David Taylor loses both his matches against Mountjoy and Griffiths but John Spencer pulls off the surprise of the match by beating Terry Griffiths, who has previously been the Invincible of this tournament, not having lost a match in the whole three years.

Spencer's win takes the tournament to the best possible climax, an England-Wales final decided by a play-off frame between the captains, Steve Davis and Ray Reardon. In the past Reardon has been revered for his ability to emerge alive from closed rooms but there is a school of thought which considers that his days as a great player are over, that he might be left for dead in there. His position as Welsh number one has already aroused mild controversy in the press though Doug Mountjoy and Terry Griffiths may be glad to be relieved of the responsibility of having to beat Steve Davis to win the tournament.

And for all the team spirit and team pressures, this tournament has come down finally to man against man, just Steve Davis and Ray Reardon, trapped as surely in the glare of the TV lights as in any closed room. The watching team members are tense as first Steve Davis and then Ray Reardon makes a mistake. Will England win? Will Wales? In the end who else but the Invincible could win?

I Just Love It, The Applause

The downstairs entrance is like an old-fashioned Odeon, pillars and huge swing doors and a little ticket kiosk sitting in a great stone desert of floor. You expect a commissionaire to ask whether you want stalls or circle, and it is a star we've come to see, though not on the screen. This is Willie Thorne's Snooker Centre in Leicester, the centre of Willie's working life, such as it is.

Willie doesn't actually like work very much so he's not always there. The professional snooker player has various ways of making a living open to him but few appeal to Willie, whose droopy walrus moustache and clubbed-seal brown eyes belie his fun-loving nature. He won't coach. That bores him to tears and he reckons only a fee of about £30 an hour would be sufficient to ensure his concentration. He won't do exhibitions either, not unless they pay him a lot of money. After all it's about a fiver in petrol just to go down the road these days, he thinks, which may say something about his car. Willie does love match play but that doesn't pay very well unless you're right at the top of the tree because most of the big events are by invitation only. Willie will earn less than £2500 from tournaments this year unless he does well in the World Championships.

But he always has enough money to indulge in his favourite hobby of gambling and he's just bought himself a nice bungalow outside Leicester. The reason is this snooker centre. It's a family concern, co-owned by Willie, his elder brother and his mother, who took out mortgages on their houses to help buy the place in the beginning. Willie just happened to have about fifteen grand lying around at the time. With a loan from the bank and help from the brewery to put in Willie's Bar, the centre was valued at £90,000 then, only a couple of years ago. Now the family has opened a new top floor, there are 2,000 members and the place is worth £530,000. Willie's younger brother works there now too, mainly, says Willie, because in true Thorne tradition, he likes time off when he wants to do things.

Willie is not one of the highest ranked pros but it is not his own self-acknowledged laziness that has kept him from reaching the very top. He is an attacking player, generally regarded as one of the most talented people in the game. But he's never had enough control of his nerves to be able to control his opponents as well. He's just not cool enough to win the big ones. He wants to win too much and wanting can get in the way of winning.

He started off as a teenage whizz-kid in the days when teenage whizz-kids were less commonplace than they are now. He was then the youngest person to turn pro, the youngest player to be invited on to 'Pot Black'. He had always been precocious, was barred at fourteen from the Conservative Club where his parents were stewards because he was too young. After a year of being allowed about two frames a day he started going to billiards halls. 'I was turned off with the Conservatives' standard too,' he says. 'It was no big shakes because they can't play anyway.'

The man who taught him to play properly, amateur Brian Cakebread, now works at his club as a coach. Willie sits there facing the gold letters of his own name painted above the bar. It's a solid comfortable room, all rich dark browns and reds, with a restaurant section next to it that has those dark oak tables and chairs with anchors on the back that you get in Berni steak inns. 'There's that many people want to play now and they all think that with coaching they can turn pro,' says Willie. 'It's sad really but it gets Brian plenty of work. Considering he's not very well off or anything he probably earns fifty or sixty quid a week from coaching, which is nice for him. He can have a few more pounds on the horses. Like me.'

Willie's enjoyment of gambling goes beyond the mere equestrian. He'll gamble when he's playing golf, gamble when he's playing cards and he would gamble when he was playing snooker if he had the opportunity. Just a few years ago the top professionals still played money matches and Willie Thorne was known as one of the best money players in the game. Now we have entered the era of the Persil-white professional snooker player, and playing money matches is regarded as the equivalent of being the boy in the grimy grey shorts. Willie Thorne does still play for money but he doesn't let people know about it. 'I'll probably ring up and say I'll be there in half an hour or they'd have crowds there. I mean, it's not good for one's image, is it?' he asks

Willie Thorne behind the bar at his Snooker Centre in Leicester

puckishly. 'Gambling with a local player or whatever? I'd never do it at night when they'd get people in. I just go in the afternoons when it's half a dozen or so. I give them a big start as a pro but I still don't want people watching me if I get beat. It's not good, is it?'

He moves upstairs to show off the new top floor of the club. 'Rates Rebates. Sundry Debtors,' points a sign on the wall but Willie Thorne is not about to make any losses. The club has been built in what used to be, not a cinema, but a council rents and rates office. The new snooker room is pale and airy, the rich mahogany of the tables gleaming red in the sunlight that's so unexpectedly streaming into the room. Snooker is a game for night-time, for artificially lit rooms, brightened only by the excitement and applause of the audience. This sunny room may be Willie Thorne's living but the applause and the excitement provide his real motivation. He's extrovert and witty in private conversation, bold on the snooker table. A more retiring player like Terry Griffiths will get embarrassed just making flash shots in exhibition matches. Willie *loves* pulling off the spectacular ones and tells you he's made more 147 breaks than any other pro. He gets a real tingle from applause, even if he's just watching another sport.

'If I watch a rock group on television or anything like that — the golf when they're walking up the eighteenth and the crowd are giving them a standing ovation. I mean, I'm sitting there watching it and it gives me a tingle. I just love it, the applause. It's nice to have so many people wanting you to do something, and that's probably what made me realise I wanted to be a professional, whether it was snooker or whatever. But snooker was the only thing I was good at.'

That and running his club effortlessly, even when he's not there. When he is, he's affable to all the people he meets, answers endless phone calls with endless patience and moves things along quickly without ever seeming to be in a hurry — though you suspect he won't stay there very much longer today. Lunches are over and there are only a few people on the tables, but it'll fill up again later in the evening and in the meantime, there's always the Chinese from the hot food takeaway to swell Willie's coffers in the afternoons.

Just Another Game, Just Another Tournament

Up the moving staircase past the posters with Steve Davis's picture slapped on them, into the lift. It's like going into another world, a rarefied world cut off from the busy shops, the crowds of people in the precinct below. Inside Preston's Guild Hall, where the Coral UK championships are being held, there is silence as the audience focus their attention on the matches before them. It seems as if there are no windows into the outside world, only into the enclosed precinct below. Not for the first time it feels as if snooker is completely self-contained, existing independently of all those people outside.

It's not so of course. Millions will watch this tournament on the television; thousands are declaring their interest in its outcome by betting in the Coral's shop in the Guild Hall foyer. And within the snooker world this is the first tournament of the season that has felt really important. The Jameson's and the Lang's were both in their first year, with no traditions to fall back on. The State Express was a team tournament with a three frame format, and while there was tension it was not the same as this, where one man will be the winner at the end. Maybe it's just that this is the first major title that Steve Davis has defended. This was where it all started for him, this his first big championship win, right here in the Guild Hall a year ago.

It has the look of a railway station, the Guild Hall, how you imagine Brunel would have designed one of British Rail's best were he alive and well in 1982 and had hundreds of tons of concrete at his disposal. The roof is so high that the lights are almost lost in it, its huge squares of unvarnished wood supported by great concrete girders. This is a main line station with matches being shunted in and out like trains coming in on different tracks. In some cases the results are a little slow in arriving, in standard British Rail tradition.

There are two match tables in use simultaneously and only a black drape between them so you can hear the sounds of the other match, hear the special sounds of a Higgins crowd, the sudden roars, the excitement that seems to set up its own sound waves, the shouts of 'Come on Alex.' From the press box you can actually see the two matches. You can see the Hurricane making a century break in the time it takes Rex Williams, with his curious mixture of flamboyance and pomposity, to make thirteen.

The glass fronted press box is provided with all the phones, Coral UK pens and typewriters necessary to satisfy the needs of the snooker scribes, but Corals, with uncharacteristic lack of foresight, have omitted to soundproof the box, so every time the *Daily Mirror*'s Smithy (Terry Smith) enters or exits a low thundering noise shakes the auditorium. The Corals people came scurrying in halfway through the first week, measuring up the tables and floor for carpeting to deaden the sound.

Corals were one of the first sponsors to come into snooker in a big way and they pride themselves on their style, the buffet lunches they provide every day, the lavishly stocked bar. 'We like to think that we set the standard,' says their press officer Malcolm Palmer. 'We showed the other sponsors how to treat people. A lot of them just used to shove the press off into a little room by themselves.' Here, he implies, they are allowed to mingle with real people.

'We like to think we're all one big happy family,' says this man whose eyes are as steely as the frames of his spectacles and frost over whenever they light on a freelance member of the press rather than the correspondents for the Fleet Street dailies.

He is loath to disclose the figure that Corals spend on their hospitality, merely points out that when Corals began in snooker four years ago they were offering £12,000 in prize money and this year are offering £40,000. A more forthcoming member of Corals' management admits that a sponsor has to reckon on spending one hundred percent of the up-front money on the backup. As the up-front money in this case is the said £40,000 Corals are obviously throwing in a matching £40,000 in free food and drink, press facilities and the courtesy of the Coral girls.

Apart from a hospitable setting in which to do business, Corals are gaining a great deal of coverage from both television and the daily papers, and a sizeable amount of revenue from their betting shop in the foyer. 'We came into snooker because it's the same type of people watching it as bet in our shops,' says Malcolm Palmer. 'C2 men. Maybe a couple of C1 punters.' According to Mr Palmer the average

C2 man is going to come home at three o'clock on Sunday afternoon after a pint at the pub, slump into a chair and watch whatever's on the telly. This week that will be the Coral UK on BBC 1. Mr Palmer says it doesn't even matter who's playing. C2 man will just watch what's on.

C2 man is being ripped off by Corals, according to Geoff Lomas, who, in spite or perhaps because of his eleven years in the business, shares the ordinary punter's belief that the bookies can't lose. The odds that Corals offer are, he says, 'diabolic', a favourite word of his. He would like to see C2 men being offered a greater choice of odds as at the moment Corals have the monopoly at all the big snooker tournaments.

Geoff is also about to own a piece of Alex 'Hurricane' Higgins and Jimmy 'Whirlwind' White, a prospect that only a very brave man could look on with equanimity. Geoff Lomas is brave to the point of heroism, having allowed the Hurricane to live with him, in his own house, for two whole years. But he does not regard the prospect of being part of the maddest management team in snooker with equanimity. Geoff has managed Alex Higgins before and he doesn't want to repeat the experience.

He has, though, become a director of a new company, Sportsworld Ltd, and has to abide by these damn group votes. He's managed the Hurricane before and knows that the man is bloody unmanageable but the other directors — Harvey Lisberg, a rock impresario, Roy Speake, a cabaret agent, and Fred Summers, a director of Wigan Athletic Football Club — all reckon he's a very good commercial proposition. 'You sign Alex,' Geoff warns them, 'you sign Alex and you'll have the biggest enemy you could ever make in Del Simmonds. We don't need the aggravation just starting off.'

Del Simmonds is the Hurricane's current manager and a very powerful man in snooker. Having helped lead a players' revolt away from the world governing body, the WPBSA, he has now been given a highly paid job as the WPBSA official tournaments director. It's one of these jobs nobody's quite sure how to define but he gets thirteen grand a year for it anyway, though he's a director of a well-known snooker equipment firm in Bristol and manager to a whole horde of players so can't be said to need the money.

Bearded and genial, with a penchant for jokes and a great interest in people's lives and personalities, Del Simmonds is not unique in having an abrasive relationship with the Hurricane. The story currently circulating the press room is that he and the Hurricane actually had a fist fight a couple of nights before the tournament started. As the Hurricane doesn't actually have a written contract with Del Simmonds the general opinion is that he's going to be mad as fire that he can't break it.

The Hurricane in fact has come to the Sportsworld offices with his wife Lynn and sworn blind that he and Del have discussed the matter like civilised human beings. All that remains is for the public signing ceremony which is set for the first Wednesday of the Coral UK.

On the Saturday night before the tournament begins the Hurricane is on the phone to Barry Hearn, begging him to be his manager. On the Tuesday night he goes to the dog track. An acquaintance of his is waiting in the hospitality room to take him home. Because the Hurricane can't drive he has a whole support system of people to give him lifts. This one, who's an anxious-looking man disguising himself in a self-assured beige suit, says that his business is selling cane furniture but he also gets a lot of video tapes. 'They're not all legit,' he says meaningfully.

He tells a story about how he went to Sammy McIlroy's testimonial dinner the other night. He was dead drunk when he got home and didn't realise he'd left the front door open. It just so happened that he had a whole load of marijuana and cocaine lined up along the mantelpiece. Well, he's in bed, out for the count at five in the morning, when there's this light flashed in his face. A copper's standing there. The man says he thought it was a raid, but the copper just told him he'd left the door open. He thanks the copper. 'Oh shut it behind you when you go will you,' says he.

The man clearly likes mixing with the stars but he won't go to the dogs with the Hurricane any more because they always spend too much — his income doesn't match up to his star's suit. He has a few drinks at Corals' expense while he waits for the Hurricane to come back but after a while he gets bored and decides to go home to Manchester by himself. The Hurricane must find his own way back. That's the least of the Hurricane's worries. In the early hours of Wednesday morning, somewhere around 2.30 a.m., he decides he's not going to sign with Sportsworld after all.

At six o'clock on Wednesday evening the press assemble in the celebrity-covered restaurant, which has pictures of Johnny Mathis and Roger Whittaker and Ken Barlow of 'Coronation Street' on the walls. Harvey Lisberg, the rock promoter who is rumoured to have dreams of an empire in snooker, is conducting the proceedings. He is plump and pink and boyish and asks the press what they'd like to drink with extreme politeness.

The two wild boys of snooker sidle into the restaurant, as shy and nervous as two skittish racehorses being led on to the track. Jimmy White gives his goofy little grin except that it's not goofy any more now that they've straightened his teeth out. The Hurricane is pale, anxious to a point so far past hysteria that he has come full circle and is very still. He looks as if he might vomit on the plush red carpets of the Starlight restaurant.

Harvey Lisberg and Geoff Lomas regard their charges with smooth smiles whose blandness is pricked every so often with little hints of anxiety. Apart from that the two men seem to have little in common. Whenever Harvey appears at the tournament he is dressed in the smart but casual gear you would expect of a man who has promoted Manilow — snappy blazers, well-pressed slacks, open-necked shirts. Geoff, who in his private life appears to favour blue jeans, adheres strictly to snooker-type three piece suits.

Harvey of course is new to the game, an exotic import from the world of show business and as such regarded with much suspicion by the snooker cognoscenti, who think he's trying to take over the game, build himself a second fortune on a pile of broken cues, players and promoters. His first fortune consists of half of Kennedy Street Enterprises, one of the largest show business agents in Europe, who in their time have promoted Meatloaf, Abba, Queen, Doctor Hook, and 10CC as well as publishing a great deal of music.

Harvey is a winner. Always has been. Back in the sixties he spotted a little group he thought had potential. The singer was only fifteen at the time, but in his cheeky small boy face Harvey saw something, an image perhaps for the times. Harvey was about to take his final exams in accountancy when Herman's Hermits hit the number one spot. Even he couldn't study *and* manage a blockbusting group at the same time. He took the group. 'I've never known any failure,' he says. 'It's funny. Ever since I started I've been associated with tremendously successful acts. I've been so cushioned it's ridiculous.'

That's eighteen years of cushioning, the number of years Harvey's been at the top of the rock business. Now he may appear to be the suave sophisticated urban winner but behind the plump softness, the ever-ready smile, is the hard fiery brain of the competitive animal. Eighteen years of winning is very nice, but in the end it has to be admitted, it's just a little bit boring — which is why Harvey decided to

Geoff Lomas, a director of the new company Sportsworld Ltd

The Hurricane signs for Sportsworld.
Left to right: Geoff Lomas, Jimmy White, Alex Higgins, Harvey Lisberg

seek some excitement in his life, and why he has made his entrance into the green baize jungle.

He's a great sports fan anyway. The spectacle of competition, of people clawing and fighting their way to victory and discarding their broken victims on the way, clearly satisfies his own competitive urges. Sport is the way he thinks the world is, and snooker one of his favourite sports. He is a fan.

Being a fan has already helped him in rock music, because the people he likes have been people the public liked too. And he is one of Jimmy White's greatest fans. 'I don't think people realise how good Jimmy is,' he says. 'He's brilliant. I believe he's brilliant. I believe he's above everybody else. He's just got tremendous ability.' But that enthusiasm for his client's skill has not prevented him from completely changing him.

Harvey Lisberg is an unabashed image-maker. You walk into his office and he starts making you over before you're halfway across the room. People aren't fixed personalities to him. They're exciting raw material to experiment with, and if, as in Jimmy White's case, some material happens to be a bit rawer than others then that just means more happy hours he can spend pulling him apart and putting him back together again; giving him new teeth, new hair, French suits, silky shirts; making him look nice.

He's got Jimmy's image to the point where women want to mother him, he thinks. 'He's too rebellious for the women to love him yet,' he says, a comment which says at least as much about how he sees women as how he sees Jimmy White. 'It's a funny thing,' he says, 'Jimmy's just a good looking lad. I don't think he's got a strong sex image, just a bit of an Artful Dodger image at the moment, cheeky. He does cheeky things.'

He ponders Jimmy's image, weighs its essential pleasantness against the known facts of the White history. 'If you wanted a real image for Jimmy White it wouldn't have been *nice*. Not if you wanted to portray him as he really is. He's lovely on one side but he was involved in so many scandals before we met him. I just don't see that side. I only see the nice side. But he's been up to mischief in the past that's totally unbelievable.

'I've not seen it, fortunately. Everybody tells me how bad he is but I've never seen it. To me he's good as gold really. He's respectful, he's nice, he's courteous. "Thank you very much for coming over." Blind drunk, he doesn't know where he is, but he still says thank you. That's the side that I see.

'But he's got a lot of very strange — the word isn't "friends" — acquaintances he seems to mix with in the London area. They take him off on these rides and get up to no good generally. That's the side where people say, Oh he's terrible. You've got to watch him.'

He ponders his other, more famous client and sighs. The Hurricane's image is more than even he will tackle. The hair perhaps. It's a well known barometer of the Higgins psychic state — if it's plastered to his head it means he's probably come straight from some revelry to the snooker table without having a night's sleep in between. 'That's bad news,' says his manager. 'I'd *never* let the public know what I was doing last night.'

But it is clear that he wouldn't really know where to begin with the Hurricane. 'He astounds me. Higgins represents everything an image shouldn't be, yet it works. That is just an enigma. You can't work it out. It's like McEnroe. He's terribly popular however badly he behaves.' He shrugs. 'At least Jimmy really looks good. Oh I know he doesn't look after himself. You can take a horse to water but you can't make him drink. But I still think if he hadn't been looked after he would have been just . . . *diabolical*.'

It's a Lomas word so maybe he and Harvey Lisberg do think in the same way really. Geoff Lomas is a man who's done a lot of things. He's been a bookie, he's run a cosmetic surgery company; now he has a computer firm and one that makes 'spy in the pub' optics, as well as a number of other activities. But no matter how many other ways he has of making a living he is a snooker person, with snooker jostling along-side the red and white corpuscles in his bloodstream. He is a snooker person in a way that even some of the top stars are not. Terry Griffiths, for instance, while he might always play snooker, is apart from the seething inner life of the game whereas Jimmy White, say, or the Hurricane, are not. Snooker is a part of him, rather than he a part of snooker. He could, if he had to, walk away from it. Geoff Lomas, you suspect, would always be trying to sneak back in.

His current involvement with snooker has developed from a point in his life when he was at a fairly low ebb — bankrupt in fact. The company he ran was, he says, one of the first in the country to provide plastic surgery on the HP. A three week holiday in Majorca and a nosejob executed by a top European surgeon cost less than a few days in a private hospital here for the same operation, he discovered.

Unfortunately a number of people less scrupulous than he came into the same business, and it was these cosmetic cowboys that the formidable fangs of Esther Rantzen sank into. The resulting fall in the facelift market forced Geoff Lomas out of business.

He went into a local billiard hall one afternoon to while away a few of his unoccupied hours in a game of snooker, only to find that the larger proportion of his time was spent in waiting. 'Christ,' he thought. 'This is a business. This is a business to be in.'

From opening Potters in Salford — the club which is famous for having barred the Hurricane more times than any other club in Britain — he moved on to running pro-am tournaments. They attracted most of the players who were to become today's top stars. Doug Mountjoy used to sleep on the Lomas couch, Steve Davis helped paint the Lomas lounge and dig the Lomas garden. Lomas used to get Terry Griffiths exhibitions at £10 a night. 'I used to give them a good time,' he recalls. 'In those days Duggie Mountjoy was a packer in a factory. Terry Griffiths was a bloody bus conductor. John Virgo was out of work — most snooker players are out of work. Jimmy White was only fourteen at the time. They didn't know anything. Now all these people are big celebrities. They're welcome anywhere. In those days it used to be a struggle getting them into night clubs. You used to say, This is a friend of mine up from South Wales, and get them in for nothing. It was a completely new world to them.'

To Geoff Lomas, as well as being a game he loved, snooker provided a world he could function in, a world whose politics and intrigues he has often been involved in, a world which satisfied the most basic needs of his nature. As well as being a snooker person he is also a gambler, as indeed many snooker people are. 'I have gambled thousands and thousands of pounds on snooker,' he confides in his whispery voice. 'Plenty of times when I didn't have it. It's not good for the nerves if it's 9-7 in the other bloke's favour and you've got to find two grand if your man loses.' His voice hushes even more impressively than usual. 'And the two grand's *not there.*'

All Geoff Lomas's distinctive gifts as a narrator come into play as he tells the story of one of his most nervewracking gambles. His voice is pitched so low that you have to strain to hear it, as if he wants to convince the hearer that what he is saying is profoundly dramatic and significant. This story, then, roller-coasters along like a series of crescendos played on muted instruments.

'I'd backed Alex against Patsy Fagan for 3,000 quid, giving Fagan a seven start. Alex was a certainty. He *could not lose*. And at that time, a good few years ago now, (before he got married), he was playing out of his mind. We went down to London, the group of us who'd made the bet.'

He now launches into a discussion of the odds being offered on the bet. In his opinion the odds were extremely generous — evens on a player who *could not lose*. For the £3,000 investment he would receive a matching £3,000, a total of £6,000. Had he himself been making the bet, taking into consideration that here was a player who could not lose and who was playing out of his mind as well, he would have had to offer only three to one on, in which case he would only take home £4,000. Still, the second rule of the gambler is not to turn down gift odds. The first is not to assume you've won until you have.

'Alex turned up *absolutely legless*. With a gipsy bird with bloody big gold earrings and one of these bandannas round her head. All ringlets, her hair down to here and one of these kaftan things on. Stoned to the world and Alex was the same. Tickets were going for £20 each on the black market and he's legless.

'It's over two nights and all through the first night's match he's got his bird sat on his knee. And the referee's nudging him and saying, "Alex."

"What? Eh?"

'It should have been ten-nil that night for Alex. The match could have been over. We'd have had the money and been back to Manchester.

'We sobered him up the following day. We made a mistake because we said, "You're not drinking." And he had the shakes. That was a mistake that we made by not letting him have a drink. And he lost by the odd frame. Really that was 6,000 quid that the booze cost us.'

His sigh stretches back across the years to that day of loss yet Geoff Lomas is an inveterate gambler. Why else is he in a company with the Hurricane and Jimmy White? Jimmy, for all his genius, is one of the biggest gambles around in snooker. Watching him move around the table you could think that snooker was an easy game. Jimmy can slam them in as hard as anybody but he can whisper them in, stroke them in, joyfully send them rattling off three cushions before they roll in, flourish them in with the panache of a magician. He's as fast as the wild Hurricane was ten years ago, like the Hurricane and yet not like him, like no-one else in snooker. If watching Steve Davis is like watching a snooker computer, watching Jimmy — as with the Hurricane — is like watching a wild snooker animal whose cue is just another part of his body, who looks at the balls and instinctively knows what he can make his prey do. Jimmy doesn't have the Hurricane's electrifying unpredictability, that sense of danger he carries with him, as if anything could happen, as if he will strip away the civilised surface of the game and reveal the ferocious currents swirling around beneath. With Jimmy the excitement comes from his virtuosity, the astonishingly prodigious gifts that seem to him to be as natural as breathing. When Alex pulls off the impossible it is always astounding. You are always aware of the achievement that has just been made. Jimmy pulls off the impossible and makes it look easy.

But for all his flair, his potential he is still a risk. Really he's a roaring boy, young and irresponsible. Winning at the highest level requires more than skill. It requires an emotional discipline that Jimmy White may not even understand yet, still less possess. He's an unknown quantity for Lisberg and Lomas. They know he can play snooker as well as anyone in the world. But they don't know whether he can win as well.

That question is the one underlying the whole tournament. Steve Davis, after a year of winning, is surely due for a loss in a major and Jimmy White looks the only one capable of doing it. Twice in the past month he has inflicted defeats on the Invincible, at the Lang's Supreme Scottish Masters in Glasgow and more recently in the Northern Ireland Classic, where he was nine-seven down and then charged off with the next four frames to take the title from right under Steve Davis's nose. If he can do it a third time Steve Davis's reputation is going to take a hard knock.

That of course would please many of the players. Steve Davis is the hate factor built into the snooker circuit and it is not uncommon to see little groups of his fellow players watching his matches and laughing aloud whenever he misses a ball. The effect of his domination of the game has been destructive to many others, whose confidence has been leeched from them by Davis and his surgical skills. Ex-World Champions are particularly susceptible and some of them are playing worse snooker now than they have done for many years.

Cliff Thorburn formerly snooker's hard man and a player of relentless patience, plays now like a lost soul, a man being sucked down into some awful quicksand. He goes out in his first match to Tony Meo. The Hurricane has recently completed a head-to-head tour of Scotland with Steve Davis, where the atmosphere became so acrimonious that the players were barging each other out of the way to get to the table and rules had to be laid down to prevent it from becoming a farce. The Hurricane had to stay in his seat till the Invincible had played his shot *and* sat down before he was allowed on to the table. As he also lost more than he won the Hurricane's confidence is low and he too goes out to Tony Meo in what is said to be his worst ever performance in a major championship. He is generous to 'the kid', but he looks wan and ill.

It's up to Jimmy then. He's started off the tournament with a flurry of publicity in the papers and a dirty stain all down the white suit that Lichfield took his picture in. He then nearly loses to Ray Reardon, taking the match only on the last frame. But his semi-final against Steve Davis is being built up as the match of the championship, because there *is* that possibility that he might vanquish the Invincible. And these two losses in a row have put more pressure on Steve Davis than he has had for a long time. It's a grudge match, a needle match, a match that finally gets people interested in Steve Davis again, especially when Jimmy expresses the opinion in print that Steve isn't actually the best player in the world and that there are five or six players who're all of equal ability and who can all beat each other on the day.

The night before Jimmy goes on the telly to be interviewed by David Vine. After all the excitement the match has generated he nonplusses Mr Vine by his nonchalance. Even if he beats Steve Davis he still hasn't won the tournament and that's what counts, he says. David Vine comes as close to irony as a man of his palpable blandness can. 'Just another game?' he says. 'Yes, just another game.'

A look of shock flits across the knowing face of the interviewer. 'Just another tournament?' he gasps.

'Yes,' shrugs Jimmy. 'Just another tournament.'

Steve Davis doesn't think so. His manager says he's all wound up for this match. Steve himself looks pale and tired. His dad says he's really been building himself up for the tournament. They head for the door. 'We're ready,' says Barry Hearn, exulting in the prospect of the battle to come. 'We're *hot*.'

The match turns out to be more painful for Jimmy White than anyone could ever have predicted. As Steve powers ahead, frame after frame, Jimmy sips at his drink, lights up numberless cigarettes, wipes his cue, anything rather than watch. He gazes round the Guild Hall in desperation but from every pillar in the hall the face of Steve Davis, advertising his column in the *Daily Star,* looks implacably down at him.

Up in the press room the one-sidedness of the match is turning it into a joke. 'He's beginning to believe he's the best player in the world,' says Smithy. 'Well if people keep telling you you're the best I suppose you do eventually believe it,' says Ted Corbett of the *Star*. He glances down at the scoreboard. Six-nil. 'I suppose there's even some evidence of it,' he says. Clive Everton is looking thoughtful. He is the game's leading commentator, owner and editor of *Snooker Scene* magazine, owner of the news agency that covers the major part of snooker reporting in this country, and possessed of an encyclopaedic knowledge of snooker facts and history. 'It's how you sit out this game that counts,' he says. 'You can get mesmerised by the other fellow. You can feel so low that when you come to the table you're hoping there's nothing on so that you can't make a fool of yourself.'

As the score creeps inexorably upwards, with not a frame on the board for Jimmy White, the younger player sits huddled up against the big green and red Corals sign. He looks just like a little boy.

Whitewash, say the papers the following day. Jimmy has fled into the night but the battle of the managers is not over yet. Barry Hearn takes the opportunity to voice his opinion of Sportsworld. It is not complimentary. Steve Davis does too. What he thinks isn't complimentary either. Geoff Lomas is unrepentant. He is indignant at the Invincible's reference to 'cheap newspaper articles.'

'Nothing to do with us,' he says in an explosive whisper. 'We can't tell the *Sun* what to print.' He resents the Davis opinion that Sportsworld have put too much pressure on Jimmy White and ascribes it to the World Champion's pique at Jimmy for saying he's not the best player in the world. 'Davis has never been criticised like that before,' says Geoff drily and then shrugs. 'It could have gone nine-nil the other way you know. The first four frames Jimmy should have won. Steve Davis couldn't pot a ball . . .' The table . . . The shaved cloth . . . what might have been.

The following night Terry Griffiths despatches Tony Meo so speedily in the evening session that he and Dennis Taylor agree to play a short exhibition match. Shot after magic shot flows from Terry's cue. It's subtle and smooth and powerful all at once.

'Who do you think you are?' says Dennis Taylor. 'Steve Davis?'

'He's better than that,' shouts someone in the crowd.

Dennis gives a wry smile, and raises his eyebrows. His next shot is an easy one but he misses it.

'Are you Jimmy White?' asks another member of the audience.

* * *

Terry Griffiths is one of the few people in the Preston Guild Hall who believes he can beat Steve Davis. He feels relaxed now, for the first time in almost a year. He takes the first frame of the final, but in the second one he misses an easy shot after a break of only fifteen. 'This is the losing shot,' says Clive Everton. 'Oh dear, there goes my four quid,' says Ted Corbett, and with it apparently goes Terry Griffiths' confidence. Steve Davis makes a break of eighty-seven to even the score and after that the Welshman just never seems to have a chance.

It seems almost incomprehensible that one missed opportunity so early on can turn a match, but then this is the game you have to sit out. This is snooker and this is Steve Davis and once he gets that first frame on the board he becomes so physically relaxed that his arms are dangling loosely down over the arms of his chair as he waits for the table to be re-set. Unlike the other players Steve Davis takes every chance he's offered and if the chances aren't there he waits till they are. He'll patiently play a long bout of safety till the table looks the way he likes it and only then will he embark on the flawless potting that underpins his game.

'Steve's game *is* potting,' says Geoff Lomas. 'He won't admit that but he's as good a potter as Jimmy White, as Alex Higgins, because he never misses. He'll not go for the pot unless he's one hundred percent certain.' It's not the usual view of Steve Davis's game but it's certainly true that Steve is as fearless a potter as the more flamboyant pair. When he goes for a shot he is sure in his own mind that he is going to get it. His lack of doubt has made him a champion but it has often needled his opponents — who think he's arrogant — and it appears to alienate part of his audience, the part that writes him off as a snooker machine. It's perhaps a symptom of the times that people can find perfection boring. We're so used to looking in sport for the stress points, the characteristics that make one person win and another lose. We wait for McEnroe to throw a tantrum, for Nicklaus's hand to tremble on the putter. We like it when the human machine breaks down, pore over its workings then. Steve Davis comes as close to perfection probably as any sportsman has ever done, is cool, competitive, patient, accurate, courageous, skilful, intelligent. And it is still not enough. People want the machine to break down.

It is not about to in this tournament. Steve finishes the day twelve-three ahead. The Davis camp is jubilant. Barry Hearn's face is flushed with excitement as he leaves the Guild Hall. Later in the bar of the big hotel in Preston where many of the players are staying, he and his wife Susan play a game of pool with another couple. It's a curious parody of the game we have just been watching. Smaller table, bigger balls, enormous pockets, ordinary players. More than anything it demonstrates the supreme skill of the professional players we have seen, the strenuous demands put upon them by competitive snooker. Barry Hearn halts mid-shot as his wife issues instructions. 'How can I play with all this verbal?' he asks tragically. 'Do they have this in the world championships or what?' His ebullience spills over to embrace all the people sitting around in little groups, drinking quietly. Standing up and waving his arms about enthusiastically he launches into a football chant. 'Twelve-three, twelve-three, twelve-three . . .' He pauses momentarily for breath. 'And what is it going to be tomorrow? Sixteen-three, sixteen-three . . .'

It is. And right now you wonder, how long can this go on? Steve Davis holds the golden cup aloft. He even puts the lid on his head so that the photographers can get their daft picture for the morning editions, same as he did last year. It's as if snooker has got into a tape loop and this scene is just going to go on repeating itself. No-one else will ever win again. It will always be Steve Davis standing there holding the trophy, putting the lid on his head, winning and winning and winning . . .

Alex Higgins

The Hurricane Goes to Hospital

Steve Davis has hardly got his bright new trophy through the door of the family home in Plumstead when the Hurricane hits the headlines. Phase one of the Higgins rehabilitation programme has begun.

Alex, say his new managers, is in a state of exhaustion, and they book him into a posh nursing home in Rochdale for a rest. He's burnt himself out, they say, after years of hotels and travelling and bad food and too much pressure. He needs to get away from snooker and all the

Alex 'Hurricane' Higgins

people making too many demands on him. All the people except the press, that is. The one thing they don't think he needs a break from is publicity.

On the principle that any publicity is good publicity the Hurricane gets a good spread in the papers, but the press are less discreet than the Sportsworld management team and allege that he has landed in this nursing home in Rochdale for two reasons — physical exhaustion, yes, but from the strain of lifting his vodka glass to his lips too often; and an acute attack of Davis-itis. He is still the most popular player in the game but the Hurricane can no longer think of himself as the best. Like the other top players he has lost too often and too badly to Steve Davis. The pain of that loss has eaten into him physically as well as mentally and he's lost more than a stone in weight.

He is, says the *Mirror*'s Noreen Taylor, 'a small bewildered boy wondering what has gone wrong with his world.'

It seems he will stay bewildered. There is another visit to hospital in February, more defeats by Steve Davis. Who knows how many more glasses of vodka? There are rows in clubs, rows at exhibitions, a series of lacklustre performances on the table. And it seems so sad that this man, who through his snooker has shown so many people that it is possible to live dangerously, should be so desperate, so very low in hope. 'Three years,' says one of the tour's regular journalists. 'I can't see Alex being alive in three years.'

January 1982:
The Lada Classic

A Small Piece of Sporting Perfection

Ted Corbett of the *Daily Star* is in the bar of Oldham Civic Centre, where the Lada Classic is being held. The bar is a standard journalistic haunt, not only for the cold hard mental stimulus of the alcohol that can be consumed there but also for the fact that people talk in bars.

Ted is conducting his customary thorough research into the scandals, love affairs and political machinations that underpin the game of snooker.

In the midst of his investigations, however, Smithy of the *Daily Mirror* comes bursting into the bar in his usual subtle fashion. The bar's foundations shake. Smithy says that something interesting is actually happening on the table for a change — in fact, something special. Steve Davis could be on target for the first televised 147 maximum break. Plenty of players have done maximums in practice, but nobody's ever done it in serious competition on the telly. John Spencer nearly did it once in the Holsten Lager tournament three years ago. That's to say, he did the 147, but the cameramen were too busy having their tea break to record it for posterity.

If you were to nominate a player to achieve the first 147 break on telly it would have to be Steve Davis, who doesn't immediately appear to be one of your flash players but who does seem to function best in front of an audience of several million people. He's dominated the game in such a momentous way that it seems only justice he should make the first TV maximum. But this week? After he's been halfway round the world and back? Through the tortuousness of negotiations with Eddie Charlton in Australia and then over to the mad heart of the American Dream, Las Vegas?

Conquering jetlag is perhaps a minor achievement after his year of conquering the might of the snooker world, but to conquer it so completely? He makes the first fourteen reds and blacks seem easy. He's into the colours now and he realises that he's got a chance of the maximum but he can't let himself think too much about that. He's got the worst angle he possibly could on the yellow, has to screw back across the brown ball for green without touching the brown. Then he ends up with an awkward angle on the blue and has to bring the cue ball off three cushions for the pink. He fancies getting it but with so much at stake it's easy to miss.

The final black is the hardest one of all but he isn't as nervous as he thought he would be though his legs feel curiously wobbly. He dreamt about doing the maximum a few weeks ago so maybe he's been preparing himself mentally for this moment without even realising it. He'd thought he wouldn't be able to hold the cue but somehow everything falls into place for him, as it has done so often this past year.

'I wanted to jump up in the air but I didn't know what to do,' he says later, sipping at a glass of champagne. 'I shall remember it for a long long time. Very exciting,' and his voice is almost a whisper.

Steve Davis — a perfectionist in all things

The break, a mixture of precision and courage, is like a Steve Davis sonnet, summing up the man in the most economical way possible. If, in later years, people were to ask, 'What was Steve Davis like?' a video of the 147 would be the perfect remembrance of him. His performance at the beginning of the actual Lada final, though — against Terry Griffiths — is the very antithesis of what we all think Steve Davis is. It is Terry Griffiths who takes control, Terry Griffiths who looks consistent, Terry Griffiths who's leading eight-three by the final interval.

Terry Griffiths is within sight of achieving his overriding ambition for this year — to beat Steve Davis on the telly. He's one of the few players that the snooker world knows to be capable of beating the champion — 'and there are only a few that can beat him,' says Terry. Terry isn't the only one who wants Terry to beat Steve. The rest of the players, standing behind the psychological barrier that separates Steve from them, want him to. The public wants him to. Terry's been practising and preparing himself mentally and he knows he's getting closer all the time. He desperately wants to beat Steve.

Only Steve isn't so keen on the idea. He comes back after the interval and starts pulling the frames back. He's enjoying himself. We haven't seen these impressive fighting qualities from him before because he hasn't been behind before, and Terry Griffiths is the only spectator in the hall who's not enjoying the sight. Steve takes him not only to a deciding frame but to the final black in that frame. He gets first shot at it but hits it just too hard and the ball rockets back out of the pocket.

The tournament has come down to a single shot, and one which Terry Griffiths has been practising without success all week. He too must have been preparing mentally for this moment without realising it for he sinks the final black and takes the Lada title. And beats the Invincible on TV. 'Eight-three up and I almost bloody lost,' he says later. 'Oh that was terrible. It's going to take me three days to get over this and I won. I'm a wreck, a wreck.'

Barry Hearn says that Terry deserved to win and he deserves some recognition. He says to Terry's dad that he's very pleased for him, and he is. He's just not to make a habit of it though, adds Barry.

And Terry gets a case of Mumm champagne as the *Observer* Sports Personality of the Week because it's the first time Steve Davis has been beaten on nationwide television for two years.

But if there's one enduring memory of the Lada Classic it's not that final black. It's not even Steve Davis's final gutsy fightback. It will always be that small piece of sporting perfection, the 147 break.

Steve Hasn't Got a Heart

At the Arena it's Robin Cousins in 'Holiday on Ice'. Next door at the Wembley Conference Centre it's the Benson and Hedges Snooker Masters. Sport as performance art in both. While film stars today have become like yesterday's tycoons — living in fortresses, driving in armoured cars and never going anywhere unless surrounded by a platoon of bodyguards — today's sportsmen are like yesterday's film stars. They're paid fabulous sums for their performance, the press record their opinions on all sorts of things outside their area of expertise — or in other words, all sorts of things they know nothing about — and they manage to maintain a lifestyle beyond that of their audiences while still being available to make personal appearances and sign autographs.

Wembley Conference Centre is the perfect setting for performers in sport, these snooker players whose struggle for supremacy creates its own fierce drama, as interesting for its intensity of human emotion as any play or movie. It's like a theatre, all burgherish comfort out front where the public are to be amused, with its wide glass-fronted foyer, dark-walled corridors hushed with thick carpet, cocoon-like bars and cloakrooms and snack stands. Backstage where the performers are — be they sportsmen or entertainers or indeed high-powered business men — it's bare and brightly lit. Like a theatre there's a feeling back here of work going on, of efforts being made to produce something. The magic of the spectacle the audience will see does not just materialise.

Snooker *is* theatre — the elegant costumes, more formal than the clothes the performers would wear in everyday life, the gracious manners, as stylised in their way as dramatic speeches where people's words have a beginning, a middle and an end. Most of all snooker shares with theatre the excitement of the live event. It's a high risk business where people stand or fall on what they can produce on the night, and its most satisfying performers are those who can impose their will on the proceedings, dominate with their character as much as their skill.

In snooker, unlike theatre, you get a result. You're supposed to be able to tell who's best by who wins. But the real champions can win even when they're not playing at their best. Even when their opponent should be able to beat them, somehow, just by force of their character and their will, they manage to dictate what happens. The element of will in the success of a champion is difficult to quantify, but it's there all right and often can be the vital factor when two players of equal skill meet.

The field for the Benson and Hedges Masters is composed almost entirely of people who have proved they have the will that makes a champion. Half are world professional champions — Steve Davis, Terry Griffiths, Cliff Thorburn, Ray Reardon, Alex Higgins and John Spencer — another quarter world amateur champions — David Taylor, Doug Mountjoy and Jimmy White. The final invitations have gone to three great fighters — Eddie Charlton, Dennis Taylor and Tony Meo.

But the will to win is not a constant. Supporters of one particular player always want him to win and can't understand when he doesn't seem to share their desire. It's not that players don't want to win, but sometimes the effort of transmuting desire into the positive will to win is too great. Sometimes the desire is so great that it takes over completely, filling the place where will, the hard channelling of desire, should be.

Is that what has happened to Cliff Thorburn, the 1980 World Champion? Is that why he has failed in tournament after tournament to produce his true form — because he so badly wants to win? These days he never seems convinced that he is capable of it and accordingly he never is. His opponent is Tony Meo who has no such doubts and wins every frame they play, five in a row, with a total clearance of 136 in the third.

It's sad to see a champion going down, they say in the press room, though Clive Everton is more acerbic. 'The score wasn't as close as it looked,' he says.

Tony Meo joins the three dominant personalities of the game in the semis. In the quarter finals Terry Griffiths has beaten Ray Reardon, the Hurricane has beaten Eddie Charlton, and Steve Davis won against Doug Mountjoy in a repeat of last year's world final that draws the biggest audience of the tournament. The Welshman is not at his best but even so Steve Davis makes it look almost like a practice session.

Eddie Charlton

Doug Mountjoy

Where Alex Higgins in his greatest matches raises the atmosphere in such an extraordinary way that his opponent raises his own game, Steve Davis at his best drains the atmosphere of tension. He makes it look as if he will never miss a ball, never tire in his relentless pursuit of perfect position. Where the Hurricane can inspire his opponents — a self-destructive quality if ever there was one — Steve Davis numbs his. They forget that they're good players too.

Without ever hurrying Steve Davis gets to three-nil in no time against his management partner Tony Meo. Tony almost has a chance to make a high break in the fourth frame, but just as he is about to take his next shot on twenty-two, a child cries and a little voice is heard. 'I'm tired. I want to go to bed.' Tony laughs along with the rest of the audience — he's got a little baby of his own at home after all — but he misses his next red and lets Steve Davis in. Steve doesn't need two chances. Four-nil. Five-nil.

There's often a point in a match, when the losing player gets just about as far down as he can go. Touching rock bottom releases him and gives him the impetus to move upwards again. At five-nil Tony Meo has reached that point. 'When you get that far behind you don't give up, but you think, what's the difference now? You might as well have a go, seeing nothing else is working' he says and does.

He pulls one frame back with the aid of a spectacular fluke that rolls right round the cushions like the ball in a bagatelle game. Even Steve Davis laughs. He is not quite so amused when Tony wins a second frame, and by the third, when he leaves an opening from which Tony wins the frame, he is looking determinedly nonchalant. His alter ego comes to his rescue, the mythical Steve Davis who never misses a shot and doesn't even possess sweat glands. Steve often plays as if he's acting the part of that other Steve Davis, and he takes the role on now, looking deliberately insouciant as Tony Meo bustles round the table.

Wembley audiences love a fightback and somehow their fervent desire seems to breathe new inspiration into the losing player, for this venue has been the scene of some remarkable turnarounds. Kirk Stevens went home for a sleep during last year's semis with his compatriot Cliff Thorburn leading the Hurricane five-one. By the time he woke up several hours later Cliff had just lost six-five. That same year Terry Griffiths fought back to win by one frame after trailing two-five to John Spencer. The belief in today's audience that Tony Meo can turn this match around is so strong you can almost see it dancing in the motes of dust in the air. You can hear it. 'Come on my son,' the Londoners are shouting, though surely they can't all lay claim to the paternity of the players.

Tony Meo has now taken four frames in a row and is only one frame behind Steve Davis. The Invincible is the one under pressure now. He has, his opponent notes, begun to get nervous. 'It's happened to me,' says Tony wryly. 'They come back at you. It's a horrible feeling.' But unlike other players, who are at their worst under pressure, Steve Davis is at his best. The desire to win freezes in those marble veins and solidifies into will. It seems inevitable that if one of these players makes a mistake in this crucial frame it will be Tony Meo. Obligingly he pots the cue ball, which allows Steve Davis to make a break of forty. His next visit to the table is a seventy-five clearance, which wins him the frame and the match.

He looks relieved as he heads down Wembley's brightly-lit corridors to the press room. 'Steve found a little bit of heart and it nearly cost him,' says one of the Romford people behind him. His companion snorts. 'Steve hasn't got a heart. It's well known.'

Steve's manager Barry Hearn claps him on the shoulder in relief. *He* is a man commonly presumed to have no heart but he says his heart was going. It's as if he is the repository for all Steve's emotions for the duration of the match, for he shows more signs of agitation than the player. 'You get used to people coming back,' says Steve insouciantly. 'You get used to coming back yourself. Tony had nothing to lose and started to play the way he can. But I've been in that situation so many times. You just try a bit harder and pull yourself together. I wasn't panicking.'

'Did you feel slightly different against a stable mate?' someone asks him. 'No,' he says, in flat tones. Barry Hearn laughs out loud. 'I knew he was going to say that.' There is not a flicker on the champion's face. 'You don't give chances away,' he says. 'If I beat him six-nil I'm much more on top next time I play him.'

'I think he took the chances rather than Steve let him have them,' says Barry Hearn. 'But you can't give the World Champion a five-nil start and expect to win.' Barry is standing on the outside of the group of press, but his identification with his charge is so strong it's almost as if he were in the centre of the group looking after Steve. His concern goes beyond the merely managerial. He's like a boxing second waiting with the damp cloth to dab at his fighter's eye, the towelling dressing gown to throw protectively round his shoulders.

He has managerial duties too towards Tony Meo, though. This is the young fighter he's got to build up, push before the press, get a name for. 'It would have been nice for a great player if Tony had won,' he says with that graciousness that is clearly natural to him and yet which always comes as something of a surprise, just because he has the reputation for being hard and ruthless. The cynical would say, of course, that he had nothing to lose if either of his clients had won, and he certainly doesn't misuse press attention by being modest about his players. Tony, he says, is going to be number two in the world, and very soon. There's a gap between Steve and the rest of the players and then another gap between Tony and Terry Griffiths and the rest.

'Alex could prove me wrong tonight,' he adds. 'But I think six-four on Terry Griffiths is a bloody good bet.'

Alex can always prove people wrong and that is his fascination. That night he is trailing one-four to Terry Griffiths by the interval. He's standing waiting in the stairwell to go on before the second half, a frail pale figure, beleagured. He looks as if everything's falling away from him, in his life as in his body, which looks thinner than ever and he's always thin. People passing ask him how he is. 'Alive,' he says but he hardly looks it.

And yet even when he's below par, as he is now, he is still capable of making up a three-frame deficit. Three frames? That's nothing compared to some of the leads he's made up. It's as if at some point during a match he moves from being Alex Higgins to being the Hurricane. He's rolling, the crowd are with him, he carries them with him. But it's not the demonstration of power that his soubriquet would suggest. If he resembles any natural phenomenon it really isn't the Hurricane sweeping everything before it by force. It's an electrical storm, incandescent, erratic, ripping the air apart in unpredictable bursts. Other players channel their desire to win into will but the Hurricane goes beyond that. His desire becomes will in the white heat of inspiration.

Any player who chooses inspiration as his protection, the quality he relies on most when he is threatened, is a gambler, a real high-roller, and of course that's why the public love the Hurricane. He conducts his professional life in a way most of us would consider too dangerous just playing Monopoly. With him it's for real. But when you do base your whole working practice on taking risks you have to accept the fact that they might not come off.

Tonight they don't. The Hurricane pulls one frame back, then another, but he does it by hard graft, by sheer dogged will. He and the audience are waiting for inspiration to take over but it remains elusive. Some of his individual shots are quite brilliant but for the most part he is chipping out small breaks by his standards — twenty-seven, twenty-one. He looks paler and paler under the big canopy of light. For once he makes snooker look like work as he progresses to four-five with a sixty-nine break.

A miscue in the following frame produces one of those Higgins dramatic interludes that are becoming more and more common as his game declines. He is fouled for a jump shot, in accordance with the rules, but not in accordance with his idea of what the rules should be. In fact many of the players theoretically are on his side. The rule was devised to prevent players deliberately using jump shots to get out of snookers. As the Hurricane's was entirely unintentional and not to his advantage he feels it's wrong he should be penalised further by having a foul declared against him. The argument over the rule goes on a long time during the match, and when Terry Griffiths finally wins the frame, and with it the match, continues down into the press room, where the Hurricane sits obsessively discussing the incident and not the loss of his title.

There will be a new Masters Champion then. Terry Griffiths won here in 1980, but this is the one title Steve Davis hasn't won — he went out in a shock first round defeat to Perrie Mans last year — and he is determined to take it to complete his unique feat of having won every major tournament in one year. He isn't playing as well as he has in the past, though his not-quite-best form is still awesome in its intelligence and control.

The match is hard fought and although Steve Davis finishes the afternoon session five-three ahead, Terry Griffiths pulls back in the evening to just one frame behind, five-six. In the players' hospitality room Tony Meo is watching the action on television, a drink in his hand. Well you have to do something with your hands. It's good exercise for the muscles. Tony's got to wait till the end of the evening session to see whether his break of 136 against Cliff Thorburn still stands as the highest of the tournament, so he has several hours of muscle exercise ahead. It's by way of a celebration for him here anyway. His fightback against Steve Davis yesterday has made him the toast of the tournament. People keep coming up and telling him what a great match it was. The best television he's seen for years, says one man. 'That's nice,' says Tony with his big soft shiny-eyed smile. 'Does that mean I'll get more money?' The man grins. 'Oh, at least twenty-five percent.' 'I'll get a tenner instead of £7.50, then,' says Tony. His snooker's better than his arithmetic.

The red-flocked walls of the hospitality room make it look tinier even than it is. It almost overflows when Jimmy White comes in showing off a new suit. They all finger the material and tell him how fine it is and yeah, it's a really good cut. Tony gazes at the television screen as if staring might put Steve Davis off and prevent him from equalling Tony's 136. He really wants that Golden Award for the highest break.

It would take more than mere thought transference to deflect the World Champion from his course. He's missed a lot of shots that he might have got and, as he did against Tony, is almost beginning to look as if he might be capable of human error, but to those watching there just seems no way he can lose. It seems unfair to Terry Griffiths, who is giving him such a hard fight. It seems more than generous to Steve Davis himself, who has made more faults in this tournament than in any other major televised one we have seen him in so far. But his will is so strong it commands belief from the spectators. In the twelfth frame, seeking good position on the next red, he goes for a long pink instead of the safe and available black. 'God he's so brave,' says Tony Meo with a kind of shocked admiration. 'I wouldn't have gone for that pink. I'd have potted the black. That was really brave.'

It's only the interval but in the press room many of the journalists are already writing their 'Steve Davis wins' stories. They've done it so often it's easy — just hard to write well. Desmond Lynam's on the phone, giving over copy about 'Steve Davis's first Masters title.' It's only seven-five in a best of seventeen frame match. Why are they all so sure? Terry Griffiths is a great player too. Might he not pull something out of the bag? Well, he might, but inevitably you feel that whatever Terry did Steve Davis would be ready.

At least the audience get excited when he wins. They whoop and cheer, and when the Benson and Hedges promotions girls come simpering in for the presentation ceremony they all break into wolf whistles. 'Go on Steve,' says some comic in the crowd. 'Take your pick.'

Somehow the organisers manage to start the presentation without Terry Griffiths who's gone off to the toilet. When he comes back he sits looking all around, as if this is nothing to do with him. Steve is loaded with a garland of flowers, Waterford crystal, champagne and a cheque for £8,000, but the flowers that Terry's given drip water all down him. Peter West interviews Steve briefly for television and then turns to Terry. 'I always think it's nice on these sporting occasions when the loser says something,' he says with his urbane smile. Terry looks mischievous. 'Well, I'm not going to say anything,' he says firmly.

Tony Meo, the other London boy, gets a great cheer when he comes on, a grey fedora pulled over his eyes at a most gangsterish angle. He struts over to receive his award for the highest break and the audience look as pleased as he does himself.

They are loud and long in their applause for everyone. Just as theatre has its ritual of bows and curtain calls to end the performance and allow the audience to express their participation in it, so the Wembley audience welcomes the chance to applaud the players. It's a sign that they themselves have been there, that they've really seen the great players. And by god it's saying that they're a bloody good audience too.

Steve Davis approves of them anyway. 'It's very nice to win in London,' he says. 'When Mountjoy won it I stood up and cheered with everyone else when he potted the pink.' He looks thoughtful. 'I've come a long way.'

Terry Griffiths is over in a corner wishing he was young again so that he could always enjoy his snooker, the way Steve does. But what comes across from Steve's own words is not enjoyment, but the sternness, the discipline of his will. By his own high standards he has not been playing well, but he has still won, and that is one of the marks of a great champion. 'I wasn't really hitting the balls too well. I was getting, not lethargic, but just not really playing the game. The concentration was there. It was the pressure. What I tried to do was gee myself up inside. I really try and say, Go. Sometimes you kid yourself you're playing well. That's almost as good as playing well actually,' says the champion without a heart, who doesn't want to talk about snooker anyway. He wants to talk about learning the piano instead. He doesn't know the words to any London songs so he'll be able to play the piano at parties instead. 'I'm going to enjoy the scales,' says the most inexorable worker at the game that modern snooker has known. 'That's what I'll really like.'

Robotoid Man Meets the Late Developer

The Assembly Rooms in Derby are deserted. It's ten o'clock on Sunday morning and the Yamaha Organs final will be played here this afternoon, but for the moment there are only a few cleaners picking up Saturday night's fag ends and crisp packets, and the bar manager trundling through behind a great metal trolley laden with dirty glasses. And there's Terry Griffiths' dad wandering disconsolately in search of a cup of tea while his son practises.

Terry's dad's name is Martin but no-one ever calls him that. He's 'Pops' to everyone, from Terry himself to the other players to the journalists who're regularly on the snooker tour. He was a steelworker for forty-eight years but retired at sixty-three through ill health and you can still hear the breath wheezing in his chest now. He's not as slim as he once was and he doesn't get around so easily any more but he loves watching snooker. 'I go up the local billiard hall every night,' he says. 'I have a cup of tea, have a chat, but I never play. I still like to watch the local league. It's rubbish after the big tournaments but I enjoy myself there. And it's always given me great pleasure going round with Terry too, even when he was a young boy. It gives you great pleasure to see him rise from nothing.'

Inside the hall Terry Griffiths is patiently practising away to rows and rows of seats with no-one in them. The big lamp over the table is on and the house lights, but none of the lamps in the futuristic white lighting grid, so the theatre looks darker than usual, and colder too, as if the absence of an audience takes away some vital element in maintaining the temperature of the place. The only sound is the methodical crack of the cue as it hits the white ball and the gentle swish as the balls drop into the pockets. It's interesting how fluent and natural all the players look when they're practising. You watch them in a match and they're twitching with nerves, their bodies are tense, they look as if they'd like to be a million miles away, anywhere but at this mild green table where the balls are like bombs ready to blow up in their faces. But when they're practising, they move round the table with ease; they seem in command, they display their virtuosity with the grace of animals moving in their natural environment.

The morning is still grey when Terry Griffiths finishes practising, as if it can't quite make up its mind to break into a new day. Steve Davis doesn't arrive with his dad till twelve-forty. He's only got time for half-an-hour's practice and his dad's grumbling because he *will* not go to bed early. 'His mind's that active that he can't sleep,' says Bill Davis. Steve's manager Barry Hearn says *he* goes to sleep late but Steve's ridiculous. He was up till three last night watching video films. He and Bill go in together to watch the final but Barry stays near the door so he can be free to make little business trips out to the bar. Bill clambers up the back clutching a plastic tumbler of beer in one hand and his customary cigar in the other.

★ ★ ★

Steve Davis and Terry Griffiths — two great players but not necessarily a great match, as the Coral UK proved. Despite press reports to the contrary there aren't that many great players around, nor great matches. There are lots of excellent ones and of course anyone who wants to become a professional at any sport has, at the least, to be very good at it. But greatness is rare and not something that can be turned on and off like a tap. The player may have a constant well of greatness within to draw on, but he can't always reach it when he wants it and certainly not when he needs it. You mightn't think so if you just listened to the TV commentators and didn't watch what was actually happening on the screen in front of you, or if you just read the ecstatic outpourings of the sporting press and didn't see them yawning as they wrote their stories. Ah, if only all play were superb, all victories fantastic, every night glorious and every finish a storming one.

But they're not, which is why one awaits the Yamaha final with some cynicism. There have been an awful lot of matches that were not great in this tournament. In fact there has, if the truth be known, been some terrible snooker here at Derby this week, including possibly the most ghastly match of the year, between Cliff Thorburn and Graham Miles. The format at Derby is a three-frame round robin, but the three frames of this match seemed never-ending and the idea of either of these players meeting anyone else was as entrancing a prospect as the idea of public toe-nail plucking. They took so long and missed so many balls and were so damn sporting about the whole thing that it became unbearable to watch and most of the press at least ceased to do so. The TV people had three slots that day but not even to fill up the time did they show the match.

Down in the depths of the building Clive Everton was steaming up and down the press room eating one chocolate biscuit after another and swearing that his head ached and his back ached, and this job made your brain like cottonwool. He glared balefully at the closed circuit television screen. 'I'm doing this for a living,' he said. 'But things like this make you feel as if there couldn't be any other reason for doing it. You feel as if you're part of some great commercial enterprise and this format is just another gimmick to bring in the punters. I can understand why so many journalists drink so much.'

The format has been unpopular with just about everybody except the punters. The press don't like it because they think it's highly confusing and what's more nothing is ever decided in time for them to file their stories. The players don't like it because they have to play out every frame to the bitter end, often long after one or the other has actually won it. And of course over such a short match it's not necessarily the best man who wins. Even Steve Davis, in one of his frequent visits to the press room, reckoned that any one of the top amateurs could beat him over three frames on ability. 'After that,' he said earnestly, 'the brain takes over.'

A loss in this kind of match though is easier for all the players to dismiss from their minds, all except the Hurricane, who takes no loss easily. On the Tuesday night of the tournament he was enbroiled in yet another of the disputes that seem to have accompanied all his matches this year, as if he can't bear to lose just because he's not playing well. Other players lose because they play badly, they choke, or else they just give up. Not the Hurricane. He has to have some drama to pour all his frenetic energy into and distract him from the snooker.

Tuesday's was a miss by David Taylor that the Hurricane thought was a professional foul. Len Ganley, the referee, agreed with the Silver Fox that he had no other way of playing the shot and had in fact made a genuine attempt to hit it. But the Hurricane phoned up Barry Hearn afterwards and said it was the first time he'd cried at a snooker match. 'He was in floods of tears,' said Steve Davis, telling the story.

His audience in the press room that day was Tex Hennessey the *Daily Mail*'s snooker correspondent whenever the *Mail* sports people

Terry Griffiths . . .

and chatting to Bill Davis

decide they can no longer go on ignoring the facts that snooker exists and that a lot of their readers would like to hear about it. Tex is gentle and generous in his assessment of players' characters — the more cynical of his colleagues use harsher terms for these qualities. He asked Steve that day if there was still friction between him and Alex. 'No,' said Steve. 'Apart from the fact that we hate each other.' Tex looked indulgent. 'No,' he said, as if Steve was a naughty boy who'd just told a little white lie. The World Champion snorted with laughter. 'Of course we do,' he said briskly. 'I like playing against Alex though. He really makes you play when he's on form.'

Steve Davis and Terry Griffiths, the two best players in the game just now, are also the two who come most often into the press room. Is it a coincidence? Terry's Welsh, of course, and has compatriot company in Clive Everton and as good as compatriot company in Janice Hale who holds loyally to Everton policy and is very fond of Terry anyway. But Steve? He seems to have no very close friends among the press. No close friends among the players either. Is that the price of being World Champion?

★　★　★

This is the fourth time this year that these two have faced each other in a major final. Steve Davis has won twice before, in the Coral UK and the Benson and Hedges Masters at Wembley, Terry Griffiths once, on the final black of the Lada Classic. Apart from Jimmy White, no-one else has had a look in this season. It's as if some computer somewhere had jammed and just kept flashing up the same two names all the time — Steve Davis and Terry Griffiths, Terry Griffiths and Steve Davis.

The final starts at 2 p.m. which should please them down Llanelli way. Pops Griffiths shakes his head. 'Down home all the old men, since snooker's been on television, they're all moaning about late nights,' he says. 'I said to them, "That's how Terry didn't win last year. You were all moaning about snooker." Terry has never changed, you know. He's the same now as what he always was. They'll all tell you that down home.

'Before when he turned pro he often wondered if he was doing the right thing. It was a big decision to make. You can struggle for years. He had a hard first year. He did the Butlins camps. He'd have a six-hour drive, play the professionals in the camp, and move down the line, Skegness, Bognor, he was doing over a thousand miles a week. It was a miracle for him to win the World Championship in his first year. When he was playing in the local league the wife used to take all the cuttings out of the local papers. I've got them all in the house now. But I lost the wife eleven years ago.' His old face creases. 'She would have been thrilled to see him winning the World.

'Terry's a proper family man too. I always remember him telling Ray Reardon, who plays seven nights a week, "If I get a chance I won't play seven nights a week. I like to get home on a weekend. Your boy's sixteen and you haven't seen him grow up." He likes home, Terry. In this game — I was just telling Steve's father — you've got to be good living. You've got to look after yourself. Steve's a good living boy. Terry says even when you're playing exhibitions people pay to see you and you've got to give of your best or be at your best. It's a hard life, with the travelling, but Terry's a good living boy.'

Though their sons display about as many domestic virtues as the SAS when they meet on the snooker table, their dads see them as family men. 'We're the same sort of people,' says Bill Davis. 'Terry's a family man and family life's got a lot to do with it. We've both got the same sort of very close family.' Steve's mum, Jean, can't get to the tournaments as often as his dad, mainly because she's a teacher and doesn't like to ask for more than her already generous holidays. Bill is a stores man with London Transport and comes to as many of Steve's matches as he can fit into his holidays and days off. He grins and waves his cigar. 'I work for a living,' he says, 'not like Steve.'

Out on the table Steve Davis's computer-like skills have clicked into action. He takes the first frame with breaks of seventy-four and forty-one. Barry Hearn folds his arms in satisfaction and grins his most puckish grin. 'He'd be a good player if he played well from the start,' he says. But the usual Steve Davis victory punched into the computer, no suspense, just a demonstration of his flawless skills and no openings for Terry Griffiths, is not what this audience wants. Even snooker purists who admire Steve's game find the basic element of sporting spectacle — suspense — missing from the standard Davis matches. 'Robotoid,' said Janice Hale of him earlier in the week. 'That's the word to describe him.' She said she was definitely going to use it in her next *Observer* article and that she once wrote a piece about Steve saying he was like a machine and he came up and thanked her. He said it was the best piece about him he'd read. Janice was really surprised. She'd thought she was knocking him.

But robotoid man is not having things all his own way. Terry

Griffiths makes up his first frame deficit and moves to a three-one lead. It's interesting to consider that at twenty-four, the age Steve Davis is now, Terry got to the final of the Welsh championships for the first time and lost because of inexperience. It's a different game now, a different world. Young players are reaching heights that perhaps only the Hurricane reached at their age in the past.

Terry Griffiths in many ways was a late developer, a man who was only beginning to realise his potential at an age when nowadays he could perfectly possibly have been a professional for four or five years. 'If Terry wanted to play with the best players we had to travel sixty miles up to the Valleys, that's where they all were,' recalls Pops. With his tufty eyebrows and keen eyes, his broad face and strong nose, he looks exactly like an owl wearing a suit, and surely a wise owl at that, with his pleasure not only in his famous son but equally in the daughter he lives with and his other son, who got his council house when he moved in with his daughter.

'When Terry turned pro I was always wanting him to win something,' he remembers. 'But when he won the World I changed. He'd achieved something. He was right for life. I was happy then. I thought he wouldn't be struggling then. Before he won it he was only £60 or £70 a night. When he was in the Crucible I was in the dressing room with him when a call came from Kilgetty, down Tenby way. Terry was booked to play at the RAOB club there. They were wondering if he was going to come there. Terry told them, Yes, certainly. Of course it was a big day down there. They were having the World Champion for £60. That night when we arrived there was everything there — television, the lot.'

His whole upper body moves up and down as he wheezes with laughter, just like a Walt Disney owl before it takes off. But he stays where he is, watching his son yet again take on the World Champion. Steve Davis pulls back the next three frames to even the score at three frames each, with Bill, his dad, enthusiastically applauding Terry Griffiths' great shots. Still when Terry makes a break of fifty to move one single point ahead of Steve in the next frame he drops his cigar case in the excitement and it goes clattering to the ground down the back of the stands.

Not that Bill's nervous, of course. Maybe in the past he would have been, but not now. Or so he says. 'I used to get very tense watching,' he admits. 'My old heart used to go pitter patter. I used to want him to win everything. But now he's made it it doesn't matter so much. He can afford to lose a tournament and he's still up there.'

One of the reasons he's up there is Bill Davis himself, who taught Steve all that Joe Davis knew. The classic cue action, the flawless positional play came straight out of the Joe Davis' instruction manual. Bill was the one whose perfectionism drove Steve and whose commonsense helped steer him away from the normal path of the young Londoners, paved with gold. 'Steve never played for money,' says Bill. 'I think that's a mistake the young lads make today. He didn't play in competitions either. I was amazed how good he was without competition. He just plays snooker. Most other people play the other player. But Steve's purely concentrating on cueing and potting the balls, not on his opponent. That's why he's such a good player.'

He renews the beer in his plastic tumbler, chomps through yet another cigar. He is tall and spare with hair that shoots energetically up from his forehead and eyebrows following close behind. His features have never stopped moving long enough to settle into the classical mould of his son's, but the two share a habit of straight talking. They both say exactly what they mean in a flat definite way that isn't dogmatic but sounds as if they know what they're talking about. They do. Steve's Dad says there's not much between the two of them at this level and for the first time this year that sounds a reasonable proposition, perhaps because Terry Griffiths has just forced a play-off on black in the eighth frame, which he wins. They're four frames each at the interval.

Pops shuffles slowly out, shaking his head. 'We're still sweating,' he says. The Griffithses head back to their hotel but long after they are gone Steve Davis is out in the foyer signing autographs and copies of his book. He is there early in the evening too, his ginger hair just visible over the top of an army of children. In another part of the foyer a man is demonstrating a Yamaha organ to prospective clients. It hardly seems a sensible way to prepare for the closing stages of a major final but we've seen Steve Davis doing it time and time again this year and he doesn't seem to lose many. He really is the perfect professional, fulfilling all the demands the public could possibly make on him and more. He gives so much out you wonder how there is anything left for himself, or if there is.

He seems more nervous than usual tonight but still manages to take the first frame of the session, watched by a full house and Derby's Lady Mayoress in her black velvet suit and gold chains of office. Terry Griffiths breaks back immediately to level the scores for the fourth time this match. Five frames all. 'What I like about this match,' says Bill Davis, 'is that Steve's made a couple of very loose safety shots and he's been punished for it. Terry's got in and made a break every time. This is the way it should be. It's good for the game of snooker. Just as it was a good thing that Steve lost the Lada. That was good for the game.'

Not good for the nerves, though. The Welshman looks as if he's finally going to regain his early lead in the match — a fluent break of forty-two to start off with, then he's on fifty-four-nil, when, suddenly, he miscues. The chance is there, just one chance, and Steve Davis takes it. Other players have been known to falter at such a point, their rhythm and confidence upset by their opponent's fluency and skill. Steve Davis makes a break of seventy-three. The frame is his and suddenly, after a see-sawing match, he looks too good to be beaten. Barry Hearn is exultant. 'This is one of the great matches,' he says with his own jubilant brand of reverence.

Pops looks solemn. 'You've got to play well to beat Steve,' he says. 'He's a great champion, he is. A great champion.' But his son isn't beaten yet. A break of sixty-nine gives him the twelfth frame and a respite that turns out to be but brief, as Steve Davis takes the next two frames. He's eight-six ahead now and it looks all over — except somebody's forgotten to tell Terry Griffiths, who claws back yet another frame to be just one frame behind.

It's best of seventeen, so the next frame is crucial. The two jockey for position at the beginning but somehow it is Steve Davis who seems to get the first chance of a break. And this is the heartbreaking bit for his opponent. This is the moment when he sees his last chance slipping away from him and not a thing he can do about it. It's how you sit at this game that counts, said Clive Everton, but all Terry Griffiths can do in what is to be the final frame of the match, is compose his losing speech. Steve Davis, making the difficult look easy, clears the table with 135, the highest break of the tournament.

Terry's speech is as witty and gracious as ever. He says he's aiming for much higher in the game now because Steve's gone higher and that there's a few matches to come before the World Championships. He's got the Llanelli Handicaps next week. Pops is proud. He says his boy's a great fighter but they're getting used to being the bridesmaid and never the bride. 'Down our way,' he says, 'nobody likes Steve because he's always beating Terry and they think he's big-headed when he gets interviewed. But Steve's only twenty-four. He's a very nice boy. Down home, see, they think that Steve is on Terry's mind, because he keeps beating him all the time. But Terry plays harder against Steve than anybody. Steve's very nice. There's a lot of envy of him. They're all jealous of him. But if you can't take defeat with glory,' he sighs, 'you might as well forget it.'

Bill Davis looks relieved. He says he's disappointed with the way Steve played, though his air suggests he knows the outrageousness of what he's saying. 'He should have been more clinical,' he insists.

Terry Griffiths is looking cheerful still, but Pops is wistful. 'If Terry'd won he'd have been a hero,' he says. 'He'd have been the toast of Llanelli.'

Terry Griffiths

First Llanelli, Then the World

The corridor to Room 503 is dark and functional, its only adornment a half-eaten salad expiring on a tray outside somebody's door. Inside the room the curtains are drawn, making an already small room appear even smaller. There's the usual telephone, television, double bed, and bathroom en suite. A piece of apple pie and half a cheese sandwich are perched by the television. This is one of the poshest hotels in Leeds and the furniture looks as if it came out of MFI.

Terry Griffiths is staying here tonight. He's driven up from his home outside Llanelli in South Wales for an exhibition at York University, but it's better for him to stay in Leeds as he has to get to Birmingham in the morning and Jersey for the evening. He washes his cue down, leaves his hairdryer sprawling on the bed before he leaves the room. His big gold Mercedes with its TG numberplate is waiting for him downstairs, its windscreen spattered with mud from all the lorries on the road up.

As he slides into the sheepskin covered driving seat he says he usually undoes his clothes when he's driving to exhibitions, as it prevents his trousers from creasing. He won't do that tonight. Once he forgot he'd done it and stopped the car to ask this lady in the street if she'd tell him the way somewhere. No, she said, she certainly would not.

Rain is smearing the windscreen and making it difficult for him to see out as he tries to navigate his way out of Leeds city centre. He sighs and says he can't be bothered with the driving. His friend Peter used to do it for him but he didn't like that so much as it meant you were never on your own, and he likes to be on his own. 'It's the only chance I get to be by myself, really be by myself,' he says. 'Once you go out to the people you're theirs. Once you go home you're theirs. When I'm away I'm alone and I need that sometimes.'

The travelling, the emotional demands made on you are just part of the price of success, a calculable part. Before he turned professional Terry Griffiths looked long and hard at the snooker player's life and decided he didn't like what he saw. For two years he pondered it, weighed the life he had against this new life. 'Two years it went on,' he says. 'I'd think, Ah, I don't think I'll bother. Annette wasn't keen on me doing it because of the type of life it is. It's not a very good married life. You don't see your wife like you do when you're working. A lot of people were telling me snooker was going to become a big sport. There was going to be a lot of money in it. Finally, I talked it over with Annette, over a long time, ages really. If she'd been really selfish she'd have said no. She'd never stop me having a go at something. But deep down I don't think she really wanted me to. She did for me but not for her. In the end I just wanted to give it a try really. It came down to the point where I didn't want to look back in ten years time and say, I might have done that. I didn't know if I was going to do any good. I knew that there was a lot of potential there for me because I never used to practise much. I knew if I went full time there was a good chance then that my game would improve a lot. I just wanted to have a go.'

The year was 1978, and Terry Griffiths had been playing the game seriously for about six years. He had played since he was fourteen but only in the casual way of a good local player. Then, in 1972, when he was working as a postman, there was a seven-week postal strike, and he started playing all day. There was nothing else to do in Llanelli. He made his first century break then, at the age of twenty-four. From that point on he rose steadily through the amateur ranks, achieving his great ambition, to win the Welsh Amateur Championship, in 1975. He nearly gave up the game altogether after that. 'I was forever playing snooker and I wasn't getting anything out of it,' he recalls.

But in 1976 he was offered the opportunity to play in the World Amateur Championships, and his experiences there were to change his whole life and attitude to the game. The tournament was held that year in Johannesburg and the South African authorities made it one of the most lavish events ever seen in snooker. Terry Griffiths had never been abroad before, had hardly been out of Llanelli on his own. He was twenty-one before he even went to London — on his honeymoon. 'I'd led a very closed sheltered life,' he says wryly. 'It was my first time away from home for any length of time. We stayed in this five star hotel, a really nice hotel. You're walking into the room and there's this big balcony outside. There was a swimming pool down there and God, Jesus, it was all so strange to me. We were looked after and it was luxury stuff. They spent a lot of money. You could have anything you wanted at any time. Everything was rich. They really laid it on.

'I played well there the first week — won my first three or four matches in the group — but then I just collapsed. I got very homesick, and I had trouble with the air being so thin. We were pretty far above sea level, and on the twentieth floor in the hotel. You'd go up there and your head would go round and round. Annette and Doug Mountjoy's wife Yvonne went to Spain the same time on Doug's Pontinental holiday and that was strange to start with. You couldn't phone. We tried the girls once and couldn't get through and that alone cost us £30, which was a bloody fortune to us then. You were disconnected from the world as far as I was concerned. I just couldn't eat. I was very homesick. All of a sudden it hit me and my game just disintegrated. I did get to the quarters. Doug won it and I was pleased that he won at least. But I was a whole week there without playing and it was just another world to me. There's no other word for it. South Africa wasn't another place. It was another world.'

That glimpse into another world was exciting though, and gave the Welshman another target to aim for in the amateur game. His next chance was in 1978 but he was beaten in the Welsh Amateur after supposedly being a cast iron certainty to win it. He wouldn't have another chance for two years, and in September of that year he finally made the decision to turn professional. Annette Griffiths was working in the local British Leyland car factory, which helped financially, though when Terry left his job in Pearl Assurance their mortgage rocketed from three to fifteen percent. A thousand letters went out from the Griffiths household, and the phone bill soared.

There were one or two exhibitions a week, at £60 a night, but nobody had heard of Terry Griffiths outside Wales. He was making enough to keep the family ticking over, but there were only so many clubs in Wales and he reckoned he would have been round the lot by the time another season was out. His first professional tournament was a disaster, an eight-nine loss to Rex Williams in the qualifying round of the Coral UK after he's been leading eight-two.

What Terry Griffiths wanted was a miracle — but only a small one. To win the World Championship at the first attempt, as he did, was beyond his dreams. He just wanted a modest little miracle. He had to play one of the top eight seeds in the first round and he wanted it to be Perrie Mans. He'd played the South African several months before and knew he had a good chance against him. The draw was made on BBC's 'Grandstand' and it came down to the last two seeds — Reardon and Mans — and Terry's watching at home hardly able to look at the screen. And the miracle happens — it's Mans. Reardon, he thinks, would have been a different kettle of fish altogether.

Well this modest miracle is a two-part miracle, actually. Terry wants to play Perrie Mans, but it's got to be on the telly. That's where your bookings come from. The thing is, the BBC sports department are threatening to strike on Bank Holiday Monday, which is when the match is scheduled. 'I'm still convinced to this day that if they'd gone on strike I'd have lost that game against Perrie Mans,' says Terry. 'It would have put so much pressure on me to win so that I'd get on the box in my next match, it would have gone against me. I'm convinced of it.'

As snooker history now records, Terry Griffiths got his two-part modest miracle and more besides. He beat Mans with BBC's Bank Holiday audience watching, and then he beat Alex Higgins in one of the finest matches ever seen in the championships, both men on form at the same time. Oh, and that was on the telly too. 'When I'd won that I went back to the hotel, and after it had all gone, all the emotions, I sat down and thought, I could win now. I knew I could win because I was playing my best snooker. I produced better snooker than I'd ever produced before — under the television lights and in the World Championship, and against Higgins on form. I knocked two centuries in in the morning in two frames. I knew then I had the equipment to win if I could keep the form. I didn't say, Oh I'm going to win the championships now. But I knew I *could* win, if I kept game together.'

The car stops at a set of traffic lights on the York road, the kind you

Terry Griffiths has a last cigarette . . .

before snooker and trick shots at York

get in France with the lights spaced out in an arc above the road like a fairy grotto. Terry Griffiths perks his head up above the wheel to look at them. 'That's unusual,' he says. He is a man of innate curiosity, a bird-bright intelligence pecking away at the objects and people that come across his path. He prefers to be an observer rather than the observed and this has made his public life difficult in the past.

His World Championship year went from being a fairy story to being a horror story. 'Wherever I went that year there were people in a queue. You were going all twisted up inside all the time but you had to be yourself as well, say hello and all that. This was happening every night of the week. I went from doing nothing to playing every single day. Then I was coming home and doing letters. I didn't have any back-up, starting off. No right accountants, solicitors, agents. It just slowly and slowly bit into me. In the end I was a bloody nervous wreck. I didn't know whether I was coming or going. I was on the road all the time trying to perform and in the end it just eats away at your game. I was getting to the stage where I was just hiding all the time from people. I'd go to a show and I'd want to hide and I'm performing. It was bad. I used to ask, Is there a door I can get out of at the end? If he says there's a door I'm right then. It didn't matter if I ever got to it. If he says there's no way out I used to go, Oh, and tighten up then. It was all a reaction to not being home where I wanted to be, with the kids and Annette.

'I used to go to bed and I'd think, Jesus, what are you doing? But I'd have to get up the next day and do it all again and again and that went on for months and months. I just could *not* get over it. I couldn't get myself mentally to accept it. I wasn't used to being recognised. I felt the people were like woodpeckers pecking away at me all the time. Annette never even knew what I was like. Nobody did. She knows now but I'd never tell her then because I like to sort my own things out. I just wanted to get through it myself. It makes it harder but it's more satisfying when you come out the other side. You're much stronger then.'

He is a man whose intense individuality and personal pride are sustained not just by his achievements on the snooker table but by his feelings of esteem for his family life. Unlike many modern champions, who give themselves single-mindedly to their sport, he gives equal value to each part of his life. His family are closely involved with his success and when he suffered the pressures of being World Champion, inevitably they suffered too. He had looked after his sons Darren and

Wayne when his wife went to work. When things changed overnight for him it was an awful wrench not to see them, he says. The older boy was very emotional and used to hate it when he went away, but there was nothing he could do about it because he had all these bookings lined up. He felt it was like being in a cage then.

A cage, no way out. The commonsense solution would be to take a break, get away from it all, but Terry Griffiths preferred to stay at home. He had never liked holidays. 'If someone had said to me, Why don't you just take a break? It'd do you the world of good, I'd have laughed in their face,' he says. 'I hate holidays. But Annette and I went to Pontins in Teneriffe for a week. I read for the first time in my life. I do read now but I never used to. Last time I'd read a book was in school. I don't drink so there was no night life. Me and Annette just more or less laid in the sun all day. We went back to the chalet early in the night and either made love all night or bloody read a book. There was nothing else to do, no TV or anything. Annette and I aren't ones for nightlife anyway, coming from Llanelli.'

The holiday was a turning point for Terry Griffiths. Never again would he allow the pressures to dominate him. Now he says he thinks he can handle them better than most. That's what marks out the top professionals from the merely good, or from the top amateurs. 'They're all good players but they haven't got the stomach, the guts to be at the top. When you watch them practising they're all much the same. It's when you get the pressure they can't handle it. That's why Steve's so good. He plays his best shots when he's under the most pressure. With everybody else it's the opposite. I seem to be able to handle defeat better than the other fellows,' he says with a grin. 'I don't go out and get pissed or anything. It doesn't take me long to recover.' He swings the big Mercedes smoothly through the network of roads around the university campus. 'I just go home and stick darts in my Steve Davis poster.'

The hall where he is to play is a floating island in the middle of a web of water. Probably in the daytime it's some soulless concrete structure but in the darkness, with its light illuminating the water and the sound of talk and laughter filtering across from the students' residences, it seems a magical place. Inside there's a beautiful polished wood floor and spacious seating, but Terry Griffiths says they ought to have a mat on the floor as he gets embarrassed when his shoes make a noise.

He is met by Jeremy, the students' union entertainments secretary, a young man wearing jeans, a tan leather jacket and a pained expression.

He says this is the second night in a row he's going to lose money. Last night they had a poetry thing with John Cowper Clarke and there was hardly anyone there. He's sold 330 tickets tonight but he'll need to sell a few hundred more before he can make a profit. He holds his plastic glass of whisky like a lifeline. Being entertainments secretary, he says, is driving him to drink.

The hall gradually begins to fill up more, though one very important person hasn't yet filed through the door — Terry Griffiths' opponent Kirk Stevens. The Welshman offers to play someone in the audience to start the evening off but Jeremy looks doubtful, so Terry sits in the narrow dressing room, fretting about when they'll finish now. They're billed to play more frames than he was told, so he's not pleased by the delay. When Kirk breezes in twenty minutes after he's billed to start Terry tells him he's late, but Kirk's companion, top referee, Len Ganley, says *he* thought the match just started when the players turned up.

There is a curious lack of tension in the atmosphere of any exhibition match. It's not the way tennis exhibitions used to be for instance, when Hoad and Laver, say, would take each other on in head to head tours where every single match counted. Here both players receive a fee that's independent of the outcome and reflects only their status in the game either as entertainers or as past winners. It doesn't really matter who wins just as long as the audience see the players, rather than their play. Although there is no lack of effort, somehow there is a lack of emotional tension. They're just playing snooker, that's all.

Kirk Stevens wins the match. He doesn't like doing exhibitions because he says they make him feel like a prostitute, so Terry Griffiths ends up doing the trick shots afterwards. Although he's keen to get away early he exchanges good-natured banter with the audience and performs as if he has all the time in the world. It's mainly a family audience, the kind of audience that many of the hardline snooker people think should stay at home. Top stars like Terry welcome the changing audiences, largely because they're bigger. 'People turn round and say, Oh the clubs have supported it all these years, which is right in one way. But they don't support the individual. When I started off and was charging £60 a night nobody booked *me*. I wanted the shows. I wanted the money. But the clubs didn't support me. Then when I won the World Championships everybody wanted to book me. Then I was charging £200 and they'd say, Christ. That's a lot of money. Now it's gone up and up. People say Steve's ridiculous charging these fees. "We used to book him when he was only so much." Well that's fair enough but at the end of the day they don't really care a shit for you. They don't care anything for you. None of them. I came to believe after a while of being on the circuit there's your family and your close friends and the rest you can forget about, because they don't care a thing about you when it comes to the crunch. You've got to look after your family and yourself first. Then the other things come after. So the fees are so high it's got to go out to the leisure centres? So what?

'Now the game's being presented as it should be, with the right image. If you went along five years ago it'd be in the local club and it's bloody noisy and they're drinking pints of beer and they're smoking. That's what I was brought up on. OK I love the game. I'm part of the game and always have been. But if somebody comes in to that for the first time they wouldn't bloody come back in a hurry. Who would to that sort of atmosphere? There'd be a certain band of drinkers and roughs and toughs and people who like to shout and bawl and that sort of crowd, but that's a very small part of the world that is.

'Nowadays you've got all the people sitting in their houses watching television and they've been caught now by the sport. So when Steve Davis comes into their town, to them he's a bloody superstar. They've only ever seen the guy on television. They've seen what he's done. The superstar now is only a hundred yards down the road in their leisure centre so they all come out and watch it, and they've got a nice seat where they can get up and go to the toilet when they want to or go to the bar when they want to and there's nice flowers on the match table. And now instead of just the old man coming out you get the wife and the two kids.'

He smiles and chats to all the wives and kids waiting for autographs, a great long line stretching across the hall. Jeremy is clutching his plastic drinks glass a little less desperately now. He won't lose tonight after all. Terry says he's knackered and could do with someone to drive him home now.

The thick sheepskin seats in the Mercedes make it seem warm, though outside the air is fresh. The sound of some drunken students sings its way across the water. And Terry Griffiths is back on the road again, just twenty-four miles to do tonight, but Birmingham in the morning and the flight to Jersey. As soon as he comes back from Jersey he's supposed to be doing an OTT programme with Steve Davis. He says, isn't that the one with all the swearing and everything? Yes, and he's likely to get a flan in his face as well. He laughs and says he doesn't think he'll do that then. Snow is falling now, great big soap flakes swirling in front of the window as the car plunges through the blackness. The headlights make a central point of light ahead and the snow streams past the car headlights and it feels as if we're in a moving tunnel and will never get out. And of course Terry Griffiths will do the telly show, because he's said he will and if he says he'll do anything, be it exhibition or interview or charity show, he'll do it. Just as a top professional should.

Pat Houlihan

An Honest-to-God Hustler

The billiard hall is up a flight of stairs above Burtons the tailors, but had you not been told so, you might never have known it was there, might well have thought that British Home Stores and the cheery stalls of the street market were all that Lewisham High Street had to offer. You might never have known that the inhabitants of this small complete world were going about their business, as indifferent to the bustle below them as if the High Street were another planet.

The door swings open at the touch of the buzzer but this is no extra-terrestrial device. The people nearest the door open it to let you in. Pat Houlihan comes forward, with a cup of tea he's just bought at the counter selling hot drinks and squash and sandwiches. There are raucous shouts from some boys playing at a table nearby. 'Eamonn's just come to the door Patsy,' they catcall.

Pat Houlihan smiles uneasily, a small formally polite man in a neat jacket and heavy horn rimmed glasses. In the days before television made snooker a game people actually knew about, Pat was a hustler, a real live honest-to-God hustler who travelled all round the country pretending to be a worse player than he was and relieving people of the trouble of having to carry their money around with them. That

98

Pat Houlihan at rest and work

lasted only as long as people didn't know him, and being a player possessed of that rare quality 'the flair', Pat was soon being recognised all over the place. 'After a while they got to know you,' he says. 'It was just a matter of time. So then, they started putting the local champion on to you. When I got well known I just used to go in and ask for the best player.'

He looks wryly round the snooker hall with its lowered ceiling, the new tiles, the wood panelling. 'This used to be such a dive. The chap that's bought it now is putting new cloths on all the tables. That floor was all wood boards and some was out,' he says regarding the new brown carpeting on the floor. 'The place is really nice now.' But for him much of the heart of the place has gone, as much of the heart has gone from his own snooker. 'It used to be unbelievable,' he says. 'All the barrow boys used to come in and speculate. You'd always get people walking in wanting to play someone. Good or mediocre, they'd always want to play for money. There was so much money in those days it was unbelievable, £200 or £300 bet on a single game. It's much more comfortable here now but in those days there was so many comedians up here you used to have a right laugh. People'd come and they didn't play but they could get a living just marking up. That was how much money there was in them days.'

Those were the days when the clubs were open all night, carrying right on round the clock from ten o'clock one morning to eight or nine the following one, with only an hour to clear the empty beer bottles and the cigarette ends, to brush down the cloths in readiness for the day's play, to mop the floor where puddles of unprepossessing liquid might have solidified on the bare boards. 'There was a club in the west end famous for money matches,' recalls Pat. 'People just used to walk in with their cues looking for action. There was more in the night than there was in the day though that club was always packed. All the tables would be going all night. I've been pulled out of bed to go and play people at three in the morning years ago. I was good in them days,' he says sadly. 'I always produced it. I was playing more and more matches and that keeps you up all the time. These chaps today, I know for a fact that I could still be up there with them now if I could get the right opportunities.'

He was up there then in the sixties, London's top amateur at a time when the amateurs were the game's real competitors. While the World Professional Champion, John Pulman, languished at home un-challenged for his title from 1957 to 1964, down there in the amateur arena, supposedly less bloody than the professional, people like Ray Reardon, John Spencer, Gary Owen, Cliff Wilson and Ron Gross were fighting it out for the top titles. Pat Houlihan's best year was 1965. 'In '65 I won the lot,' he recalls with relish. 'Five major tournaments in all. In the final of the All-England I beat John Spencer eleven-three at the Blackpool Tower Circus — plus I won a lot on bets. I used to always beat John in them days. After I beat him he went on and won the World Professional Championships in 1969. I went to Earls Court to play a challenge match against him and I still beat him.'

Spencer of course went on to become a three times winner of the World Professional title and one of the top stars of the modern game. Pat Houlihan's career was built on playing matches around the London clubs, many of which at that time were frequented not only by snooker enthusiasts but also by gamblers, con men, gangsters, people who might not have been willing to admit how they made their living, either to the Inland Revenue or to the Metropolitan Constabulary. 'That west end club when it was in its prime,' remembers Patsy, shaking his head at the memory. 'All the tearaways, all the lads came down there. The Krays even had a snooker club, a place down the east end, I don't know its name now. I played in there lots of times. You knew what they were and what they weren't. They didn't take any liberties as long as people just played snooker and paid for their tables.'

In that half-lit world Pat Houlihan was a name. He had the flair. 'I was the draw in them days,' he says. 'I remember once playing in the Burroughes Hall in Soho Square. They had to have two police cars to control the crowds. I couldn't even get myself in. I had to force my way through the crowd. I always got a good living then. If I didn't in London I went elsewhere. Once someone suggested going to Jersey but when I got there I was known. There wasn't nothing for me in Jersey. But I used to have a good life going round. You always ended up in the pub. You'd play snooker in the afternoon and then have a nice drink in the evening.'

That life — the travelling, the betting, the money matches, the tatty clubs — was the only way Pat Houlihan knew then of making a living at what he did best. In the end though he has been condemned to it for life. Today when snooker means big cars, big houses, big money for its top stars, Pat Houlihan is still playing money matches and a few exhibitions when he can get them. He's struggling to get through the qualifying rounds for the major tournaments. The reason lies right there in the sixties, when he was in his heyday. Even though Joe Davis had played and won his last World Championship in 1946, he still controlled the professional game, such as it was. There were only six pros then, at the beginning of a decade which was to prove itself indifferent to professional snooker. There was Joe himself, and his brother Fred, but Fred had the income from his farm and didn't just rely on the snooker. There was Rex Williams, whose family had a printing firm, and Jackie Rea, who turned himself into a comedian as well as a snooker player in the end. John Pulman and Kingsley Kinnersley scraped a living from exhibitions though there were few of those. In that economic climate it was Joe Davis who dictated what happened in snooker.

And Joe Davis, whose reputation for invincibility had rarely been put to the test over the past fifteen years, and whose finances were secure after a career of unparalleled success in snooker's palmier days, decided that there was no room in the game for newcomers, especially if, like Patsy Houlihan, they were known money players. Joe would have appreciated the game in the eighties where image is all-important and the players, as well as being good at snooker, must show themselves to be gentlemen, stainless steel gentlemen, ruthless in their will to win but well-mannered, respectable, and controlled to the point of blandness in their emotions. Pat Houlihan represented a more dangerous world than that and paid the penalty. 'It was sewn up in them days,' he said. 'It was very very hard to turn pro. Joe Davis was the kingpin. His word was bond. When he said yes or no that was it.'

Joe Davis said no and Pat had to wait till 1970 before he could turn pro. By that time it was too late. Somewhere, probably in some less than salubrious club on a less than perfect table, for not much money, Pat Houlihan had passed his peak. He was never to succeed in the professional game as he had done in the amateurs and now, with only two and a half weeks to go before the qualifying matches for the World Championship, he is plagued with a recurrence of eye trouble and worried about the amount of money involved just in getting himself to Stockport.

Snooker like all competitive sports is cruel to those it leaves behind. Pat Houlihan, having been in the sport all his life, is now struggling to make a living from it, victim of our devotion to the media — if you haven't seen it on the telly it hasn't happened. People like Pat Houlihan exist only for the real snooker people. He is hardly even a name to the casual fans who switch on the snooker if there's nothing better on the other side. Even those who do know about the game want to see the

102

winners. They want to see Steve Davis and Terry Griffiths down at their leisure centre, not Pat Houlihan, even if he did used to make century breaks in four minutes before anyone had ever heard of the Hurricane.

He is in serious mood as he looks ahead to Stockport and the seemingly mammoth task of trying to qualify for the Sheffield stage of the World Championships, the important bit, the bit that's on the BBC every night. It will cost him £150 in travel and accommodation even if he loses in this first match and none if it will be paid back in expenses. 'And yet the top people are paid £1250 for just walking in,' he says. 'Something should be done about that. They could have taken a couple of thousand off the top prize and then given the preliminary round chaps their expenses. Last year we had to win five matches before we came across the top eight. It's better now. We've only got to win two or three matches more than them, but you're playing people like Willie Thorne and Jim Meadowcroft in the qualifying — you can beat them or they could beat you. It's very close. In the seventies I hardly got to play the top men at all.

'You know my hardest match? It was against Ray Reardon, and it was the last time I played him. That was 1965, just before I beat Spencer in the English Amateur. Reardon was five-one ahead and I had to win the last five frames. He was a copper then. Said I should be locked up.'

The green fringing round the table lamp throws an unnatural pallor on to his face. Beyond him Lewisham's lads are practising on the snooker tables, each in his own small world, some dreaming perhaps that, one day, snooker will bring them fame, fortune. Playing for a future. 'I don't fear them when I go there to Stockport,' says Pat Houlihan. 'That was my strong point once. But I overtry now. Getting on the table once a year you do, because you know you'll only get one chance. I've had some people beat me that they just couldn't have done. I just overtry.' His face is sombre. 'I've got to try and tell myself it ain't just this tournament once a year. I've got to try and take it in my stride.

'It was a lot easier mentally when I was younger. I was a Steve Davis in those days for coolness. I used to love playing matches. I was very fast. I had the flair. I still have as a matter of fact. It seems funny that John Spencer went from amateur to professional champion. Ray Reardon went from amateur to professional champion. Gary Owen went from amateur champion to professional runner up. I think if I'd lived up north I'd have made more of a go of it. Jackie Rea said if Pat Houlihan had lived up there he'd be turning work down. Because I had the flair you see. I had the flair.'

Alex Higgins

The Hurricane Quits

There are only three weeks to go before the Embassy World Professional Championships begin in Sheffield and the Hurricane wants to quit Sportsworld. To a snooker public inured to the unpredictable from the Hurricane this is unsurprising news, but it is the cause of some controversy among the directors of Sportsworld.

Matters involving the Hurricane it will be remembered have caused disagreement among Sportsworld's directors before. Not all were satisfied that signing him was a wise choice in the first place, though Harvey Lisberg is still convinced that it put Sportsworld on the map in snooker. 'It got everybody scared,' he remembers. 'It was unbelievable.'

Since then however Harvey has had to cope with the Hurricane's customary contempt for the idea of being managed. The scene generally goes something like this. Harvey arranges some event for the Hurricane to participate in. It could be an exhibition, it could be an invitation to a social event, it could be an advertisement. He tells the Hurricane. The Hurricane is not grateful. 'What's in it for me?' he says. 'Get double,' he says. 'Get treble.' Harvey tells him he's got him £5000 to do such and such but the Hurricane turns round and says, No. He wants ten. And he wins in the end. The Hurricane gets what he wants. 'He *won't* be managed,' cries the perplexed Harvey.

In the circumstances it's hardly surprising that Harvey votes for the Hurricane to go. Harvey doesn't think he's capable of being managed. He doesn't think the Hurricane shows any respect for anybody. He is *not* the sort of person that Harvey wants to manage. Harvey doesn't want to represent people who demand money from the press for giving interviews. He is aghast at the very idea. He wants to manage somebody who appreciates what's being done, someone who'll listen to reason. Roy Speake and Fred Summers both agree.

Geoff Lomas thinks they're all crazy. From the start he's been under no illusion that managing the Hurricane is anything but a ticket to trouble. But there's only three weeks to go before the World Championships and if the Hurricane happens to win they're in Klondyke country. He tells it to Alex straight, on the phone. No way he's getting released from that contract. The Hurricane is furious. He says right, he won't do any exhibitions. He won't sign any endorsements. Geoff Lomas's silky voice comes back to him, unperturbed. 'That's your business Alex. Our business is you're under contract and you're staying under contract.'

But then the Sportsworld directors have to go and have a meeting, and that's it. The other directors know the Hurricane a bit better now and they decide that if he doesn't get what he wants he'll cause them a lot of trouble. They decide it's not worth the hassle. They vote three-one in favour of releasing the Hurricane. They don't really think he's got a hope in hell of winning the World Championship anyway.

Cliff Thorburn

The Most Difficult Game in the World

It's two o'clock in the afternoon and the good citizens of Walton-on-Thames, lunch over, are busily going about their business in the shops and offices, buzzing about in their cars. In the house in Ashley Close, though, it is the early morning smell of bacon and eggs that creepy-crawls its way along the hall to greet you at the door. Cliff Thorburn greets you too.

His house is the house of a successful man, in a town which, even if it does feel like a suburb without a city to belong to, is a town for successful people. The street is quiet, filled with white prosperous looking villas like the Thorburns' and lined with apple and cherry blossom trees whose fallen petals are making the April air smell warm and punchy.

Cliff Thorburn *is* a successful man, the 1980 World Champion and always an invitee to the major televised tournaments. Unlike the Patsy Houlihans of the world he doesn't have to worry about qualifying for the World Championships, and Sheffield does not represent his one big chance of the year. There will be time, there will be tournaments for him, and even if he should fail in the first round this year, there is money enough in the bank to cushion the blow.

And yet, in the most basic way — his form on the snooker table — Cliff Thorburn ceased to be a successful man perhaps as much as a year ago. Apart from the Lang's last October — where he was a finalist — and the Yamaha — where he won a qualifying group though where the matches were only over three frames — he has lost his first match in every single major tournament this year. His high seeding position has meant that his defeats have often been as far into the tournament as the third round and that he has always been well rewarded financially. But defeat, especially to a champion, can be nothing other than failure.

It's always difficult to anatomise failure. Where do the defeats become a pattern? Is there a point at which success ceases to be a possibility? When does the mind finally give up and acknowledge the fact of failure? This year Cliff Thorburn has played probably the worst snooker of his career. Before he won the World in 1980 he was known as a player who lost from winning positions. This season he's just never been that far ahead, and yet, ironically, his greatest success contained in it the seeds of failure. The pressures of being a modern world snooker champion can take away the pleasures.

'Snooker was my whole life the year that I won the championships,' recalls Cliff. 'That was almost forced upon me, to be all my life. I didn't have time to play golf. I was playing five, six, seven times a week for eight months. I got to a point in the end where I just used to be like a robot. I could drive from here to Burnley, get to Burnley, and not be able to remember anything that happened in between. When you play that much — I shouldn't have played that much anyway — that's how you get sometimes. You're talking to yourself and you're thinking about things on the way up and when you get up there you don't know what you were thinking about.'

106

That crazy World Champion's year was over, though, before the beginning of this season. Steve Davis had the title and the pressure and all the rushing about to do, and still it hasn't gone right for Cliff Thorburn. The solution, he has decided, is to go home to Canada. He thinks now he should never have left. He missed his chance to capitalise on winning the title and never was able to in Britain, where Steve Davis's run of success just afterwards was greeted by the business men with the fervour Mark McCormack would bring to the coming of the Messiah.

Cliff's future now appears to be secured — a lucrative contract with a large Canadian billiards company, the chance of making as much money as he did in his title year all over again, perhaps an eponymous club in Toronto, home of Canada's big money. His return home too will help the Canadian game, something he has not been able to do before. 'Every time I go back people always want to do interviews and things like that — radio, television, newspapers. But then every time I'm leaving. I've just never followed through with anything because I'm always coming back here. Here I find that I just get involved in too many things. It's way too political here for me. There's too many guys wanting to grab. The game itself, it's like a big business now.'

But it's still the business he loves and makes his living in, and losing hurts, especially when the most business-like of all the players is doing all the winning. The story of Cliff Thorburn's loss boils down to one thing — Steve Davis. You can disguise that fact by saying that the two periods — the one of failure, the other of unprecedented success — have just coincided, but Cliff Thorburn is not the only player to have been demoralised by the Londoner's relentless efficiency. 'Snooker is ninety-nine percent in the mind,' says the Canadian, a proposition that sportsmen from all disciplines believe of their own sport, but which is particularly true in snooker, where the pattern of the game is dictated more by the brain than by the body, and where the signals that the brain must send to the body under stress are minute, moving a muscle at a time, just like Popeye's bulging shoulders in the cartoons.

'In actual playing terms there's not much difference in ability because everyone's got their own type of game,' says Cliff, another proposition believed by the majority of competitive sportsmen, except the champions, who *know* they're better, and the audiences, who can see they are. In snooker there is actually more justification for the statement than in other sports, because if one man gets an opening — whether by luck or by his brainpower — he can give an exhibition of his own type of game to his opponent, which is precisely what Steve Davis has been doing most of the past eighteen months, of course.

The Canadian is a deeply private man who prefers the public to see him through the gauze of image rather than in the light of what he really is. He is reluctant to go through the pain barrier of talking about his feelings in public, and when he does, he expresses them hesitantly, as if they're hypothetical feelings really, and don't actually belong to him. 'Everybody's not playing well and that might have something to do with one or two people doing better than everybody else. You might get bogged down a little bit and I'm sure that there are quite a few guys going through what I'm . . . what I *went* through, not playing well.' Are we talking about Steve Davis? 'Yeah, or Terry Griffiths. Steve's young. He's got a zest for the game. We've all had it. I certainly won't have the same as what I had when I was twenty-two, twenty-three, playing a lot every day. You can't maintain that all the time. He's going to get tired of travelling around. He'll charge more money and play less.'

It is hard to avoid the feeling that, in spite of his neutral demeanour, Cliff Thorburn feels defensive about Steve Davis's success, which punctured his own period as World Champion. Before Cliff's reign had passed the halfway mark it was already becoming apparent that he was unlikely to retain his title. Now, even when he is not being specific, the image of Steve Davis is present in his conversation, hovering behind the words. Preventing Cliff Thorburn from acknowledging that he has been suffering from a loss of confidence. 'Over here,' he says, 'if a snooker writer has a favourite player who loses he'll say he lost his concentration. But for somebody else he'll say that the fellow's got no confidence. And yet they're both feeling exactly the same way. I think that it *is* concentration. Even if you slip from thinking about something to negative thoughts, that is loss of concentration. Like, a snooker writer's favourite player, when he loses his concentration instead of loses his confidence, what is that guy thinking about? Is he thinking about taking his dog for a walk while he's playing in the World Championship? While he's down on a shot? What *is* a loss of concentration? The whole thing's a joke. You're thinking about the game, totally. But the correct way to say it is loss of concentration, because *everybody* in this game chokes at times. Why has Terry Griffiths beaten Steve Davis two out of the last three times? Because Steve Davis had a loss of concentration? Or is somebody finally going to admit that Terry Griffiths was actually a better player in the tournament?'

What may be hard for Cliff Thorburn to admit is that Steve Davis

Elegant Cliff Thorburn

has developed a similar type of his game to his own at a much younger age. Their careers have been so different they could have been living on different planets and not just different continents. There was no competitive structure in the Canadian game when Cliff Thorburn started — still isn't — no amateur league, no international competition, no televised snooker to show the young people what the game was like at its highest level. The only way to learn how to play snooker competitively was to gamble, and Cliff Thorburn was doing that only six months after he took up the game at the age of sixteen.

At an age when Steve Davis was playing the top professionals — Higgins, Virgo, Dennis Taylor, Griffiths, Mountjoy — Cliff Thorburn had never even seen a world class player. Eventually, six years after he first took up snooker, Rex Williams and Fred Davis came on tour to Canada and the twenty-two-year-old Cliff saw them play. 'I really had no yardstick to go by,' he says. 'I didn't know what the best players in the world played like, let alone looked like. Rex and Fred wore suits, which impressed me of course.'

He had learned his snooker on his own, with no television image to guide him. He had to build up his skills slowly, painstakingly, by himself, practising eight hours a day to get it right. People now make comments about the slow speed at which he plays but care was the only safety net he had when he was learning snooker and he has relied on it ever since. 'I felt like quitting a thousand times when I first started to play,' he says. 'It's tough. It's probably the most difficult game in the world to learn. The average person starting out will be a lot more discouraged playing snooker than any other game. In golf only ten percent of everybody that plays can break a hundred, that's of all the people in the world who play. The same thing in snooker. Except it would have to be one percent of all the people who play snooker have made a run of a hundred or more points. The game is so fascinating people are just happy to knock in *one* ball the way somebody else did on TV the night before. It's a hard game to get hold of and then once you learn how to play you've got to learn how to be a competitor as well, how to handle yourself under stress.'

Cliff Thorburn had been a sportsman all his life so he knew about that part of it. His father, a municipal worker in Victoria, had always encouraged him to take part in sport. 'He was a sanitation officer — a garbage man,' grins Cliff. 'He didn't have very much, but he was very sports minded and he just pushed me into sports.' Cliff's parents had been divorced when he was only two so he was brought up by his grandmother and his father. For years he thought his mother was dead, and only found out she was still alive when he was himself an adult. 'I know now that my father loved me and everything, but the only way that he showed it was to do good things for me, not to talk to me. He pushed me into sports and that was a good thing. It took me a long time to figure our relationship out. It's very nice now.'

Then, it was a little strained. Cliff had tried all the tough guy sports — football, baseball, basketball, tennis, rugby, lacrosse — but he eventually realised that his thin lanky body was absorbing more physical punishment than was compatible with his personal safety. Snooker was less drastic in its effects and he immediately became obsessed with it, and made it his living. His father was not impressed with the idea of his son in an occupation that at that time was held in Canada to be reserved only for bums. He told Cliff to get a job and get a haircut. His uncle told him he had a different solution. 'What's that?' asked Cliff. 'Join the Army,' said Uncle.

Cliff didn't. Instead he set off on his travels, criss-crossing the North American continent in a search for the competition that would improve his game. He knew all the towns where there was snooker action — Oklahoma City and Phoenix, Arizona, Detroit and Jacksonville, Los Angeles, San Francisco, Duluth, Minnesota. 'Just one or two nights and I was gone. Normally you just cleaned them all out and left town.'

Glamorous though it sounds, the travelling life was monotonous, and the diversions that broke it usually unwelcome. The Thorburn on the road adventures are well-known — the Japanese fisherman who went berserk in Campbell River and chased him round the snooker table with a huge fish knife, the fifty-four hour non-stop match with Dead-Eye Dick in San Francisco, where he knew it would be a long match when he saw that his opponent had two pairs of socks and a bottle of pep pills in his cue case. Just like *The Hustler*. 'We were like two hard-hitting heavyweights in the last round of a title fight. Punch drunk, swaying on our feet.'

Cliff Thorburn never was a hustler, though, and wouldn't like anyone to think he was. A man of great natural dignity, he is regarded as one of the toughest players where discipline and snooker's image and traditions are concerned. His only concession to hiding his professional status was in southern California where the tables were smaller than full size. 'You'd have to go in and act like an American. I'd wear an old mechanic's uniform and dirty my hands a bit. But then I'd play as good as I could. I wouldn't hustle. It was gambling. I never held back or took advantage of people. I had too much pride for that I guess,' he says, and then grins. 'Also I was stupid.'

The flash of self-deprecating humour cannot disguise the depth of his desire for respectability. He has always wanted snooker to be socially acceptable in his native Canada. 'I've always wanted to be a straight player,' he says simply. Now that he *is* a straight player, he is very straight, and yet he is a man of contradictions, often aloof and unbending in public, but one of the wittiest players on the circuit in private. He's cool, urbane, controlled, but when something pierces the carapace, there are glimpses of a more passionate and aggressive man underneath. His altercation with Steve Davis in the 1981 World Championships is the most obvious illustration, sparked off not just by Davis's assumption that his opponent was powerless, but also by the breach of etiquette involved.

Doing things the right way is very important to Cliff Thorburn, perhaps because he spent such a large proportion of his working life being regarded as an undesirable. Anger is not far away when he talks about Steve Davis's retinue, though perhaps he might not be as angry if the vocal Romford crowd followed any other player. 'Well if that's big time snooker then that's the way it is,' he shrugs. 'Maybe I'm a little bit old-fashioned. I used to think that people have a lot of integrity when they're actually watching the game. But if you're going to whistle and things like that when one guy's playing then that means you're an absolute idiot, because you just don't understand what's going on down there. You might as well go to school for two years and know how to conduct yourself, learn the game a little bit as well. If a guy's got five pounds he can go and do that if he wants. It's all part of the game. But it took a little bit of getting used to.'

He stretches long legs out on the oatmeal-coloured sofa. Even wearing jeans he is elegant. He was once called the Rhett Butler of the green baize and he has the strong, cynical good looks of that American hero, overlaid with a contained world-weary charm that is more European in style. If he were to choose a time to live other than our own it would be Paris in the 1890s, strolling down the broad pavements of the Champs Elysees with his blonde wife Barbara on his arm.

He says that when he thought of the World Championships he imagined they would be played in a room with solid gold fittings and chandeliers hanging down. He's played in a place like that now, he says, the Cafe Royal in London. It has chandeliers. But the first World Championship he saw was something of a disappointment in its setting

112

— John Spencer and Alex Higgins fighting it out in 1972 in Selly Park British Legion hall in Birmingham, and the audience sitting on upturned beer crates. The following year was City Exhibition Halls in Manchester and rain coming through the roof. No glamour left then.

The glamour of snooker, if ever there was any for Cliff Thorburn, has long gone now. 'I've now had to realise that it's my living,' he says. 'It's past the novelty stage now. Whatever my goals and my ideals are I don't dream any more. I may have an idea but it's not a dream. If I think of something, then I'm going to go out and do it, whereas before I'd just think, That would be nice. Now I have to do it.

'A lot of people who I'm around, they only think of money. I didn't start playing the game for money, but I know now that the more I make now the less I have to do when I'm a bit older. I'm just very heavily obligated to be involved with the game in Canada. Because it's almost my life you know, something that I have to do. It's not really like a sacrifice, because I miss my family and friends and my lifestyle from before. People who are my best friends have just had children and we've had our son. We were all really good buddies and interested in each other just for what we are and not because you're a snooker champion or anything like that. I miss that . . . I just miss who I am over there. I've been the best player there for about twelve years, so to come over here I was a big fish in a big pond whereas over there I'm a big fish in a little pond. I could do a lot more for the game in general over there than I could here. A lot of people here think I should still be over here slogging it out and doing exhibitions all over the countryside, but it's not my idea of what I want from the game. I don't want to be playing all my life.'

He and Barbara have been renting this house ever since they first arrived in Britain eighteen months ago, so maybe deep down he never really meant to stay here, would always have gone home in the end, even had he won the World title three times over. There are only nine days to go before this year's championships, and he says he's feeling quite good. It's the first time he's felt good for a long time. He's been given the use of someone's billiard room and he can go over there and practise every day for hours at a time. Before he had to use the Kingston Snooker Centre and he'd never get private practice at all. People were always coming up to say hello.

'But you never know until you get to Sheffield,' he sighs. 'You never know until you pot the ball to win or the other guy pots the ball to beat you. You can't know.'

Really, though, he's looking beyond the World Championships, looking forward to going home, looking forward to his new life in the Canadian game. He says he feels sick at the thought that he left the country just when he'd become World Champion and that might have had anything to do with the decline of the game there and the demise of the Canadian Open. What he would like to see back home is a nationally televised snooker tournament with 2,000 people comfortably seated and the best players in the world competing. Preferably with himself in the final. 'That would just about do it for me, I think. And then to win the World Championship five or six times,' says the man who says that the dreams have died.

April 1982:
The Highland Masters

Defeat is for Tomorrow

Steve Davis says it's the first time he's going to be able to go to bed by 11 p.m. for oh, it must be a year. He's playing in a tournament in Scotland, staying at the Kingsmills, one of those hotels that's like a country one but which the proprietor proudly claims is only a mile from the town centre — though the rest of us may find it a little difficult to think of Inverness as urban.

The date today is 16 April, the day the qualifying rounds for the World Championships start. While the World Champion is up in Inverness the onslaught on his title is beginning. In four different venues — Sheffield, Bristol, Stockport and exotic Sutton Coldfield — players are converging in hopes of winning a chance to take his title away from him. Out of the surging mass of Englishmen, Irishmen, Scotsmen, Welshmen, Australians, Canadians, South Africans and people from Grimsby, one man will earn the privilege of facing Steve Davis in the first round. For them it's a chance for immortality, the one opportunity they will have in the year to join the top pros, the men who can get match practice practically all the year round, the men who can play in Inverness just two weeks before the championship.

The tournament is the Highland Masters at the Eden Court Theatre in Inverness. It's by invitation, with Davis, Higgins, Reardon and Spencer facing four Scottish pros — Matt Gibson, Eddie Sinclair, Bert Demarco and Murdo McLeod. There's a first prize of £5,000 so it's worth the players' while in financial terms, even if it does mean the season gets ever longer, ever fuller.

Steve Davis's season bears witness to the theory of the ever-expanding universe. On top of his tournament schedule Steve has crammed in exhibitions, challenge tours, *Daily Star* snooker nights. He's opened supermarkets and talked his head off for his weekly column in the *Daily Star,* and even written a book, albeit with a little help. He works so hard he is in danger of not being able to stop ever, like a planet spinning on and on into infinity. It's common practice to blame Barry Hearn, his manager, for the frantic pace of the World Champion's life, but Steve Davis does nothing he doesn't want to do. 'Anything Barry does is all right with me,' he says firmly.

He's won his first match against Matt Gibson, but only after the Scot has been ahead for the whole match. He says he's never going to win this thing if he doesn't play better than he did tonight, which doesn't sound very hopeful, coming only two weeks before the World Championships start, but he sounds chirpy and confident, as he always does. He's not given to self-examination. 'I just try to play snooker a lot,' he says.

Tomorrow, though he does not know it yet, he will go out of this tournament by the astonishing score of nil-six to Ray Reardon, who's hardly been travelling at all. He's been at home taking his game apart. The Hurricane will go out too, again by the astonishing score of nil-six to John Spencer. These are such curious results it is hard to imagine what they portend for the World Championships, if indeed they have any significance at all. Snooker is such a mixture of skill and luck, of character and courage and pure chance. 'It's gone beyond sport,' Steve Davis himself once said. 'It's not just a sport. It's more like a serial. That's why a lot more families watch it these days, older women and young girls that might not know a lot about the game but are interested in the people. It's like Coronation Street with balls.'

For the moment, though, defeat is for tomorrow, the World Championships two weeks away. All Steve Davis wants to do is snuggle down into his duvet. Not many hotels have them so it's an unexpected luxury. He's comfortably installed in a family suite, with more beds than he can get into at once but lots of space and a huge window stretching almost the length of one wall. You can see into the owner's back garden, all daffs and bright tulips at this time of year. And it's got all the things that snooker players always want too — a colour telly, coffee making equipment, the telephone.

Just in case he can't get to sleep at this unexpectedly early hour Steve's got a book to read. He's usually up till the small hours of the morning. 'You play a match and then can't go to sleep immediately so staying up becomes a habit,' he says. The book's all about how Darwin's theories were wrong and how there are no fossils to support his ideas about some of the supposed stages of evolution. Turtles come into it somewhere too, he says. He's impressed with his own intellectualism in reading it but says he's just showing off. Normally he reads Tom Sharpe.

By eleven o'clock tonight at least two people know they are out of the World Championships, that their chance has gone for another year. Steve Davis still has two weeks left of being the champion, two weeks before *he* must take his chance. He relaxes in the warmth of the room, with its cream shag pile carpet that you can sink your toes into and its glowing autumn colours, old gold and cream and rich orange. 'I want to be like a cat,' he says. 'Sleep fourteen hours a day.'

April 1982:
World Championship Qualifying

It's a Cruel Game, Pat

It's Stockport again and yet another qualifying tournament. Only this time it's the most important one of all, for the World Championships. One chance a year for the understudies to step out of the shadows, one chance a year for the young players to make their mark. If they're good they'll break through whatever the system, Steve Davis said at Wembley. But is it true? Could one chance a year really be enough?

Pat Houlihan is in buoyant mood as he prepares for his match against Australian Ian Anderson. He came up a day or so early with his pal Derek and they went over to Blackpool for the day. It's so nice in Blackpool, one of Pat's favourite places. They had a walk on the beach and a nice drink. He played his greatest match there in the Blackpool Tower Circus when he beat John Spencer for the 1965 English Amateur. 'That was the best experience I ever had in snooker,' he says. 'And not just because I won it. Up there in the Tower with 1,500 people in front of you. You could hear a pin drop.'

Now he's in the Romiley Forum in Stockport with maybe thirty people there and a silence that feels dead though it is broken by the hum of the air conditioner. The atmosphere here is austere, as though the audience will have to be convinced they are watching something worthwhile before they will get emotionally involved. There is no sense of drama or tension as there is at the big tournaments, as there will be next week at the Crucible itself. It would be easy to forget that for the players this is a moment of supreme drama. The outcome of this match could, for the successful one, change the course of a life.

Both Pat Houlihan and Ian Anderson are edgy, missing shots that should be straightforward for any professional. They normally would be. Although spectators often write off players who are not at the very peak of the game, all the professionals are highly skilled at what they do. They would not be here otherwise.

Pat Houlihan is five-three up by the interval and reckons he'll play better tonight. He is chirpy, buoyant. Ian Anderson is subdued. He says he was frightened even to pot the balls at the end there, in case something went wrong. He goes back to his hotel in between sessions for some coffee. It's a big rambling red brick place with heavy dark oak furniture in the lobby and an old-fashioned sense of solidity about everything. Ian reckons it's costing him about £50 or £60 a day to live in Britain, what with accommodation and meals and everything. And we've got the worst hotels in the world, he thinks.

He has come 12,000 miles from his home outside Sydney to be here and he has to make it through to Sheffield just to break even. Without match practice though he doesn't see that he's got much of a chance. He came over on the plane with Paddy Morgan, the Australian number three and Paddy told him he'd never played better in his life before, then went out and got beat nine-one. Ian says he's the same. He practised the other day with Rex Williams and Rex won the first frame and not another all day. Ian says he's playing so bloody well, *he* thinks, and then he gets here and can't knock a bloody ball in. Can't get a damn thing right. Getting the bad run on the balls hurts, especially as the same thing happened in last year's qualifying when he played Dave Martin. He was the one that was getting Dave into trouble and then he couldn't take advantage of it.

He says you try to tell yourself it's not mental but deep down he thinks it must be. He is as blond and bronzed as you expect your typical Aussie to be, but his lifestyle owes more to snooker philosophy than to the national mania for physical fitness. He looks as plump and prosperous as any businessman and he wears his track suit strictly for jogging down to breakfast in his hotel.

At thirty-seven he is one of only three professionals active in his country — the ubiquitous Eddie Charlton, Paddy Morgan, who's really from Northern Ireland, and himself. His life could not be more different from that of people like Pat Houlihan, who, if they get exhibitions at all, are likely to be playing in the smoke-filled beery atmosphere of working men's clubs.

Ian Anderson travels up to 100,000 miles a year chasing the exhibitions that are his main source of income. He has played in only three actual tournaments this year and only in this one are the matches full-length. When he first started as a pro he had to work as an administrator for a transport company, then for a billiard company though there were several snooker tournaments in Australia then. They have gradually all fallen away till now he finds himself criss-crossing a continent to play 'local yokels', as he puts it.

The yokels in Australia, though, are much better catered for where entertainment is concerned than our British yokels. Their clubs are like palaces, says Ian, especially in New South Wales. They're fantastic places. You might have fifty or sixty thousand members in one club alone and it only costs five or ten Australian dollars a year to join. There might be ten billiard tables, indoor tennis courts, a gymnasium, swimming pools and, as befits the land that gave us Foster's lager, countless bars. They run on the revenue from fruit machines, so just to make sure there are enough chances for the members to hand over their money to the proprietors, there are usually about 500 machines in every club. Best of all for the snooker players who are part of the entertainment, though, is that the clubs are large and spacious and always cool because of the air conditioning, not like the poky, smoky, eye-watering clubs in Britain.

For all the gorgeousness of its settings and the vastness of the country, snooker in Australia is not the success story it has been in Britain. There is only one television tournament actually made out there — the Winfield Masters, won last year by Britain's Tony Meo — because it's cheaper for the Aussies just to buy from the Brits. They can't even be bothered to show their purchases half the time anyway. There's footage of last year's World Championship and this year's Yamaha that's never been seen on Australian telly, even though it's on twenty-four hours a day and there are five television stations in Sydney alone.

That's why Ian Anderson, along with all the overseas players, dreams of a world circuit. He's stopping off at Singapore on the way back home to set up some shows there later in the year. Maybe that way he'll recoup some of his losses on this. A thousand pounds he reckons it's cost him, not to mention the five weeks he's had to pencil out of his working year to make the trip.

He stops at the hotel reception desk for some chocolate, muttering about blood sugar levels. He gets into the car he's had to hire to drive himself around while he's here. 'If Pat loses tonight OK he's going to be disappointed,' he says. 'But he just gets in his car and drives a couple of hundred miles and goes home. I can't go home tonight. It's 12,000 miles away.' This gentle courteous man is away from home for forty weeks of the year and he's missing his wife, he says. His daughter's five years old and he's never been there for her birthday. He wonders sometimes if his way of life is really worthwhile.

'You come over here and you've got to perform now,' he says. "If you don't you've got no chance of showing anyone what you can do for another twelve months.

'Lose and it affects your rankings, yet without match practice you've got no chance.'

He goes into the final session immaculate in his evening suit. Pat Houlihan doesn't have a proper evening suit but he's put on a bow tie and his hair looks specially combed, though the parting is about as straight as a fork of lightning. Chirpy and comical as he is off the table, on it he looks grim, hard, and his face has the adamantine planes of a Red Indian. Two bright spots of red burn on his cheekbones as he steps under the light.

Ian Anderson is softer, less competitive looking, as if the manager of the club had wandered by mistake into the tournament lists. He strikes the ball softly, almost tentatively at times, without producing that satisfying crack that is the sound of a ball being hit firmly. As he plays there is a constant smile on his face though whether he is trying to propitiate the gods of snooker or placate the audience in case they are not enjoying the game, is uncertain.

He takes the first frame of the evening and Pat Houlihan wins the second and third. In the fourth he is only seven points behind with blue, pink, and black on the table. Without aggression, still smiling, he has suddenly reached a crunch point in the game. He can win this frame. He can bring them back to level terms again. He has a real chance to win the match.

He misses the blue.

It is one of those moments in a match when you suddenly see beneath the facade of mildness, the correctness, the decorum of snooker into the harsh competitiveness that the players channel into the game. Snooker's image makers would have you believe that it is a civilised game, played only by gentlemen who remain gracious whether they win or lose. But beneath the elegantly cut suits, the snowy white embroidered shirts, beat raw red hearts that are pumping blood into the players' veins at an alarmingly rapid rate.

Ian Anderson, the calm, the gentle Ian Anderson concedes the frame in a torment of rage at himself. In that single demonstration of fury the match slips away from him. After the interval he gallantly chips away at the cocky Londoner but Pat Houlihan, with almost twenty years more experience behind him, knows how to hang on to an advantage and takes both frames and the match. Pat Houlihan does not tell himself there is nothing mental in snooker.

Ian Anderson sits in the bar later, dejected. 'It's a bloody long way to come for one day's snooker,' he sighs. 'I could have been up on the Gold Coast and played a day's snooker there. And lain in the sunshine afterwards.'

The following day Pat Houlihan is to meet Dave Martin, the man who put Ian Anderson out in last year's qualifying. Martin has been a professional for only two years and although he did very well in his first major tournament, reaching the semis of the Jameson's Whiskey tournament in Derby, he has had little chance to consolidate that success. Most of the big events are by invitation only and how you did last season counts for more than this one — until next year, of course.

Dave Martin at thirty-five is a dark solid male-looking man who takes possession of the snooker table with the proprietorial air of a landlord at the bar of his public house. But once on it his game has a boyish kind of energy, like a kid playing keepy-uppy with a football in the streets so that everyone can see how good he is. As he finishes his break he looks at the audience with a bright alert foxy gaze. He storms into a four-one lead but the wily Pat pulls his lead back to just one frame. They end the afternoon on five-three to Dave Martin.

If things were to continue in the evening as before, the match could be anyone's, but while Pat continues on much the same level as in the afternoon, Dave Martin moves his game up a level. In the old days, when Pat Houlihan was breaking the four minute barrier for making century breaks and had more bottle than Ray Reardon, then Pat would have moved his game up too. But he's older now and the eyes have gone, and it gets harder and harder to hold on when younger cockier players are hurling breaks of sixty-eight and 127 at you. Pat's friend Derek, a round pasty-faced man who has been following him around for twenty years, ever since the famous match in Blackpool Tower Circus, blinks behind steel-rimmed glasses. He looks so miserable that you expect two great big fat tears to come rolling out from under the frames and splash down on to his plump stomach.

Pat doesn't win a frame that evening but he looks more cheerful than Derek.

'It's a cruel game Pat,' sighs Derek heavily. 'It's a cruel game.'

Pat shrugs insouciantly. He says he'll have to get contact lenses. He'll be all right once he gets a new pair, just watch him. He says he did have a set once but he left them on top of a taxi one night when he was drunk and the taxi driver just went off with them. Didn't even see them.

Frank Callan, the man who is commonly considered to know more about snooker technique than anyone else in the world, maybe even than Clive Everton, remarks that Pat's taking his defeat well. 'I takes it well because I've had to get used to it,' says Pat. 'He played well tonight. He could go well in Sheffield.' Frank says that Pat managed to shut him off in the afternoon but in the evening Dave managed to get at the big colours, which is what he likes. 'He's very in and out, is Dave,' says Frank. 'He could be really bad tomorrow night.'

Someone standing behind them at the bar says *he* saw Dave Martin playing last night against Kirk Stevens and he was just as good as he was tonight.

But when they go back in to play the customary exhibition frames it's Pat who's knocking them in like it was easy and Dave who's missing sitters now that the pressure's off.

It's the last match of the qualifying tournament, Dave Martin the last man to know he is going forward into the tournament proper at Sheffield in five days time. They're all standing around at the bar afterwards talking about it as they drink their beer. Everybody in snooker thinks it's going to be a Davis—Griffiths final, just as the last five major tournaments have been. Everybody outside snooker thinks that too. It'll be Borg and McEnroe, Coe and Ovett, Ali and Frazier. It'll be an aficionado's final, with the two men who really are at the top of the game fighting it out for supremacy. But where everybody outside snooker thinks Steve Davis will win, the smart money in snooker is on Terry Griffiths. He's destroyed Steve Davis's confidence they say. Steve Davis, they say, has no chance.

As Dave Martin rises to leave Pat Houlihan calls out, 'Play well.'

'That's all I want to do,' says Dave.

Pat Houlihan's reply is acerbic. 'That's what you've *got* to do.'

Dave Martin leans towards him, bright foxy eyes softened with drink. 'If I play well,' he says. 'If I play as well as I can play, I'll be the only one in the world that's slaughtered Steve Davis.'

Pat Houlihan looks highly disgusted as Dave Martin glides his way towards the door. 'That's the drink talking,' he says shaking his head in outrage. He says Dave Martin's high tonight because he beat him and he used to have a bit of a reputation. But it's not the same thing as beating Steve Davis. It is just *not* the same thing as beating Steve Davis.

He and Derek have a chaser with their beer and then a few others. Pat says you can't blame people for not wanting to book him for exhibitions. People know he used to be good once but now they think he's past it, he can't do it any more. You can't blame them for thinking that way. All they want nowadays is winners. He has put his big horn-rimmed spectacles back on. He says his sleep was broken last night at the hotel. It's supposed to be a good one but the beds are very hard. His eyes weren't sore in the morning but they were very tired. He's been putting Optrex in them all day. Derek says when he gets his new eyes he'll be right back up there next year.

Derek says that Pat's match at the Blackpool Tower Circus was some match, that was. Pat says that John Spencer put in his autobiography that his match in the Blackpool Tower Circus against Pat Houlihan was the worst he ever played in his life. There was no call for him to say that, Pat says. He played badly because he was forced to. If it was just that John Spencer played badly why couldn't he beat him after that, when they played their challenge matches at Earls Court and all those places?

He and Derek stand on the pavement outside the Forum waiting for their taxi to arrive. There's nothing for them in Sheffield now. They'll have to watch it on the box like everybody else. Pat Houlihan can't stay gloomy for long. They might go down to Sheffield for a couple of days after all, he says. They could always have a little bet.

30 April — 16 May

The World Championships

The Crucible at last. The season, so long, so hard, has been building towards this moment, the opening of the 1982 Embassy World Professional Championship. This is the big one, the no-excuse tournament, every player's dream. The theatre foyer is crowded with people but it would be an event to come into the Crucible anyway, with its jewellery stall and the sweetie counter and the gift shop that feels like an Eastern bazaar with its musky scent of incense and its colourful Oriental scarves and knicknacks.

As the crowd sit waiting in the theatre, smaller than you expect when some of the lesser tournaments have been played in halls like airport hangars, there is the sense of excitement you always get at the beginning of a major sporting event, but it is muted. Everybody expects the tournament's opening match — the defending champion Steve Davis against Tony Knowles — to be merely routine. The real anticipation is for the final, two and a half weeks away, where Steve is expected to meet Terry Griffiths. They've been neck and neck over the last part of the season and a meeting in the final will settle a question that this time last year looked answered for years to come — who is the best player in the world? Even if the match degenerated into poor snooker, into a brawling, slugging, punch drunk battle of the heavyweights, it would matter. It would be important. It would provide that most longed for phenomenon of sport — a result.

The people sitting so patiently here under the gantries studded with lots of tiny little lights twinkling like starlight, aren't, then, expecting great excitement tonight. It's nice to come along to the first night and they might not get a chance to see the World Champion in action later in the tournament, when tickets are harder to get hold of. In the public mind Steve Davis has an aura of invincibility. He is the champion and many have bet on him to win again at the extraordinary odds of five to two on. If Corals can't see him losing the public can't either.

He has surrounded himself with the aura of a champion, installing himself on the whole top floor of a posh Sheffield hotel with an assorted collection of Romford supporters, video films and space invader machines. The Prince in the Tower. Under siege in his tower. His recent form has been poor. Out of the glare of publicity, without the pressure of top competition, he has been playing badly. Two nights ago he played an exhibition match in Birmingham. Top referee John Smyth was officiating and he says, 'He played two local players. And he got murdered.' Steve is still here to tell the tale, so perhaps the result wasn't that drastic, but it is clear that the champion's preparation for the defence of his title could be thought to be less than ideal and has included more book signings, store-openings, exhibition matches and public appearances than most people would consider advisable.

His opponent, Tony Knowles, is a recent recruit to the ranks of Sportsworld. Geoff Lomas likes his snooker and Harvey Lisberg likes the strong sex appeal of his image, and between the two things they reckon he's going to be a big and bankable star. Now Tony isn't that well known outside the snooker world but the BBC know a good news story when they see it and are keen to run the one about the first sacrificial victim to be offered up on the altar of Steve Davis's invincibility. They want to now what it feels like to be cannon fodder and ask Tony if he'll do a three minute interview on 'Newsnight'. Harvey Lisberg is delighted by the idea. Three minutes prime time network television. Who's heard of Tony Knowles after all? But when he phones Tony up, the player says no. All he wants to do is beat Steve Davis. He doesn't want to do an interview. He doesn't want to stand around in a tight suit before the game. He just wants to go out and murder him.

Harvey's suffering from shock but he doesn't believe in interfering with a player that way. 'Great Tony. Great,' he says. 'You go out there and do it.' He puts the phone down and turns to Geoff Lomas. 'We've got a right one here,' he says. 'The man's mad.'

But Tony Knowles isn't mad. He believes he can do it. Usually he gets very nervous before a big match, but not tonight. He remains composed in spite of the fact that he immediately takes a four-nil lead. Barry Hearn is standing at the back, craning to see, his face grim. When Steve complains in the very first frame about a photographer's clicking camera, he goes rushing out along with half of the Snookasport staff. The photographer later claims to have been threatened by someone though no-one's quite sure by whom, and in any case it's far less sensational than what is happening on the table.

Tony Knowles looks ruddy with health compared to the tired pale-faced boy who sits watching him. There is a quality of icy anger on Steve Davis's face, as if he can't believe his own nerves, his own unprecedented incompetence. Usually he is at the peak of his form in major championships but this time he looks as if it's all happened just a little too quickly, as if he wants to stop it all, come back next week and start again. He looks cold, as if his veins are all iced up. 'Scared to death, isn't he?' says one of the scorekeepers. And after the grind of the snooker circuit, the travelling, the demands of the public, a year is such a very short time to be World Champion after all.

Terry Griffiths, the 1979 World Champion, is sitting in bed at home with his wife Annette, watching the match on TV, and he can't believe what he's seeing. 'I've seen Steve playing off form before,' he says. 'But he isn't off form. He is just disastrous. He can't do a thing.' Terry has never seen Steve play as badly, not even as an amateur, and he's appalled. As the session creeps to a close, the champion has won only one frame. Eight-one to Tony Knowles. Terry Griffiths thinks he'll come back. He remembers when he was seven-one down to Steve himself, as defending champion, and he fought back to ten all. You save face a bit then. He wants Steve to come back.

Not many of the other players do. There's a group of them watching the match upstairs from the player's box. As the crowd buzzes with that special kind of excitement that grips an audience when a champion is about to be beaten, a number of his fellow professionals are laughing and urging 'Come on Tony.'

There is a sense of shock in the back-stage corridor as the evening session ends. 'Somebody smile,' says Barry Hearn, but the most he is offered is the observation that it isn't over yet. 'Isn't it?' says Barry quietly, before he heads down the corridor muttering about the wheels temporarily being dislodged.

In the press room one writer has just been ticked off by the *Sun* for phoning through on the special line they're using for news from the Falklands. It's early on in the crisis and among the journalists here there are rumours of greater casualties than are being reported, and Fleet Street editors suppressing information, though at the Ministry of Defence they think the press are releasing too much information to the Argentines. Here in Sheffield they're teasing the *Daily Star*'s Ted Corbett that he'll have to write his story without mentioning the fact that the *Daily Star* columnist — who receives £25,000 a year just for talking to the newspaper — is being beaten. The headline will have to read, 'Bolton Boy Gets Through' without saying who his opponent was, they say. Ted listens with his customary dry humour. 'Yes,' he says, 'there's a D notice on it.'

The following day his columnist begins the session by potting the cue ball. It is an ominous start. Under the lights his hair glints orange, like the orange thread woven into the satin of his waistcoat. He still looks pale and drawn. Tony Knowles looks tense but he's playing tight safe snooker, building up his score with a series of small breaks, and he takes the first frame of the session. 'Is it a fix?' someone asks Barry Hearn jokingly. 'I wish it were,' he says. He says he's never seen Steve touch the white ball before, as he did in that frame.

Tony Knowles looks sick with nerves as they start what could be the final frame. He chalks up a break of eighteen first, then gets another opening. 'It won't be long now,' says Barry. The break goes to twenty-four and it is Steve Davis's chance. This is the crunch for him, his last opportunity to seize hold of this match, turn it all around, recover just a little bit of his champion's form. His first long red shoots straight for the pocket, then rockets out again. Barry Hearn looks resigned. 'There's no way,' he says.

He is right. The champion makes a brave attempt with a thirty break but it is not enough. There is not enough conviction there. On the other table Dave Martin, who said in Stockport he'd slaughter Steve Davis if he got the chance to play as well as he could, has not even got

126

The Invincible is defeated . . .

but conquers the press with humour

past the first round. He loses by five frames to Graham Miles, the man they all think they can beat.

And somewhere on the M5 motorway Terry Griffiths stops at a service station and hears the news on the radio. Steve Davis has lost ten-one. It's the kind of score you expect him to inflict on his opponent and Terry Griffiths feels sad that he's crashed out without redeeming his name as champion. 'He must have gone,' thinks Terry. 'He lost ten-one, just give it up he did.'

Steve Davis walks straight from defeat on the table into the press room. There's no time for him to compose himself, no time for just a quiet moment alone before he must analyse in public why he has suffered this most bitter defeat of his career, why he has lost the championship he must have begun to think of as his own personal property — because everyone else did.

The post match press conference is a sadistic invention anyway. We're such hypocrites about modern sport, demanding sportsmanship, civilised manners, conformity to rules, when all the time what we like best are the glimpses of more primitive emotions, the Bothams and Connors of the world going berserk and winning matches on a great surge of animal aggression, the adrenalin-lifted performances of losers struggling to survive. We'd be disturbed in real life to be confronted by such raw emotions but they excite us when they're caged behind an eighteen-inch television screen. The post match interview is just another part of the fiction that sport is for gentlemen. It implies that competitors, after going through a prolonged ordeal of emotional stress, should be prepared to come in and explain themselves afterwards.

Many top sports stars have refused or been unable to talk to the press after unexpected defeats. Steve Davis has lost more than anyone else in this tournament has to lose, yet here he is talking candidly and wittily, to journalists whose main aim is to extract a good quote from him for their stories. In victory he has often seemed arrogant, almost patronising to his opponents, as if they had no chance of winning against him. Now in defeat he has the grace of a champion. Outside a couple of top players stand gleefully discussing the match. Here in this room Steve Davis is speaking with a simple honesty that is very hard to achieve at the moment of defeat. The no excuse tournament, Cliff Thorburn called it and Steve Davis offers no excuse.

He says that Tony kept him under pressure by playing tight snooker and not making any silly mistakes. All credit to him. He didn't give away as many chances as Steve thought he would. 'I did play a bit like a dreg,' he says, and somehow the casually used, slangy word has a bravura about it that is typically Romford. Defeat is accepted but as no more than a temporary setback. The wheels may have dislodged for the moment but there is no doubt in Steve Davis's mind that they will be back on course again soon.

He says that after a recent poor spell he'd been looking forward to playing well in the championships, extremely well in fact. And he doesn't think all the travelling has wrecked his game because he's enjoyed it all. And obviously he's very disappointed but you've got to take it. You can't take the winning if you can't take the losing. Everybody slags you off but at least you know that when you do play well again they've got to change their minds.

Barry Hearn suddenly darts over to where Steve's sitting. 'Just to round off the day,' he says, 'you're going to be called up, only someone's just said you couldn't hit one of those Argentinians.' Steve Davis laughs, not as if he's putting a brave face on it but as if he's genuinely amused. He laughs even more when Smithy of the *Daily Mirror* thunders in, goes to sit down and promptly lands on the floor instead. Smithy is a legend for his inability both to avoid accidents and to do anything quietly and Steve Davis nearly falls off his chair, he's laughing so much. That's made his day, he says.

His sense of humour is like a flag waved in the face of the enemy. The Romford way is to lose in style. Steve and Barry would have been the first to break open the bottles of champagne as the Titanic was going down. Steve even says that he's enjoyed the match, even though he got beaten — 'in a masochistic sort of way,' he says with a grin.

'It's a nice position to be in, eight-one down,' he adds. 'If you win you're a hero. It's a hundred to one shot to be a hero. I'm going to play it low for a couple of months. Then I'll start my hero campaign. I shall look forward to my next chance to regain the title.'

Barry Hearn watches him go. He says he's going to smile at everybody now, and no, it won't make much difference to them business-wise, five percent at most. But it's not the money. He sighs. It's a strange feeling, he says, almost a sense of release. They realised a month ago that Tony was going to be the hardest match. But not ten-one. Not that hard. He stalks down the corridor to find his charge and his irrepressible optimism re-emerges. 'Oh well. We're on the Meo-mobile now,' he shouts, raising his fist as he goes.

* * *

It's a Sunday night and the arrival of the Hurricane is awaited with some impatience. Rumour has it that he is coming from his Manchester home by aeroplane, which would mean a half-hour drive to the airport at one end and then another half hour drive back into Sheffield from the airport at the other. There is great glee among the press at the thought that supposing there was fog, would the plane have to be diverted to Luton?

The Hurricane arrives in Sheffield by more conventional methods and finally makes his way down to the Crucible practice room in the early hours of Monday morning. Because it is in the early hours of Monday morning one of the Crucible staff attempts to put the lights out. The Hurricane's disapproval of this decision is so violent that the electrician's sweater somehow gets ripped during the ensuing discussion. The Hurricane then asks the way to the nearest toilet but decides a walk down the corridor is more than can reasonably be expected of a man in the early hours of Monday morning and proceeds to piss in the nearest plantpot. There are reports that the lighting man is going to make a formal complaint to the WPBSA but the Hurricane apologises and offers to buy him a new sweater and the WPBSA fail to receive a complaint about it. No-one speaks up on behalf of the plantpot either.

The Hurricane's back on form on the table too, beating Jim Meadowcroft in a sparkling ten frames to five. He says that at night's when he feels his body's awake, that's when he's alive, though obviously not alive enough to take a walk down the corridor.

This is his first talk to the press this tournament and of course he's asked about the Davis defeat. He says Tony played very well for a raw kid, though at twenty-six, Tony might have preferred a more dignified personal description. The Hurricane says he wasn't too happy with the way the commentators described the match. They all said Steve was off when he never got into the match at all. For Tony to come in and overcome the nerves like that was monumental. He says he's frightened of Steve but not as frightened as he used to be because Steve's not being a machine any more. The freshness of him has gone and it will take an awful lot of effort to bring it back.

He is in philosophical mood as he ponders the demands of the game, the way success in it is always accompanied by a decline in your

130

standards. He doesn't even like playing snooker now. He likes playing golf. But sacrifices have to be made if you want to gain security for your wife and children — you might have to work as many as three or four nights a week. You have to be like an athlete, practising six or seven hours a day for months on end, like Daley Thompson really, though Daley only has one purpose, one track meeting and snooker players have to do a lot of travelling in between. The Hurricane says he hasn't actually brought himself to do any practice yet. He would kill to win the World Championships but there again wanting to kill to win isn't good enough — you have to practise too, though he doesn't say whether he means you have to practise killing or practise snooker.

'I'm finding it difficult to concentrate,' says the Hurricane solemnly. 'One minute I'll knock in a cracking red and then suddenly I don't know what to do. It's not familiar to me any more. And my timing's so off it's not true. It's down to the one basic thing,' he says. 'I'm not sure of myself,' and proceeds to say how he's not at all worried about his next opponent, Doug Mountjoy, though he doesn't want to be unkind because Duggie's a nice fellow.

He comes in later that afternoon with two big boxes of kiddies sweets for the press, little jelly animals and chewy pink blobs. Ted Corbett reckons it's the only way he'll shut the press up, stuffing sweets in their mouths, but it's a kind, if incomprehensible gesture, prompted by who knows what sort of whimsical or humorous urge on the part of the Hurricane.

The big match that afternoon is the final session of Terry Griffiths' against Willie Thorne. By the end of the previous day's play Willie is leading by five frames to four, but nobody believes he can win it. Willie's a loser, a man who has so much trouble coping with the nervous tensions of big-time snooker that he's had to have treatment from a hypnotherapist. Even when he gets to nine-five many of the snooker people watching don't think he'll win. He just doesn't have the mental attitude of a winner.

As it happens though Terry Griffiths doesn't have the mental attitude of a winner either. 'Yesterday against Willie I was four-two up and I was terrible disappointed with the way I was playing' he says. 'I wanted to win in style. I was thinking, This is bloody awful stuff, instead of going there and thinking, I'm four-two up and I don't care if I've got to piss in his eye to win. That's what competing's all about.

'Of course when you're wrong in your attitude everything's bloody wrong then. The cameras keep moving all the time. The table's hopeless. People keep moving up and down the steps. Willie Thorne is getting in my way. The referee keeps getting in my way. Everything's wrong. It all goes then. There's nothing wrong in all these things. It's you who're wrong.

'It just wasn't the same for me when Steve lost. I was so disappointed it's untrue. I just didn't have anything to aim for. I know it's silly to say that. It's the World Championships. But I don't really think I'd have been happy winning without beating Steve, because I knew deep down that if I was on form I could win. I knew I could beat all the other players. The only one I don't know if I could beat is Steve. I know I can beat him sometimes. Steve knows that as well. He doesn't know if he can beat me. I know the way he thinks about it because I know the way I think about it.'

When you're playing Steve Davis and yourself as well as your opponent, you don't have much chance of winning, especially when your opponent has, he says, a seven-one record against you. 'When the public see me against Terry Griffiths on the television they think Terry's a certainty,' says Willie. 'They've only seen him on the telly in the last two years and not me. But I've played him seven times and only lost to him once. That was nine-eight on the black in the final at Pontins. All the lads at home in Leicester have had a right laugh because I was three to one underdog against Terry. Everybody there knows my record against him and they've won a few quid.'

Good for the Leicester lads but it's turning out to be a bad week for World Champions. Steve Davis, Terry Griffiths and now Cliff Thorburn have spent their time ensuring that they will be ex-champions. Thorburn is unlucky to be matched against Jimmy White, whose form is breathtakingly fluent. He looks as if he'll take the whole field apart. Jimmy is not regarded with whole-hearted admiration by the snooker press, who think a world class player should have a safety game, but when he's playing such heartbreaking snooker it's hard to see why he needs it. He flashes through the first six frames like a shooting star. Cliff Thorburn tries valiantly to slow him down, but Jimmy is moving the balls around like a magician. Cliff will think he's left the table safe — and it probably would be were his opponent anyone else — when, abracadabra, Jimmy will pull out one of his astonishing pots.

Cliff Thorburn is generally held by the players to have one of the most boring games around. He's so slow, so dogged they can't be bothered to watch him, but he is one of the most intelligent players in

132

Ray Reardon relaxes . . .

but it's all too much
for Terry Griffiths

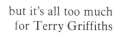

the world, and were he on form, it is clear he would have a good chance of slowing down the youngster's game. He's like a surgeon slicing his way into the contents of the other player's brain, probing the weaknesses there. He is constantly fascinating to watch and if only he were playing well this match might follow a very different pattern. But the things he tries never seem to come off and he's missing the easiest of pots, and although he never stops trying he just can't seem to make the move from guts to confidence. In the end he's playing so badly that Jimmy White's own game begins to be affected.

'It must be too many early nights,' says Jimmy with cheeky grace. Geoff Lomas, his manager, has been waking him at nine o'clock every morning so that he'll get used to the early sessions. He hasn't been drinking either. He hasn't, he says mournfully, been doing anything. It can only do you good. 'Can't it?' he asks, a bit worried about the answer to that one. He is generous towards his opponent, says he played with Cliff over at Kingston Snooker Centre and his game is not what it was. 'It's a shame really. But it's just stages you go through. I went through one.'

Cliff Thorburn has been going through this stage for a whole season now and is getting desperate, but you wouldn't know it from his manner, which is witty, if a little subdued. 'I've been playing the tournaments but not enjoying it any more,' he sighs. 'It's been like working for a living.' He says he's taking positive steps to change his attitude by going back home to Canada. He'll go home and watch some baseball, though a much-travelled journalist says he shouldn't watch his team, the Blue Jays, as it'll only depress him. Cliff laughs and says he thinks he *will* go. That might make him feel better. 'If my game gets any worse going back it'll be a bridge job,' he says and you're struck once again by the gallantry of these snooker players, who can turn defeat into moral victory with their dignity and humour.

The deposed champion, Steve Davis, is here this afternoon, giving support to his Romford team-mate Tony Meo. It's the first time he's been down to the Crucible since his defeat and he looks pale and drawn. Barry Hearn is here too, of course, explaining why he's got rid of the Lucania chain. He's sold sixteen clubs, keeping only his Romford headquarters. Not that it needs much explanation when Riley Leisure are buying him out for £3.1 million. 'You should retire,' one of the press tells him. 'Barbados is nice at this time of year.' Barry Hearn doesn't think much of that idea. 'I'd rather be in Sheffield,' he says.

He's bought videos of *Rocky* and *Rocky 2* for Tony Meo because they make him cry, but he wishes Tony didn't get so nervous. When he heard that Steve had lost, his first reaction was frantic. 'What happened? What happened?' But he immediately supplied the answer himself. 'He didn't play. I know. That can happen to anyone,' and Barry vigorously mimes the frenetic quality of the fear Tony is instantly plunged into.

Now that Steve's out, many people expect Tony to be under pressure to redeem the Romford name. Several of the press even think he's got a better chance of winning the title than his pal Jimmy White because Tony does have a safety game. He's playing the South African number one, Perrie Mans, the man Steve Davis once said was the only player who could destroy him because he could play the way he does and know what he's doing. Perrie is famed as an unorthodox player who goes for his shots without much regard to what happens to the cue ball. His positional play in fact is one of the standard jokes of the circuit, but it's one that can rebound as Perrie is a hard man to beat. He doesn't give a damn who he plays, is frightened of no-one, not even Steve Davis. 'There isn't one top player,' he says firmly. 'Not at the moment there isn't. Never mind what they say. One player will have more publicity than the other because he's got a better manager perhaps.'

Perrie treats snooker as a game, a dangerous attitude for a professional player. He's got a couple of cars, a couple of houses out of it and his life is much easier than it used to be, when he was working as well as playing snooker. 'You enjoy it,' he says. 'If you get beat you take it like a man. Crying and complaining are not going to help. You make enemies then and people say, What a bloody bad loser he is. Whether you win or lose to me it's only a game.'

As he's played it badly the past couple of years there's no pressure on him, he says, because nobody expects anything of him, and he builds up his score with his usual collection of thirty breaks and crafty safety play. Tony Meo starts off with a three frame lead but Perrie gradually whittles it back and eventually moves ahead himself, He's leading nine-eight when the young Londoner makes a forty-seven break and moves fifty-four points ahead. If Meo wins this frame he'll level the match and take it to a final frame play-off. 'And Tony will be scared stiff and the Riley cheque hasn't cleared yet,' groans Barry Hearn.

But Tony doesn't get a chance to be scared stiff. Much to the astonishment of Tony, Barry and the entire press room, who have never seen Perrie making a break of over thirty-odd in a major tournament, the South African makes a fine sixty-two clearance to take the frame and the match. There is stupefaction on Tony's face but

Barry just bursts out laughing. 'That's what I want to see from this fellow,' he says. 'A bit of class.' Clive Everton offers Tony some consolation. 'He's never done it in a tournament before.' And Perrie Mans, the object of all this amazement, gives a smile of satisfaction and says he's felt good all along, very good. 'I still lose position but I'm not all that bad,' he says firmly, and then with undisguised amusement at the bemused faces in front of him, 'I'm two feet away now where I used to be six feet away.'

Tony Meo stands at the bar looking miserable. 'How do you feel?' asks his manager. Tony looks surprised. 'Relieved,' he says. 'Yes, it's a strange feeling,' says Barry. 'It's always easier to walk away.' Tony keeps shaking his head and saying he just can't believe that clearance. It was a wonderful clearance. But Barry can't dwell on defeat for longer than about three minutes. He's already confirmed a Steve Davis booking for two and a half grand instead of the £2,000 that was Steve's fee as World Champion — 'novelty value,' he'd said — and he's already thinking ahead for Tony. 'How would you like to be a middleweight?' he asks. 'We need a good middleweight. Eat your heart out, Marvin Hagler. It's Mustapha Hamsho Meo.' He claps Tony on the shoulder. 'We'll fight back,' he says. He's heading for the exit and Romford when the happiest thought of the day strikes him. 'We're going to have a losing party,' he says. 'We've never had a losing party before.'

* * *

After the emotional stress of all the accusations and complaints, the Hurricane needs some stability in his life, so his wife Lynn drives over from Manchester with his baby daughter Lauren. As befits the child of the Hurricane, eighteen-month Lauren is a busy curious little girl who abjures the usual childish need for sleep and spends most of her time investigating the things around her, whether journalists' typewriters or heavy iron bars on the floor. She's unexcited by the Hurricane's invitation to be like him and sit and watch the snooker, but she does recognise the game when she sees it. There's a big poster of Steve Davis in the press room and she rushes over and points at it. 'Daddy, daddy,' she says. The Hurricane looks horrified. 'That's not your daddy.'

* * *

A smile walks into the room. Ray Reardon may or may not be accompanying it. It's hard to tell as the Welshman rarely drops his public image — sociable Ray, with a smile and a word for everybody. 'Ray is not the person that you see,' says Terry Griffiths. 'You don't see Ray as he really is. He does break it down every now and then, but there is that continual front. He's been in the public eye all the time but he's not a selfish person, no. He's done a lot for the sport Ray has. He doesn't do everything right. He does a lot of bad things, I think, the way he treats the referees and that type of thing. He likes to stamp his personality on people, which is just his way. He's done a lot for the game.'

Ray Reardon has just beaten John Virgo in a match where he has demonstrated a remarkable return to form after a couple of years when he was generally considered to be in decline, despite his high rank in the seedings list. He says he feels full as a butcher's dog, fantastic, and that he can do anything with his new cue. Well it's not that new, really, he found it in his own snooker room, but he can do all the things he could do with his other cue, which he had for thirty years. It gives him confidence, which is fifty percent of the battle, he says. The other fifty percent is practice and he's been getting at least four hours a day of that for the last three months.

It's the end of the first week and the big Sunday names are in. Hugh McIlvanney of the *Observer* is here, a modest down-to-earth man, patiently trying to get his questions answered. Ray Reardon keeps the Journalist of the Year waiting. When he finally manages to put a question to Reardon, the Welshman walks off halfway through and slowly stubs out his cigarette.

He says that he really felt for Steve. 'He's one of the best players in the world today, without a doubt,' he says magnanimously. 'I think the lad's been overworked.' He says he has a book out too but he's refused to help with the launch whereas Steve has been touring about all over the place and doing signing sessions at nine o'clock in the morning in big London stores. The pressure was on him from before the word go as defending champion. 'But at least you've been there. You've had a taste of the greatness of the game. You're in the records. No-one can take that away from you,' he says.

His own record, six World titles in nine years during the seventies, has not even been approached by any modern player. He is a man who has won everything there is to win and is used to thinking of himself as the best, a man who can't bear to think that modern snooker can carry on without him. His ruthlessness as a competitor was his greatest asset in his heyday. He wouldn't let go then and he will not let go now. 'You know you're playing bad, but you never realised you were on a downward slide. It's only when you get to a certain part of that slide that you realise. When you're winning you don't notice. Your choice is to get out of the game or improve. Now that I've got myself right upstairs and have been organising myself better in my private life as regards practising, I've been enjoying the game more. I don't want to be left on the shelf. I want to be up there.'

John Virgo, his beaten opponent, wishes him the best of luck for the rest of the tournament. But he's upset. He says he's playing the best snooker of his life and he hasn't had the chance to show it. A fair run of the balls, that's all he asks. 'Ray did not play very well in that first session,' says John mournfully. 'But he still led six-two when I should have been seven-one up. He won at least four of those games through flukes, which put me under pressure for the rest of the game.'

Up on the table the match between John Spencer and Willie Thorne is still toiling on. John, himself a three times winner of the World Championship, is no longer the player he was, and unlike Reardon, hasn't ever bothered to do anything about it. He's more interested in having a laugh, though there aren't many in his match against Willie — he's trailing badly. He goes off to the toilet mid-session and when he comes back discovers that the Reardon match is over. He gets down to the table to break off and then suddenly realises that the screen separating the two tables has been lifted. Up he gets and waves at the people on the other side of the theatre. And in a moment of sheer joy they all wave back and shout hello.

*　*　*

There are few such moments in this tournament. It's all about pressure, about the sick feeling inside when you can't control what your arm's doing and your cue won't move and it just seems to stick there when you try to force it. Silvino Francisco, South Africa's number two, is here for the first time thanks to the WPBSA's new policy of paying seventy-five percent of the air fare. He can't believe the pressure. 'This atmosphere,' he says. 'I'm going to take some videos home to show my brother Mannie, another top South African player. The atmosphere's electric. The easy shots you miss. I've heard about it from all the other

138

South Africans but we haven't got anything like it. It's hard out there, I promise you. I watched the world team event on television and I thought, How do these blokes miss shots like that? Now I know. You've got to have so much concentration out there — it's unbelievable. And you've got to go for your shots. You can't play too negative because if you get a good potter he's going to shoot you to pieces. He's going to break your heart.'

Silvino, big and bronzed, his dark romantic eyes in counterpoint to his child's snub nose, is a breaker of female hearts. 'At least the housewives have someone to watch,' says an Embassy official. Snooker owes its current popularity partly to the fact that so many women *do* watch it. It's the ideal form of revenge for all those years of being excluded from male sport, the perfect game for watching men as sex objects — all that strutting round the table, displaying their elegant ensembles; the bending and stretching that make clothes cling tightly to sensual bodies; the moments of silence when the light above the table falls fleetingly on to sculpted male cheekbones.

Not all snooker players can resist the temptations offered them in their new found role as sex objects. On the final day of his quarter final match against the Hurricane, Willie Thorne hits the headlines for his off-table activities. He's cited in a divorce case for adultery with the wife of one of his best friends. This story is regarded as so much more interesting than mere snooker — despite the fact that it happened at least a year ago — that the nationals ring up their northern news boys at three in the morning with lists of names and phone numbers. 'It was like a bad dream,' says the suitably elegant representative of the *Daily Mail*. The *Sun*'s man from Liverpool takes a similarly jaundiced view of the proceedings. He doesn't like snooker anyway.

The journalists display more tact than their editors, gratefully seizing any excuse not to interview Willie just yet because it's such an important day for him. Willie, with a little help from his hypnotherapist, has become calmer and more confident and has slowed his game down from his previous Hurricane-like speed. The Hurricane has too, though he manages to keep ahead most of the match. In spite of a smooth 143 clearance that turns out to be the tournament's highest break, Willie never manages to catch up and loses by three frames, thirteen-ten.

'My mind was so good this year,' he sighs. 'I just literally couldn't see myself getting beaten, and I'm very disappointed, very disappointed. I believe I was totally in control of my nerves at this championship, for the first time. And it's horrible having this in the background. It's even more horrible having a slight excuse when I feel I was playing well enough not to want one.'

With admirable restraint he refuses to take anything more than his prize money of £3500 home, though the *News of the World* offer him twice that for his story and the *Daily Star* are talking of a sum between five and six thousand for information about what snooker players do in their spare time and where they go after their matches. 'If I'd lost to Terry in the first round there wouldn't have been anything,' says Willie. 'But now I'm the centre, the focus and I've got a chance of winning it, the press have made a big thing out of it. God knows why.'

Snooker has become one great big news story these days, though today is not a successful one for pretenders to the throne. Silvino Francisco goes out to the evergreen Reardon, while Tony Knowles, after being five frames ahead at the beginning of the final session, manages to lose to Eddie Charlton, the man who has almost won this so often before. The Australian is gracious, saying that that last frame is always the hardest and that snooker is a flukey type game, let's face it, and the most exacting demanding ball game there is because of it. Someone standing nearby pats the disconsolate Tony on the shoulder and says, 'Never mind son. It's been a good championship for you really.' Geoff Lomas looks solemn. 'He's very very pleased,' he says. 'Very very pleased.' Tony Knowles nods. 'Terrific,' he says in disgust.

As experience appears to have the edge over youth this year the signs augur well for the Hurricane. He's over ten years older than his opponent, he's a former World Champion, and he appears to be more constructive this year than he's ever been, keeping a tight rein on his emotions. The only thing against him is that his opponent is Jimmy White, who has been one of the few players to shine at the tournament this year. He looks as if he could shoot anyone to pieces, break everyone's heart.

If the Hurricane loses to him it will be like losing to himself of ten years ago. Alex has deliberately slowed his game down, eschewing the crazy, spectacular shots that have so often caused his downfall in the past, but Jimmy doesn't think twice about them. Older players, as well as programming their muscles time and time again with the pattern of the right way to do things, also have built in the knowledge of how easy it is for things to go wrong, but Jimmy simply never considers that possibility. He is fast, fluent, fearless, just the way Alex used to be, and if the press who're regularly on the circuit refuse to be astonished by

140

him, it's only because they've seen it before, ten years ago, when the Hurricane first came into snooker and took the game apart.

'The Alex of ten years ago would have beaten the Alex of today,' says his compatriot Ronnie Harper of the *Belfast Morning Telegraph*. 'He was fantastic. He was out of this world. He's the best safety player in the world. The man's a genius. That's why it hurts when you hear about him peeing on daffodils and things.'

He hasn't been near a daffodil all week, though, and looks near genius level at the beginning of the first session. In the other semi, Ray Reardon V Eddie Charlton, the breaks have been of standard championship length, around twenty-five minutes each, but Higgins and White complete their first session in 110 minutes, just over half that time for each of the eight frames. The Hurricane starts off with a four-one lead and an opponent apparently intimidated by the occasion, but by the end of the session the players are level and Jimmy White has recovered his nerve and his most dangerous form. The tournament has now gone into its final phase of press conferences after every session but Harvey Lisberg comes in to excuse Jimmy from attending. 'He's not being funny but he doesn't really have anything to say. It's been a hell of a struggle but he's not unhappy about it from being four-one down.'

The Hurricane is unhappy. He's already in the practice room, tearing with ferocious desperation at the heart of his game. He says he's not going to speak to anyone till he gets his game together.

There isn't much opportunity to judge whether he has or not at the beginning of the next day's play. It's all Jimmy, Jimmy coaxing the balls into the pockets with his magic wand, Jimmy who's leading eight-four, Jimmy the crowd are cheering for. This must be a curious sensation for the Hurricane, who always has the people behind him, always makes them gasp at his brilliance. These days, he says, he has to take other avenues. 'I made the mistake of changing my game and tried to go with him. But I can't do it like that any more. He is still for the glory.' The Hurricane's only one frame behind at the end of the session, though, taking the last three frames in a row, and he's jubilant. 'After Jimmy's start he must be a little worried because I can come back. I can come back pretty strong,' he says with his usual ebullience. But later that night, up in Embassy's hospitality room, he is sitting there in tears, crying because the crowd got excited by Jimmy's shots and not his, crying because Jimmy is doing it his way.

Charlton and Reardon, in the other semi, are proceeding with far less overt agony. They present themselves as seasoned campaigners, battle-scarred veterans who can take almost anything fortune has to fling at them, though Ray Reardon says he'd rather do without the beer drinkers and the sweet-eaters and the latecomers. The Welshman is a frame ahead at the end of the first session, catching up an initial three frames deficit, but in the next two the pair are neck and neck. Their match isn't like that of the more instinctive pair, where the impetus .switches from one to the other. They're more dogged, more dour. They make no concessions. Jimmy White will often concede a frame before all the colours are cleared, setting the balls up again as if he were playing for a few quid in some little club. He would rather lose the frame than go through the boredom of safety play. But Eddie Charlton and Ray Reardon play every last ball out. Even if they've no hope of winning the frame they reckon they might break up the other fellow's rhythm. They've played each other often, know that they're going to need every advantage they can get in a match that could go on for ever, and may well be decided on the very last frame, as has happened so often before in their matches.

Unfortunately for Charlton, Ray Reardon is usually the one who's taken that last frame. He's put the Australian out of four previous World Championships and this is to be the fifth. Surprisingly, after the relentless competitiveness of their struggle, Eddie Charlton fails to take a frame on the final day's play. 'There's a lot of pressure out there,' says his opponent. 'It's the one who makes the most mistakes, isn't it?' Eddie Charlton says he's a bit disappointed, disappointed with the run of the balls in particular. Ray has had some luck, he'd say. Six or seven times he's had a wild flash and missed the pocket by a mile and it's Eddie who's ended up in dead trouble. Eddie is philosophical, phlegmatic, and underneath it all, very fed up. 'Perhaps I'm not good enough,' he sighs.

Ray Reardon has just returned to being good enough after several years when it looked as though his game would never be good enough again. During the seventies he won the World title six times and he has never been beaten in a final. He's the iron man under pressure, the man you can send in to a closed room to fight for his life. The question is, who is he going to meet? The boy who can shoot you to pieces and break your heart? Or the man who would kill to win this championship?

There's a carnival atmosphere in the theatre this evening as the two most flamboyant players in the world go into their final session at eleven frames each. Lynn Higgins is in tonight in a royal blue dress that matches the Hurricane's silk shirt — he bought several dozen from a factory in Hong Kong and has been trying to flog them to the other players. His opponent takes the first frame of the evening but the Hurricane, with an extraordinary fluke on brown that ricochets right round the table and back again, levels to make it twelve each. They're thirteen each by the interval.

As the players emerge into the backstage corridor for their brief rest, the Hurricane is drawn into a crowd of VIPs, gracing the match with their fleeting presence. 'So nice to see you, Alex,' trill voices that emerge from gooily painted lips. 'Nice to meet you Alex,' say the men, bluff and gruff and man to man. The Hurricane graciously says hello to them all, even apologising to one smartly dressed lady for the fag still smouldering between his fingers.

As the two competitors return, the audience, glowing after their interval refreshment, start calling out their support. 'Come on Jimmy,' they shout. The Hurricane looks furious. 'Be quiet,' he says, as if there is a gross breach of snooker etiquette. 'There's a match on you know.'

Jimmy White certainly knows it. He takes the next two frames. Only one more now and he'll have won. But that last frame is always the hardest. As he hovers on the brink of victory the Hurricane knocks in a gritty seventy-two break to bring the score to fifteen-fourteen. Jimmy's still got an extra chance though, and when he brings his score to fifty-nine it looks all over for the Hurricane.

There are times in a player's life when he needs to win and this is one of them for the Hurricane. He's had a disastrous year, has been harried from defeat to defeat, from one humiliation to another. He's not won a major tournament this year. He's been tormented by the ever-present image of Steve Davis winning the things he wants to win. If he does not win now he will be regarded, as he already is by many in the snooker world, as a has-been. While the other players want to win the title, regard it as a dream, a fantasy, the Hurricane desperately needs it.

And yet it would be completely unexpected for him to be the winner when he has done so badly all year. Like Cliff Thorburn he has played his worst ever snooker dazzled by the glare of Steve Davis's excellence. It seems he has even lost touch with that inner flame that used to rage through him like a brushfire, setting his audience alight with excitement and firing up his opponent as well as himself. The inspiration in this match has all come from Jimmy White but it is warm, easy, glowing,

143

flowing inspiration that thrills the spectators but doesn't necessarily move them. When the Hurricane is inspired he touches a nerve, grazes against something raw in the collective psyche.

Now he looks a little crazed. Leprechauns and pixies and rabbits' feet sprout from his back pocket and there's a Sacred Heart medal that a lady from Dublin gave him in his waistcoat. When he sits at the side he frequently stuffs his baby daughter's dummy into his mouth and clamps his lips tightly shut as if he is grinding his teeth against the rubber. As Jimmy builds up his first break though, the tension has gone from the Hurricane's face. He looks bereft. He wipes tears from his eyes. He knows it's gone now. The break ends on forty-one and still the Hurricane can't get in. Jimmy starts building again but ends on only eighteen. He's fifty-nine ahead though. It should be enough.

The Hurricane moves to the table. He misjudges his position on the first colour and has to go for a long green instead of the pink he should have had. Everything seems difficult, as he plays the slowest, bravest snooker of his life. Jimmy White is unable to keep still. He sips water, taps the table, wipes his cue, but his eyes are fixed on the Hurricane, mesmerised as the Irishman eschews the comfort of having the crowd roaring behind him and carves out a break of sixty-nine in utter unbearable silence.

Snooker is one of the most satisfying of sports because it shows the personality of each individual player so clearly. It's like examining a brain under a microscope, no great physical spectacle to distract from the laboratory conditions of extreme pressure. In some ways the Hurricane is something of an anomaly. Where many people show themselves at their worst under pressure, he is at his best. He hasn't got the coolness of a Steve Davis or the predatory instincts of a Ray Reardon. He just has raw courage, heart. At its worst that can mean he has to walk a psychological tightrope, take the match to extremes before the stimulus becomes great enough for him to pull out his last card. He has a history of taking matches to a final frame, was prepared in this tournament to go out of the championship on a single shot against Doug Mountjoy. But at its best his courage has a pure gritty grace that transcends the hysteria, transcends mere bravado. 'Higgins has always showed tremendous character in the playing of the game,' says Terry Griffiths. 'It's off the table it all goes. He's an odd one. Normally the character you've got off the table is the same on. It comes out in your play, under the pressure. But Alex isn't like that. He's different from everybody else.'

Tension and excitement on the way to victory for the Hurricane

The sixty-nine break is one of the bravest pieces of play ever seen on a snooker table and it effectively wins the Hurricane not only the match but the championship. It would be too cruel were he to lose to Jimmy after such an extraordinary feat and indeed the youngster seems crushed by the magnitude of it all. He has nothing more to give and sits forlorn as the Hurricane makes first a fifty-nine break and then puts the result beyond doubt with a thirty-seven.

The audience, Jimmy's audience, is on its feet at the end. The whistling and cheering just go on and on, a tidal wave that seems as if it is never going to break. The Hurricane's elation spills out into the corridor afterwards. He's hugging Lynn and people are jostling him and a couple of his spikey-haired punk friends are telling him he's the number one. He's the best. He knows he is. 'Isn't that the best temperament you've ever seen in your life?' he asks his journalist friend, John Dee, who's rugged and humorous and at this moment looks in need of a drink after all the emotion. 'Win or lose I think I'm the best,' says the Hurricane, and there are few in this steamy stretch of humanity who would disagree.

He hurtles into the press room to call his parents in Belfast. He's wild with glee as he shouts down the phone. 'Daddy. We're in the final. How's my mummy? Is she all right? Hello mummy. We're in the final.'

He is jubilant as he starts to talk to the press, saying that Willie told him his sixty-nine break was better than his own 143, and that he's proved that even without practice he's still the best. The press cluster round to listen but it's not like a proper interview with people asking questions. It's a rollercoaster ride through the Hurricane's emotions. 'People call me all sorts of things but when people are kind to me I can be kind in return. Youse boys haven't been that kind to me all over the years. John Dee's been kind to me and John Dee knows me more intimately than many.' But the paranoia blows away with his cigarette smoke as he goes on to talk about the seven year itch and how it's the ten year itch with him in snooker as he won the title in 1972. 'I think I've got every chance of winning the World Championship now. No disrespect to Raymondo,' he says with his puckish grin.

'The thing is the kid's got me. But at times you lose concentration and such a fast player can make an unforced error. That's what he did do. I bided my time. I got the chance. It wasn't an easy break but it's not bad for a bloke that doesn't practise.

'I felt very sad and sorry for Jimmy,' he says earnestly. 'Throughout

146

the tournament the kid's played really well.' But his voice rises with impish gaiety. 'There's no way a Whirlwind can beat a Hurricane.'

Someone asks him if he's ever played better and he says he played a bloke in Australia once for 500 dollars a game giving him a twenty-one start and only being allowed to pot the yellow. He had eleven yellows up and down the table and he lost. He played better that day, he says, though no-one believes him.

'This is important for me and my missus and my baby. Hopefully we'll have security for the rest of our lives. That'll do me. I can go out and play golf.' His wife Lynn is standing listening, still looking shaky with nerves. She asks him for a cigarette but he says sharply she should have her own cigarettes. She's got enough money. She looks tearful and he relents and gives her one of his.

And Romford's Robbo says the match was brill. You'll never get anything briller than that.

★ ★ ★

The final never quite matches it for brillness. The Hurricane makes a century break (118) in the fourth frame but still ends the first session two frames behind Ray Reardon. His big interest of the afternoon seems to be, not the snooker, but the 4.45 at Beverley. He has a £250 bet on 'Lady Justice' ridden by his best friend, jockey Peter Madden. As that comes in at 8 to 1 it sweetens his mood for the evening session and he ends the day ten-seven ahead.

After winning the first session Ray Reardon never seems to be ahead again. He circles the table like a shark, sleek black head cocked as he scrutinises the balls, his teeth bared in a wide-mouthed shark's grin. But he somehow seems to have lost his shark's killer instinct. His will to win is there, driving him on to narrow the gap time and time again, but he can't quite seem to close in when the opportunity presents itself. The mental ascendency he once enjoyed over the Hurricane has gone, lost probably when he lost his own game. It's an advantage an opponent never hands back to a sportsman.

Ronnie Harper, the Belfast writer who thinks the Hurricane was at his best as an amateur, recalls a previous match between these two at Belfast's Ulster Hall. The Hurricane hadn't been beaten there for about six years. In the very first frame Reardon started off with a spectacular long red that immediately got the audience excited and on his side. The Hurricane threw the frame away searching for a single shot that would impress as much as Reardon's. As Ray Reardon watched with a satisfied smile and the occasional puckish wink at spectators he knew, the Hurricane threw frame after frame away till the match was gone. 'Ray knew exactly what he was doing,' says Ronnie.

Ray has retained his impish humour but it's not the same Hurricane any more. He's slower now and wiser and at last seems to be winning in the fight against his own flamboyant nature. Ted Corbett of the *Daily Star* says that when he wrote his first article about how fast the Hurricane was John Spencer came to him and said Alex should slow down. It's taken him ten years but he's finally done it, with the result that whenever he makes a big break there's this intense silence as if the audience are all scared he's going to crack under the strain.

But the Hurricane knows this championship is his, is not going to crack under any strain. Friends tell him to think of Lynn and the baby but his Friday night victory over Jimmy White is his insurance. When Ray Reardon finally catches up with him to level the match at fifteen frames each, his nerve hardens. While the Welshman makes crucial errors in the next two frames the Hurricane comes up with two enormous breaks, one of seventy-nine, the other of seventy-three. In the thirty-third frame Ray Reardon pots the cue ball and smiles up at Terry Griffiths in the press seats as if to say, 'Is this an omen?' It is. The Hurricane closes out the match in the most spectacular Hurricane-like way, with a total clearance of 135, while the audience sit silent, like people bound together under a spell.

As the last ball drops, that silence is held, just for a single moment, and then chaos is unleashed into the hall. The formalities of a presentation ceremony drift on, with the Hurricane crying and crumpling the cheque and the audience sounding as wild as he is. Lynn Higgins is standing at the side with baby Lauren held against her sequin-encrusted chest and the Hurricane starts beckoning frantically to her, 'Bring my baby. Bring my baby.' She looks uncomprehending at first and the Hurricane's face crumples up with anguish till she moves across. And he's hugging the baby and hugging the cup while little Lauren stares in bewilderment at this roaring clapping crowd of people. Finally she understands and the tiny hand creeps above her head as Lauren Higgins waves to her public — and they wave back.

Champions are usually good losers as well as good winners and Ray Reardon is gracious and dignified. 'I was enjoying it actually. I had chances that went but I blew it badly there. I think the game got to me a bit. Not half,' he says in that syrupy Welsh voice, and chuckles. 'I missed some silly shots and he wasn't missing much himself. You wonder why you miss them sometimes. But I gave him a good battle. I made him sweat a bit. The 135 break, what a super way to go. After he's got past the seventy-five, eighty mark I'm on his side really. I knew then that I was out and that he'd won the title. Whoever wins it you're always pleased they won it,' he says with commendable diplomacy, though questionable accuracy. 'I'm disappointed I didn't win,' he says, and that rings true.

The Hurricane is surprisingly subdued. While Ray Reardon is still distributing bonhomie he seems almost sad. He says that he doesn't want to rant and rave about it. He's won it and he's just grateful. 'It's hard to put into words what I feel at this moment,' he says. 'Perhaps I should have won it against Cliff. I wouldn't know. But hopefully next year can look after my family — and then I can get my handicap down.' He rambles on about his vitamin pills and his crazy eating pattern and the rotten food in hotels, saying that this year he's let his mind rule his body, but he's not carried away with elation as you might expect. 'I can't believe it. I don't know why I should have done it,' says the new World Champion, bumming a cigarette off reporters.

Elation comes later, as he chats on the phone to a friend. 'People will have to show me more respect,' he says and his speech has returned to its normal torrential flow. 'I think I was cruising during the break but I have to see it again to prove it to myself. It hasn't sunk in yet. I haven't yet realised what's happened. Maybe it'll hit me tomorrow morning. The man upstairs shines on you now and again,' and his face cracks into that lopsided child's grin of his.

Inside the theatre they're already dismantling the tables, taking down the television lights and the commentary boxes. The lights are all on in the theatre and the little starry gantry lights are lost. And these World Championships are finally over. The gamblers have done their money and done their brains. The losers have gone home. The sadness, the excitement, the extremes are packed away quickly for another year so that the men can have a drink before closing time.

The Hurricane walks back to his hotel with his mother-in-law and a glass of vodka and coke, a crazy Pied Piper with a straggling retinue of teenagers in T-shirts, black boys in woolly hats, assorted journalists and a solitary man clutching a bottle of champagne. The Hurricane brandishing his glass, dissects every shot he played as the little group stravaigs through the empty Sheffield streets.

People stand up and cheer and whistle as he comes into the hotel.

Lynn has come in a taxi and is already there, resplendent in her floaty blue and gold chiffon. The journalists are already at the bar, joking about how the WPBSA may have to congratulate their new World Champion and then ban him. He's up before them in the morning for several breaches of discipline. The Hurricane parties heedlessly on into the night but Lynn can't stand the pace and goes to bed early, leaving her husband drinking with Peter Madden, the jockey friend he says is like a brother.

The Hurricane flashes from one group to another, leaning against the piano to let someone take his picture one moment — 'This is my Steve Davis pose,' he says — and the next sitting drenched in champagne as Kirk Stevens pours a bottle of bubbly over his head. At five-thirty in the morning practically everyone else has gone, but the Hurricane is still there.

He wanders into the hotel foyer and stands there, talking to the night porter. Peter Madden straggles out after him eventually, eyes hazy with drink, a gentle man with a satyr's twinkling eyes and a sweet smile. He says the Hurricane is a genius. He's like McEnroe in tennis. They'll be talking about his match with Jimmy White for years. And what about Lynn? he says. She wouldn't give him a drink for two whole frames and he lost them both. Is that the way to treat your husband, if he likes a drink? And he's a genius? He nods sagely. He'd never tell the Hurricane he was a genius, though, he says.

The Hurricane is telling the night porter that he's a modern day champion. He's glad he's done it now, in the modern day, with all the pressure. He can die happy now. An extravagantly blonde lady with an opulent figure and a kind face sashays up to him at the reception desk and says she'll read his fortune in the Tarot. And they all say he doesn't need his fortune in the cards. He's got his fortune now.

After the Hurricane

He did it. The impact of the Hurricane winning the World Championship has been felt throughout the corridors of Sportsworld Ltd, the people who let the Hurricane go. But there has been time for the dust to resettle on the leather-look chairs and the glass coffee tables, time for the building to sink back on to its smart new foundations. There has been time for the shock to be absorbed, a necessary task made easier by the canny bet the Sportsworld's directors made some weeks before the championships. They have now recovered what they reckon they'd have earned for the rest of the Hurricane's contract.

Geoff Lomas though is unconsoled. 'It's not really foresight to let the World Champion go three weeks before he's won it. Is it?' he asks, with the air of certainty of a man making a statement rather than asking a question. 'It just shows everyone what clowns we are,' he hisses. He speaks in a voice so low that it is almost lost in the rumble of traffic outside. It is what is generally called a conspiratorial whisper though in this case it seems designed to repel conspirators, as if Mr Lomas fears enemies lurking behind every door, or hidden tapes recording his conversation. And perhaps he is right. Who knows what goes on behind office walls?

Or perhaps he's just in a state of shock still, for Geoff Lomas can hardly believe that the Hurricane *is* the new World Champion. 'How he won it God only knows. God only knows,' he muses. 'During sessions, during sessions,' he says, 'when he was playing Jimmy he was sat there, *reading the Bible.*' He stares fixedly at you as if to check that you are registering as much shock as he is. He is apparently satisfied for he continues. 'While he was sitting there he was sucking a *crucifix*. I couldn't believe it. Bloody rabbits' feet everywhere. There was no way he was going to go out and win that.' He is thoughtful for a moment. Although, like most of the snooker world, Geoff Lomas recognises the essential lunacy of the Hurricane, unlike most of the snooker world, he is genuinely fond of him and accepts him for what he is. 'I'm glad he won,' he says softly.

Then he laughs. 'Snooker must be the only sport in the world where they allow stimulants. Jimmy won the first three or four frames of every session and then the vodka started taking effect and Alex has regained his nerve and started playing a bit.'

He looks like a gipsy, Geoff Lomas, with the dark curly hair, the swarthy skin, the pellucid blue cat's eyes that stare at you and through you, and he has the gipsy's sense of mystic forces at work beneath the surface of life. 'My thought is that everything's for the best. Everything always turns out for the best. I'm glad Jimmy got beat. I think he would have killed himself. He's over the top now . . .'

His opinion is not altogether shared by Harvey Lisberg, who thinks it might have been a nice problem to have to deal with. But Harvey too is not unhappy that Jimmy lost. A world title this year was not in the scenario he had sketched out for Jimmy's future. He thinks that if Jimmy had won this year everybody would have said it was just because Steve and Terry got knocked out. What he really wants his young client to do is to win and knock the whole damn lot of them out as he goes. He's scheduled that for two years hence.

If it were just up to Harvey Lisberg we might as well all pencil it into the history books already because he's the type of person who refuses to contemplate the existence of defeat in his life. He's a man who smiles a lot, which gives him the appearance of being shy, but he says he's vicious. He says he's far more competitive than any sportsman and that he gets bored if he doesn't win. He won't stay in snooker and be a loser. This means he won't stay in snooker if Jimmy White's a loser.

All Sportsworld's hopes are pinned on Jimmy. If he eventually wins the World title the company will have enormous power in snooker, in much the same way that Barry Hearn has now. 'And who had heard of Barry Hearn two years ago?' asks Harvey. But if Jimmy doesn't win, Sportsworld will be nothing, and Harvey Lisberg doesn't like the idea of being nobody. He likes to stamp his personality on whatever he is involved in.

He sits in his office in the modern building his rock firm, Kennedy Street Enterprises, have erected in posh Altrincham, outside Manchester. It's just a bit big for them and Sportsworld, so they're letting some of the offices off. When he first came into snooker Harvey wanted to do more than just stamp his personality on the game. 'I was determined to change the world,' he laughs. 'But after one week, when

I saw what happened I wasn't prepared to do it. I said I'll wait till we've got the World Champion and then we'll do what we want to do. I knew that I was right and I knew that the system was wrong. But I wasn't prepared to fight it because you wouldn't have got any thanks at the end of the day.

'There's a lot wrong in snooker but I don't think it's very sinister. I think it's kind of amateurish, that's all. I don't think it's a load of people who're wheeling and dealing and making fortunes. I do think there's slight inefficiency all round the place. I think things like the seeding need sorting out. That affects people's livelihood. Jimmy won two tournaments last year and got to the semi-final of the Coral and the World and he's seeded ten. That can't be right. There aren't nine people that could beat *him*. All right there's Alex and there's Davis and there's Griffiths — who's seeded fourteen.'

Having dismantled the seeding system, the WPBSA, Mike Watterson and the television authorities, he goes on to admit that he actually likes the people in snooker. But it is clear that he doesn't respect them very much. 'They think they know it all and they know nothing,' he says. 'They think that Mike Watterson's exploited them but I don't think he has. Nobody's exploited the game. I think the fact that there are empty seats and yet it's so popular proves there's something wrong somewhere. I don't think the British public understands what going to a snooker exhibition or championship match *is*. They don't. Unless you get in the hall you can't believe how good it is.'

Harvey Lisberg is more than a fan, he is a snooker salesman, determined to get the product across to as many consumers as possible. Where Geoff Lomas is a snooker person, he is a showbiz person. He likes stars, excitement, the live event, and he thinks that is what snooker should be selling itself on. 'If people only knew. When they go there they can get a drink and it's nicely done and they're comfortable and the players do a show and they talk to the audience and they sign their posters and everything. Of course if you start giving V signs to the audience and refusing to sign autographs and finish when it's five-nil and refuse to play any more frames and storm out blind drunk and then rape the receptionist on the way out then you can't really expect it to be good.

'Excepting these comments relating not to anybody in particular I think it could be a very nice evening out for a family.'

Excepting the particular person to whom these comments do not relate and whose image has proved intractable to change, Harvey

Lisberg is very excited by the idea of the possibilities for image-building that exist in the sport. He doesn't want to change the nice gentlemanly style of it, the suits, the quiet, the good manners. That, he thinks, makes the game look as if it's not too money-minded. 'Somebody actually said to me, Don't spoil it for God's sake,' he says. 'But there's a lot of money in it, a lot of greed in it, a lot of everything in it. Maybe it's not quite as apparent as football, which is horrific. The public have divorced themselves from football. They don't want to know about that. The footballers are so greedy and so money-minded and so over the top that they've lost communication with their audience. I don't think snooker players have. I still think the Welsh cheer for Griffiths and Reardon. The public cheers for Higgins whatever he does. The girls all cheer for Tony Knowles.'

But while the sport has a very distinctive image, individual players, apart from a few honourable and dishonourable exceptions, have no real identity of their own. They're all nice men, with quiet wives, polite children, big houses and cars and no personality. And it's that part of it that Harvey Lisberg is itching to change. 'Personally I think the image of snooker players has been very poor really,' he says, with a speculative glow in his eyes. He is clearly very fond of the image he has built all by himself, Jimmy White, even if the bold boy *did* turn up with an earring during the World Championship. The earring is on the way out. But image making has its problems, as he has discovered. There are, it appears, people who think that Jimmy White is too sophisticated. People who identified with him when he was just a scruff no longer do, now that he's gone all suave on them with his French shirts and his straight teeth.

Towards the Hurricane, the one that got away, Harvey maintains a dignified attitude. 'We could have kept him. I think other people in the firm would have liked to have kept him. But I won't keep anybody that doesn't want to stay,' he says blandly. It's a stance that's easy enough to stick to, considering the Hurricane's known inability to be managed. Sportsworld conducted their period of management in the style of the heavyweight boxing promoters, isolating their man and hyping him up in the media, but as usual with the Hurricane, they're the ones who've been floored. 'We gave Alex three months out, which was completely intentional, to enable him to win the World Championship. It succeeded one hundred percent. In the process he left us because we didn't find him any work. He'd forgotten that the whole idea was that he wasn't to play. He refused to play Davis under any circumstances and he was having nightmares. Then he said, "How can I live? I've got no work."'

He shakes his head in exasperation. 'I wouldn't say anything against Alex. There's no ill feeling. What I would say is, how can you deal with that sort of situation?'

The Hurricane situation was that he wasn't prepared to accept that Sportsworld were entitled to twenty-five percent of his earnings. It's not an unusually high percentage for a modern management team to take, but the Hurricane hadn't ever been involved with this wall to wall managerial style where the client's legal, financial and even personal life is controlled from management headquarters. 'It was difficult for him because he was worth money. Jimmy's not. Twenty-five percent of nothing's nothing. But twenty-five percent of 1000 is 250 and it's, What are these bastards doing for this? I'm doing this. I'm doing that.' Harvey Lisberg sighs. 'He was just too much in the end.

'I think he came to us in the first place because of the publicity job we did on Jimmy. And then we did it on him as well, all that about the hospital and everything. He got everything he wanted and he got the rest. I think he'll come back to us as well. Or want to come back to us.' And will Sportsworld have him back? He hesitates just for a second, then shakes his head. 'No,' he says, 'I don't think it's right.

'I think Jimmy's exciting but when we took on Alex we got more excitement than we needed. Now we're happy again. We've got just the right blend.'

And just the right property. As Harvey Lisberg says, a lot of people got very excited by Jimmy White in the World Championships. 'If you're so good at twenty,' says Harvey, 'at twenty-three you should be unstoppable. I've not tried to do anything to his game yet, but it could be my responsibility as a manager to get hold of him by the scruff of the neck, stick him into bed at nine o'clock, get him up at nine o'clock in the morning, stick him in a snooker hall to practise all day for six weeks before a major title — if he can't win in his own flamboyant way. I wouldn't do that at all at this stage in his career. But if I found he went through a season and hadn't won a tournament all season his own way, the following season there's no way he's going to get away with that. He's going to be regimented.

'He's gone into training his way but his way might be drinking till five o'clock in the morning, then playing from five till nine. I'm not saying that's true or not true because I don't know. We weren't responsible. But if we *are* responsible, he's sleeping in my house, I've got an eye on him, he's eating regularly, the doctor's checking his blood and sugar levels and all that junk that nobody does in snooker. They're crazy — the amount of concentration and sugar they lose in a match is unbelievable. Nobody ever thinks about things like that. If I bloody well had anything to do with it . . . I won't at the moment, because I don't want to be accused of interfering with his natural ability. Let's see what happens, if he can get there just through that.

'If he can't then he's going to have to be put down, like Alex was and stopped and told, Right, you're stopping drinking. Which Jimmy did do incidentally. He stopped completely for three weeks.' He bursts out laughing at the absurdity of it. 'Next time it'll be for six months, that's all I can say. He can go on a drinking spree from May to September and get into a complete paralytic state. Then no more drinking.

'You see, everybody that surrounds him is bad news for him. Everybody. They're all drinking, they're smoking, marijuahana, whatever they're on. They're on women, three women, five women, men. There's no limit in snooker. There's nothing normal about it. And this kid is there in the middle of all this.'

As soon as the words are out of his mouth the diplomatic Mr Lisberg wants to claim them back. He doesn't want to give snooker a bad name. He likes things to look nice, even if they are not. He's a very curious mixture, frank to the point of indiscretion, yet very conscious of what he sees as the public's need to retain a sanitised picture of their sporting heroes.

He has, in Jimmy White, a diamond in the rough, a player who seems destined already to be a world champion. Sportsworld's paternalistic style of management is viewed with suspicion by many in snooker, who think it goes beyond the call of duty for managers to tell a player what he's to say when people ask him questions. Many, too, think the showbizzy style of Sportsworld, the dramatic statements they instruct Jimmy to make in the press, the intense publicity, will put too much pressure on him. But Harvey Lisberg and Geoff Lomas are clearly both very fond of Jimmy and if their motives are not always quite as altruistic as they would plead, they have invested faith and commitment in a player whose life in the past appeared to be a series of black marks blotting out his skills. They believe utterly that he will be world champion one day.

'After all,' says Harvey Lisberg, 'I don't think anybody could behave worse than Alex and he's won it twice — and a lot of other things as well. Of course he's got tremendous courage, Alex. Maybe Jimmy

Harvey Lisberg

Mike Watterson

hasn't got that courage.' He shrugs. 'He'll have to develop it.

'Alex came from a very tough background and has had to fight his way through. Jimmy hasn't had to do that. From the age of fourteen Jimmy could go in a snooker hall and earn himself fifty quid. He was never short of money from fourteen years upwards. It's very difficult to teach respect for money in anyone who started like that. He didn't have Alex's background of rank poverty.'

And what of Alex, the Hurricane, the man who walked away from Sportsworld? What does the future hold for him? Can Harvey Lisberg see his future clearly? 'Either he will assume the responsibility of being the World Champion and play well without any pressure on him or he'll do what he's done so far. He lost six-nil to Reardon at Pontin's and the other night on Granada television it was announced, Alex Higgins *was* going to be on the programme but he walked out of the studio twenty minutes ago and we've got another bad boy, George Best. I don't know. That was just the first thing that happened. There could be no end to it.

'I don't think he'll be able to handle the success that's coming to him at all. I think this year is going to be disaster beyond all expectations and belief. Why shouldn't it? It was disaster last year. Why shouldn't the same thing happen again ten times worse? It's not my problem,' he says, with a certain amount of relief in his tone. 'I just think you're going to read about it.'

Mike Watterson

The Man Who Runs the World

There's a strangely temporary feeling about Mike Watterson's Chesterfield office, as if the place has been set up in a hurry and may not stay as it is for long. There's no proper shelving, so the files are stacked on the floor all round the room and there are piles of the magazine *Cue World,* of which Mike is the new proprietor, sitting at the door awaiting distribution. Even the electric kettle is plugged in on the floor.

But Mike Watterson is not about to move on. He's the man who runs the World Championship, the man who in 1977 took a gamble on promoting it when it looked as if it might not be staged that year, and has been collecting his winnings ever since. Along with lots of enemies.

On the last night of the World Championship, as the Hurricane was on the phone celebrating his victory, Mike Watterson was to be seen celebrating a victory of his own — the rout, for the moment at least, of those enemies. He was wearing a new suit that was his celebration present to himself, in a brown checked material that gave him the air of a rather muted end-of-the-pier comic. There was more venom than humour in his gaiety that night though. 'Snooker's becoming a rat race,' he said. 'And for a while there it looked as though the rats were winning.'

Throughout the championship there had been talk of changes in the balance of power in snooker. Even people in Mike Watterson's own staff thought that the revolution was coming, and that he himself was on the way out. Although he had a year of his contract with the WPBSA for the World Championship still to run, two of his staff had already been approached and offered the job of promoting next year's tournament. It seemed certain that Watterson would lose this most prestigious event, the one that keeps his promotions company, Snookasport, ticking over through the summer, when there is no real income from snooker.

But his previous success in running the championship and his good relationship with the sponsors prevented his being ousted. 'It's the man with the money who dictates what's going to happen,' he says. 'The contract the WPBSA has with the sponsor states quite categorically that the sponsors will have the final say in who produces the event. They're not going to have a lot of people trying to run something when they haven't got the expertise. When I say that I don't mean them as individuals, because they're bloody nice blokes all of them, and obviously as individuals they're very good snooker players. But I'm afraid to run a good operation you need to be a lot more than just a good snooker player that talks a lot. There's too much headbanging been going on in the WPBSA, too much talking behind closed doors and cloak and dagger secrecy and attempting to stuff people out of sight. It's not good for the game at a time when things are going so well. People should be working together instead of trying to work against other people purely because of personal envy or personal greed or whatever.'

Mike Watterson is the target for more personal envy than almost anyone in snooker except Steve Davis. 'Harry Grabbit' people call him, as if he takes all he can out of the game without putting anything back. Running the World Championship has made him a rich man, with a big house in Chesterfield, three profitable snooker clubs and a gold Rolls Royce with Joe Davis's old number plate, 'Cue I'. It has also made a great many other people rich. Mike Watterson's promotions in snooker have brought the game a new professionalism, and if he now appears to have a great deal of power — practically all the major tournaments are run by Snookasport — it is only because he himself devised many of the tournaments and brought the sponsors in. 'I used to travel thousands and thousands of miles a year talking to sponsors, trying to get them involved in the game,' he says. 'They'd say, "Snooker? No. Come back with a project on showjumping." Now I'm expected to go out in the street with a begging bowl for my living after carrying the bloody game so far. If brains were dynamite that lot wouldn't have enough to blow their noses.'

His contention that sponsors should sponsor, promoters should promote and above all, players should play, is generally expressed in just such scathing terms. He has an arrogance which alienates many people. Throughout the whole of one tournament for example the gold Rolls Royce could be seen parked almost daily on double yellow lines outside the venue, in spite of the fact that there were parking spaces provided. Make an appointment to see him and he'll keep you waiting while he has a bath and a meal before he strolls in — and then will be generous in his hospitality. He is a baffling mixture, a man who feels under threat — and is — but who is ruthless to others when he feels they're against him; a man quick to condemn others but who is himself vulnerable to criticism; a man who sometimes behaves with an imperialist arbitrariness but who has suffered for several years from such bad nerves that he has sought help from psychiatrists, physiotherapists, faith healers and hypnotists in his efforts to control them when he plays.

He is, as well as being a promoter, a player of considerable ability, who has represented England at amateur level and has now been accepted as a professional. 'I can hardly play at all now though,' he sighs. 'I've got twitches and jerks and all sorts of things and it's driving me crazy. I'll get straight on the black and just freeze. If I try to play a

160

screwshot off the cushion I just freeze and miscue. Since 1979 there's been a lot of pressure, a lot of aggravation in the game, with some of the professionals wanting to pull one way and leave the rest on their own by setting up the Professional Snooker Association. I had a sort of minor nervous breakdown over it, and I've never been right playing the game since then.'

Perhaps because the PSA interlude had the power to upset him so deeply he now ridicules it, saying that after the usual WPBSA meetings the players would all switch seats at the table and have the PSA meetings, cancelling out all the decisions they had made minutes before. 'Players aren't capable of controlling their own destiny. They're really not. They've proved it in every sport you care to mention. Look at the state of football now — just because of the greed of the players. In snooker the top players think they should have the biggest say in which way the game's going to go, because the game's all about them and not about the bottom end of the ladder.' Mike Watterson shakes his head in disgust. 'Have you ever seen a pyramid without a bottom? You've seen them without a top — where the top's flat — but you take out the bottom and the whole thing collapses.

'I remember reading in a paper two or three years ago about Vitas Gerulaitis. He said, "Tennis is all about us top five. The rest don't matter." Now that epitomises the intelligence of top sportsmen. Was he born, was Steve Davis born or Alex Higgins born World Champion? Was Ray Reardon born World Champion, or was he once a little minnow playing away in a snooker club, trying to fight his way into the amateur team and then entering the English Championships because at that time Joe Davis was the top one? The game is all about what happens at the bottom. The top is merely the projection of that. The top doesn't support the bottom. It's the other way round. But you try telling that to top professional sportsmen and you might as well turn round and talk to the panelling on that wall.'

He is one of the few people in snooker to express such altruistic sentiments, this so-called Harry Grabbit. He sits hunched up on the sofa in the billiards room that adjoins his office. He looks elfin, vulnerable. The mahogany of the snooker table gleams rich red, a contrast to the wood veneer panelling on the walls. It is testimony to his sense of history — it belonged once to Ernest Rudge, the man who taught Joe Davis — but its bright green surface is scratched with scores of tiny marks where Mike Watterson's arm jerked and sent the cue careering across the table.

The People's Tournament

It's a grey Monday afternoon in Prestatyn in North Wales. Jimmy White is sauntering up the high street with that curious walk of his which manages to be both shambling and rubbery at the same time. He has a group of friends with him and whenever a girl passes they all whoop and cheer. The woman taxi driver says that Higgins is here too. He was in the Railway Bar this afternoon and she got his autograph. She thinks he's lovely. She told her husband she'd drive him all the way home to Manchester for free if he wanted.

Uniformed guards stop her car at the gate for a security check. This is Pontin's holiday camp, the event the annual May snooker festival. By Monday the Open championship is into its third day of play. There are 1,048 entries this year, more than ever before, and almost 4,000 people in the camp. It's only a week after the World Championship and interest is running high because Alex Higgins, the new 'People's Champion,' is going to play.

There are already at least forty-five people in the ballroom though it's only five o'clock and play doesn't begin till seven-thirty. They're making sure they get seats to see the Hurricane this evening and are having their tea while they wait, eating sandwiches they've brought with them and sipping tea out of thermos flasks.

It's more democratic than most modern sports, snooker. It's not like tennis where the stars really are stars, and as such have to be protected from their public, escorted to and from the courts by muscular policemen, cocooned in swish limos to take them back to their posh hotels once their matches are over. To date no snooker player has been known to aspire to the hand of a Princess, even if her daddy's principality is only a little larger than Fred Davis's stud farm. Snooker players may stay in top hotels and wear suits that cost them several hundred pounds a time but most of them like the same things as their audiences. They stay in touch with them. There is no mystique created around them as there is in other sports. Even Steve Davis, whose manager's hype and own invincibility last year made him snooker's nearest approach to the aloof superstar, is sitting in the cafeteria here at Pontins drinking tea and signing autographs for his fans.

There are fans everywhere. Pontins is spilling over with them. The initial impression is that the camp is one vast council estate populated only by men, men carrying cue cases across to their chalets, men wandering round with pints of beer in one hand and fags drooping downward in the other, men clustering round the Corals betting shop in the main entrance foyer, men hammering frantically away at computer games. Then gradually you notice the teenage girls in their tight T-shirts and funny hats, the morose mums glaring at the Noddy train as it bears their offspring back towards them. You even occasionally see the odd woman carrying a cue case.

As the professionals are introduced on the first night of their championship it seems that all 4,000 of the men, women and children in the camp are squashed together in the big ballroom. Blonde smiling Pontins girls lead the players out by the arm as if they're incapable of walking thirty-six yards without assistance. Perhaps in the past one more temperamental than the rest has bolted at the sight of so many people joined together in mass perspiration.

The Professional tournament itself is something of a hybrid, populated on the one hand by the failures of the World Championship, rabid to show that they're really as good as they think they are, and on the other hand by the World Championship successes, who having triumphed in the ultimate competition, find it difficult to focus their attention on snooker in a holiday camp. In fact it is difficult even for the audience to focus their attention here, where the matches are played to the accompaniment of clinking glasses, rattling crockery, people shouting across the cafeteria to one another, knees crashing into glass-laden tables in the bar, and the machine-gun fire of space invader machines.

Steve Davis's rabidity quotient is at an all-time high — metaphorically speaking, of course, he isn't really foaming at the mouth — and he beats Willie Thorne six-two, while Terry Griffiths, Sheffield's other major casualty, also survives Pontin's aural assault course with a six-three win over John Virgo. The People's Champion continues the reversal of Sheffield form by going out to Ray Reardon, though as ever he has to do it in a more spectacular fashion than anybody else by suffering a six-nil defeat. Ray Reardon still hasn't realised he's allowed a week off form.

★ ★ ★

The camp is so crammed full of snooker fans that even the people who work there can't get in to see the stars. On the staff bus to Rhyl the morning after the Hurricane's whitewash the cleaning ladies are lamenting that they can't get passes for their sons to come in and watch the snooker. There are too many people inside the camp to allow outsiders in and some have even had to hand back passes they'd been issued. 'Ooh,' they say, craning out of the bus window. 'Is that Prince Charles come to Pontins?' as Doug Mountjoy's bright red Jaguar glides into the car park.

The pros may be here to meet their public but they don't actually want to revert to being exactly like them. Instead of bunking down in the self-catering chalets and buying tins of baked beans from the sunshine supermarket on site they are staying in the Grand Hotel, a couple of hundred yards away. Admittedly it is about as Grand as an extended golf clubhouse and looks like one too, but at least they don't have to mingle with the multitude there.

On Wednesday night most of them stay at the Grand to watch Aston Villa face the might of Germany in the European Cup final. Over at the camp Steve Davis faces the indestructible Ray Reardon in the professionals' final. They're all there for the prize-giving ceremony though, even the Hurricane, who hasn't heard about the presentation and is just about to watch *The Omen, Part 2* when he has to come rushing over. He's given a huge ovation as he goes out to receive his Pontinental holiday vouchers and cheque for £750. On his way he makes a point of stopping to shake the new Pontins Professional Champion by the hand but Steve Davis looks unimpressed by his graciousness. He sips at his glass of water as if it were vinegar.

The Hurricane is shooting through the cafeteria later when he is suddenly assailed by the first pangs of hunger he has felt for days. He darts across to the serving hatch of the Jackpot fish and chicken bar and grins winningly at the counter assistant. A long line of people waiting on the other side gaze at him as he asks the girl could she serve the residents first. Hugely amused, she piles his polystyrene containers high with fish and chips and a meat pie. The Hurricane looks aghast.

164

Doug Mountjoy plays the machines

Eugene Hughes signs autographs

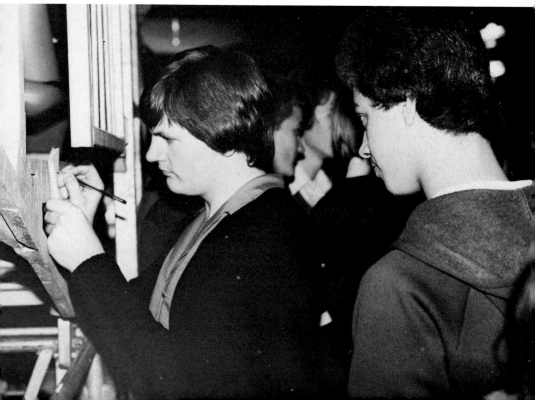

'Are there no knives and forks?' he asks, extremely disturbed when she says there aren't.

He tears at the hot greasy golden fish with his fingers, saying that even though he had to rush over for the presentation he got a standing ovation and that can't be bad. His eyes are puffy with drink and lack of sleep. Next year they might hold the World Championships in Warrington he says, his eyes crinkling up with humour. That'd be good for him, wouldn't it? and he laughs his wheezing laugh. He wouldn't have to go far for free vodka. Better than free fags, he reckons.

He hurtles through to the Clwyd Bar for a drink but it's after eleven-thirty and they're already shut. As he comes through the door a friend of his grabs hold of him, a big burly chap who dwarfs the slight figure of the Hurricane. 'Do us a favour Alex,' he says, clasping him to his chest in an enthusiastic bearhug, but the elusive Hurricane, somehow, so quickly that you don't even see him move, has wriggled out of his grasp and is off. 'The bugger,' says the man, but his gaze is half-admiring, half-amused as he watches the Hurricane go.

The cabaret in the Clwyd Bar, with its risqué jokes about Andy Pandy and Looby Loo, has ended now and one of the Bluecoats is running a disco. Steve Davis joins in the dances, even the daft ones like the Tweets and the Boat Dance, though when the compere draws attention to him shuffling along the dance floor on his bottom he gets all embarrassed and flees.

Upstairs in the billiard room the Hurricane is standing watching the action with his intent look of a child who fixes his gaze totally on the object he's studying till something new comes along to claim his attention. There are eighteen tables up here but you can still go up at two-thirty in the morning and be told there's no table free for another hour. There are people up here who haven't even seen the beach behind the camp. The Hurricane, for all that he has been a star for ten years, is still part of this world. Downstairs Steve Davis is enjoying himself on the brightly-lit dance floor, with the Bluecoat making jokes and little girls giggling as they ask him to pose for photographs with them. Up here the lights are so low over the table, the haze of smoke so dense, that you're perceiving things through a resistant film. The players' actions seem to be suspended as if they are moving underwater.

There are two worlds in snooker, the brightly-lit one of the family men, the media men. And this half-lit, half-crazy one where people play snooker and cards through the night, where livings are made by

166

keeping on the move rather than by settling into the structure of society, and ducking and diving is the order of the day when you come up against authority. The Hurricane may be a good family man now and have an army of people regulating his life, but he never will be part of the establishment. This is the world he came from and the world he will always belong to, no matter how often he may demand preferential treatment or more money for his services than he should ever be in charge of.

In Pontins the two worlds of snooker roll along together, as close as they will be all year. The stars here are not just the television names known to the general public. People are as excited here by the stars coming up, the top amateurs, the new young professionals, many of whom have been living for years off their wits as well as their snooker. Pontins is not really about the professionals. It's more about the collective dream of the real snooker people that one day they will make it to the top. The Open championship, with this year's record entry of 1,048, offers that tantalising prospect to anyone who can fight his way through the pack and then beat the top professionals.

That is what the Open *is* really. Nobody wants a professional to win. To try and ensure that they don't, they have to concede thirty points a frame to their opponents. There are people here who regularly make century breaks yet have gone out in the first round of the tournament, so the professionals are behind in the betting.

* * *

They're behind in terms of interest too. Thursday morning and Ray Reardon is on one table with maybe a dozen people watching. On the table next to him are Joe O'Boye and John Parrott, with well over a hundred people standing on chairs and tables and each others' shoulders to see. John Parrott is only seventeen and looks as if his mother has given him his Weetabix and told him to wash behind his ears this morning. He is fresh-faced, clearly burdened with perfect health and it is obvious that even if he smoked he'd never wake up in the morning coughing and spluttering his guts up. He looks as though he's got lots of O-levels.

Joe O'Boye, on the other hand, is a thin waiflike type who doesn't look strong enough for the energy involved in a morning splutter. At the moment he is trying to disguise himself as a schoolboy with his grey flannels, neat jumper and white shirt, but behind the decorous facade

167

Joe O'Boye with the man who pays his bills, Gordon Banks

Steve Davis plays chess while Terry Griffiths, Dennis Taylor and
Willie Thorne relax with a pot of tea

lurks one of the wild boys of snooker. He is also one of the biggest draws in the country in the amateur game though he will be turning pro in a few months.

In preparation for his launch into the big time Joe has acquired himself a manager, Reg Warland, and a salary as a paid employee of Gordon Banks' Promotions. Before these balmy days of regular money Joe was knocking about the billiard halls of Britain playing money matches with all the lads who reckoned they could beat an English Amateur Champion. (Joe won in 1980.) He sits in the bar after he's lost to pink-cheeked John Parrott and reflects on his last two years of snooker. He is gazing off into the intermediate distance and he seems to take an inordinate amount of time to formulate a sentence. 'I got mixed up with the wrong people for two years,' he says, after a long pause. There is another long pause before he adds the opinion that he was drinking too much last night and that's why he didn't play well this morning.

He has, it transpires, been drinking too much all this week and was observed in the men's toilets on Tuesday night slipping and sliding around the floor with Jimmy White. The opinion of the spectators was that neither could attain the motor control necessary for the act of standing up. This is not the first time the two have indulged in mobility experiments. They both went out to Tasmania together for the 1980 World Amateur Championships and were said to be so drunk before the opening ceremony that the team managers had to douse them in black coffee before they could carry the flag for the nation.

They were good pals in those days but Joe says he never sees Jimmy now. 'He's big money now isn't he?'

'Jimmy's doing very well,' says manager Reg Warland smoothly. 'It would be very nice if Joe could do as well.' Reg looks the way a manager should — crisp shirt, the sharp grey suit, layer cut hair — but behind the chic blue lenses of his steel-rimmed spectacles, his eyes are anxious with the stress of managing a lunatic. Who knows what crazy Joe's going to say next? Joe, observing Reg's nervousness with a detached but delighted humour, expounds on his reasons for not turning professional immediately he won the English title. 'I didn't think I was good enough,' he says. 'But I was wrong. It was a mistake.' He lapses into private amusement. 'When I turn pro I think I could do . . .' He considers his words carefully and gives Reg a big slow satisfied smile . . . *'quite* well.'

Managerial hyperbole may have been avoided in Joe's case. It is difficult to withhold critical hyperbole from Ray Reardon. On his way to the final against John Parrott he beats Steve Davis by an astonishing four-nil and then takes on the young Londoner Neal Foulds, defeating him in a dour struggle that the amateur is expected to win. After all, you just *can't* give these men twenty-five points start and win. Well, that's another thing that seems to have eluded Ray Reardon's notice this week, as he moves magisterially into his second final.

In the Clwyd Bar that night Steve Davis is able to relax properly for the first time this week. He's there in his jeans and a striped sweat shirt, displaying more than his usual interest in the contents of the bar. By his side Romford's Frank Mizzlebrook is mourning his loss in typically extravagant style. Mizzle has a religious sense of the drama of snooker, and meets victory and defeat in an ecstasy of sentimentality that seems merely eccentric to the outsider but satisfies some inner desire for fervour among young Romford people. 'I got all dressed up in evening dress for these two fine gentlemen,' he says, in his soft voice like the hushed whisper of a priest in the confessional. 'Two fine gentlemen, both World Champions. And we lost. Well, we've had to suffer defeat before.'

His sturdy chest and child's firm jaw are both thrown out in an attitude of pride, unquenchable spirit in defeat. Steve Davis is displaying a more flexible attitude to his loss, joking with the usual collection of young girls who want their pictures taken with him, and gulping freely at his lager. Mizzle, perspiring now in his black dress suit and stiff shirt, discloses that he referees a lot of matches for the London boys. 'But I won't refuse to referee a match because it's not Jimmy White playing,' he says, about to strike an attitude of fierce integrity when he realises that his chest and chin are both conveniently thrust out already.

'The boys all love me,' he says, gazing paternally round. 'They treat me like a father, I think.' He says that one came up to him and said, 'I love you Mizz,' and he said, 'I love you too Paul.' And nobody has to misinterpret it, but just to show how sincere it was, he kissed Mizzle on the lips. Mizzle's eyes are moist as he relays this story to the small collection of supporters gathered round him.

He says that a photographer came and took his picture for *Cue World*. He was overwhelmed. That is not for him. That, he says, with extravagant gestures towards Steve Davis, is for people like Steve Davis, who are fantastic snooker players. Who is he? He has a lot of friends in snooker, that's all. A lot of people love him, he says humbly, and heads for the dance floor. He ends up surrounded by a ring of clapping, whooping snooker boys goading him on as he clicks his fingers and shuffles his feet in an unsteady interpretation of Spanish flamenco dancing. Steve Davis grins in appreciation but his own dancing is rather more restrained and orthodox.

Standing watching the dancing with a nonchalant expression on his face is Eugene Hughes, hero of the Irish at the State Express in Reading and putative star of *Playgirl* magazine. That hasn't come to anything yet he admits, though he's still hoping. The State Express was terrific for him in other ways though he says. He's had loads of bookings at home in Ireland and he's been on television in a kind of 'Pot Black' they have there and he's doing Butlins every week on a Tuesday. If it wasn't for that now he'd go on holiday to the Grand Canaries, but he'll just have to wait till next year for that. He says Ted Corbett and Terry Smith both spent a long time trying to dissuade him from trying for *Playgirl* but when Terry had gone off Ted slips the *Star* phone number into his hand and says to let him know if he *does* do it.

Sure he's been coming to Pontins since it started, says Eugene. In the old days they used to let the Irish lads play the piano upstairs but they won't allow that now. He even had to con his way in this time. You used to be able to just roll up and get a chalet but the place is so full they wouldn't let him in. He had to make a fuss and say he had a phone booking before they let him go in with his pals.

At two in the morning Mizzle has wandered off somewhere but Steve is still sitting there in the Clwyd Bar, holding court with a small group of friends and supporters. The security guards have long since patrolled the camp with their guard dogs and now are waiting patiently for Steve to go. Once he makes a move the others will too, they say.

An hour later in another part of the camp Joe O'Boye wakes his long suffering manager Reg Warland and tells him how sorry he is for giving him such a hard time. He has the perfect solution. He'll go out first thing in the morning and go for a run to make up. Reg is unimpressed by the thought of this act of penitence. 'Leave me out,' he says. The next morning he is woken from his sleep a second time by the sound of a person crashing about the chalet. It's Joe. He's in from running on the beach, and looks shattered. He says he only ran 300 yards and then had to walk back because he was so knackered.

Fresh-faced John Parrott has already started his final against Ray Reardon when Steve Davis plonks himself down in the cafeteria. He's already had one ice cream but accepts another from a friend who stops to chat with him. The night before he's agreed to do an interview on condition that no serious questions are asked as he's not a serious person. Now in the bright hard light of the Pontins cafeteria he's changed his mind. He says that everything's been written about him but the size of his willie and we're not finding out about that. Certainly it's a subject beyond the scope of the normal investigative reporter.

The conversation is punctuated by incessantly clicking cameras and requests for autographs. One girl appears in dungarees whose straps proclaim her love for Elton John and Terry Griffiths, and Steve Davis tells her she's got some throat coming up to him with those badges. He lets her have her picture taken with him nevertheless, examines her camera to see how it goes. 'That's a term they use for girls isn't it?' he grins. 'Do they go or not.'

He seems to like talking to all the people who approach him. 'I could just as easily stay in the Grand Hotel,' he shrugs. 'For all the bother, there's lots of people here from my amateur days. It's different for someone like Ray Reardon, say. He's been out of the amateur game for fifteen years. But Pontins holds lots of memories for me. I was in John Parrott's position four years ago. I think it was in the semis that I beat Ray Reardon.'

John Parrott hasn't reached that eminence yet. As yet he's still just neck and neck with Ray Reardon, who is ferociously hanging on to even terms in the match, despite the handicap he's conceding. Russell Jarmac, a Romford regular with a sweet expression that looks constantly on the verge of dissolving into neurosis, emerges from the match with a look of transportation on his face. 'I want to go up to Ray Reardon and tell him what a great player he is,' he says solemnly. He shakes his head in wonder. 'I forgot how *good* he is, what he's *done* out on that table.'

'Well a great player doesn't lose it,' says Steve with understandable acerbity, for in the eyes of the public might he not himself be said to have lost it? A ten-one defeat to Tony Knowles and the Hurricane the new World Champion? 'He's fought to get it back and you've got to give him credit for that,' he says, as though someone in the company were denying Reardon's feat.

He and the Welshman are actually very alike, both sharing an intense pride of performance. In Reardon's case the dislike of playing badly in public has driven him on to his extraordinary recovery of skills that most people thought were gone for ever. In Steve Davis's case, pride provides the motivation lacking now that more normal

172

considerations such as fame and fortune have been satisfied — he has been acclaimed as the greatest snooker player in the world and could retire tomorrow if he wanted to. 'But there's no way you want to play badly when there's people watching,' he says.

In the Pontins cafeteria *everybody* is watching him but he manages to share a pot of tea with his friends with commendable normality. Rob and Alexis are like male and female versions of one prototype, plump round-faced people whose eyes are permanently crinkled up with good humour. Rob works in the markets while Alexis is a fashion consultant with her own garment business specialising in pure silk. She says she dresses people like King Khaled's daughter and Princess Michael of Kent. Steve says he's met Princess Michael and she's a good sort. She's a goer, he bets.

Rob produces a new cue for him to have a look at. He's been given it by some bloke who's trying to flog a whole lot of them and wants him to show it to a few people. Rob runs his hand, chunky with rings, along the smooth surface of the piece of wood. He says his game has gone since he had his own cue stolen. It's just never been the same. Not that it was that great anyway. Steve Davis looks at him sharply and says you've just got to work harder if you lose your cue. He tries the cue out along the tea cups. Yes, he says it's very nice. Ebony and ash, very nice. 'I'd have it, but I've got no reason. You get like that,' he says. 'You think, I'll have that . . . ' His voice trails away in the vocal equivalent of a shrug.

Rob says there's a club near where they live called the Green Baize and they've got stickers saying 'Snooker players do it on the Green Baize.' Steve Davis is aghast at such sacrilege. 'If you're a snooker player don't even say it,' he says. Like almost all the top players he is very concerned that the right image of snooker should be projected to the public. He thinks the dress is very important, for instance. It keeps the game a gentleman's game. Nobody's going to start kneeing somebody else in the groin if they've got a dress suit on.

Second cups of tea have been poured out now and the two men are busy recalling memorable shots. Alexis asks Steve how he remembers individual shots like that but he says he usually only does if they were part of a pattern. Take the Benson and Hedges final against Terry Griffiths, he offers. He was six-three ahead there and then Terry's fought back to six-five and he's gone, he says. Steve Davis admits he'd gone. He gets this one red right up the bottom cushion. He hadn't potted a ball for two frames, but he gets that one and it wins it for him.

Rob says you can lose a game on just one ball too and he says yes. In this against Ray Reardon it was the brown. If he'd have got that he'd have fancied himself.

Alexis says it doesn't matter, this. It doesn't matter at all. Steve Davis looks at her in mild exasperation and says he wanted to win the double. He wanted to win the Professional *and* the Open. Alexis says there's always next year, but that doesn't console him. He says he might not be here next year. You never know what will be on. Mind you, he concedes, for all that it can be a pain, you do get a good laugh here. Rob looks solemn. 'This is your roots Steve,' he says. 'This is your roots.'

★   ★   ★

In the big ballroom Reg Warland is wistfully watching nice John Parrott against Ray Reardon. He says he's worn out. Joe is wild, he says. He can't understand it, as he comes from a very loving family, really stable. It's not as if it's a broken home or anything like that. John Parrott is moving round the table like Just William, all healthy and fresh but with his shirt hanging out the back. Reg looks mournful and says he's got a great image. He'd love to manage him. That's the image you need. He sighs wearily and says he just can't understand why Joe's so wild. He should be mature by now. He's twenty-two after all. You should be mature by twenty-two, shouldn't you?

On the table John Parrott is refusing to be intimidated by the occasion or the sharklike smile of his opponent. With the crowd solidly behind him he closes out the last three frames to win seven-four. John Virgo's wife Avril looks approving. Her hair is drawn into a severely sophisticated chignon, her features into her characteristically acid smile. One of her companions says that John Parrott is a good looking boy. She says yes and he's got his three piece suit, all the business. 'He's good potential professional material,' she says judiciously. She and her companions all agree that it's good for the game when somebody like that comes through.

The Mayor and Mayoress of Prestatyn present the prizes though they can't give anything to the Hurricane because he's not there. Then they draw the raffle tickets — Ray Reardon has suggested that all the pros donate a cue in aid of the Falklands benevolent fund — and the entertainments manager congratulates the campers on their good

174

behaviour throughout the week. There's an end of term gaiety in the air.

People are still chattering as John Virgo begins his famous impressions, kicking off with a sarcastic apology for the absence of the Hurricane who has hardly been seen in the camp all week anyway. 'Unfortunately,' says John, 'his arm was aching from signing so many autographs.' A constant ripple of chat accompanies his act in spite of the efforts of Avril who keeps shouting in a stentorian voice at the audience to shut up. She is wearing a chic black silky jacket and fine gold chains and looks the image of restrained femininity, but she is uninhibitedly vocal in her attempts at crowd control.

Unconcerned, John pads his way through his routine, even telling the joke about Ray Reardon and the beauty competition where the contestants offer ever greater inducements to be judged the winner. Where John says he stopped at number forty-eight, Ray is supposed to have stopped at number two because a kiss and a cuddle is the best offer he's had in ten years. Terry Griffiths says Ray Reardon doesn't usually stay for this joke but he's sitting there as usual, smiling his shark's smile throughout. John's Terry Griffiths impression follows that one but he declines to do Cliff Thorburn as well as otherwise the bars would be closed. 'We're often asked if we're still playing snooker when it goes out on television,' he says. 'Well *we're* not but Cliff and Terry might be.'

He ends with his Alex Higgins impression, complete with new piece of business where the Hurricane appropriates the nearest plantpot for his own personal purposes.

The next morning the cleaning ladies are throwing piles of laundry on to the balconies as they prepare the chalets for next week's guests. People are queuing for their last cups of tea and Cornish pasties in the cafeteria. And the lady taxi driver, on the way back to the station says she's furious. The Hurricane did want to go all the way back home to Manchester by cab after all but she had her day off and those rats in the office didn't ring her.

Terry Griffiths

It's Better Than Working

It's a hot sticky day outside the Holiday Inn in Slough, but inside the temperature has been held to an artificially cool level. This hotel is just one more in the anonymous series of top hotels that snooker players' economic status induces them to live in. To compensate for its lack of character it has a swimming pool, its own hairdressing salon, and king size beds and colour television in the rooms, but living here, even for a few days, must be the institutional equivalent of having a holiday in Harlow New Town.

Terry Griffiths stumbles down to the reception area after eleven this morning. Usually he's up by eight but he didn't even get on the table till eleven o'clock last night and he was signing autographs after that till half past one in the morning. 'The queue never seems to end then,' he shrugs. 'They say, "Will you sign it for Louisa or someone?" and you think, Jesus Christ, why can't you just ask me for my name? I thought next one I'll say, Do you mind if I just sign my name else I'll never get through the crowd. Then I thought, No, I mustn't say that. It's wrong. They're talking about their kids. It's their children. If you tell them you don't want to sign that, it's an insult. So I just kept signing and all of a sudden you go through it. A chap comes along and says you played well and you start chatting then. I enjoy that side of it. It's still half past one and I'm absolutely shattered. I'm worn out. And it was so hot there. But now I've started to enjoy it. The end of the queue comes and you think, Oh there's no more. With these people *they're* queuing up till half past one. Christ, they don't want to have to queue there till that time. They've been sitting there all night. We're all going through the same type of things and if you see that it helps you a lot.'

His patience in signing autographs stems from one night just before he defended his World title when he was grumbling at being tracked down by a group of fans after taking elaborate precautions to avoid them. There was an old woman in a pinny standing watching — he says he can see her face now — and she asked him, wasn't he proud that the children were asking for his autograph. It was the darkest period of the Welshman's life and he says he almost wept when she said it. 'I went inside and if someone had put me in a room on my own I'd have cried my eyes out. These are the things that are important in life, the little things that you're told at certain times that hit you hard for one reason or another. All these things have got to be meant to happen. Why were those kids there? Why did that woman say that one thing? Why did I listen to that one thing when I knew that all the way along?' Ever since that night Terry Griffiths has been proud that people ask him for his autograph.

He is one of the most philosophically-minded players in snooker, a man constantly seeking to find a balance in life, involved in an endless search for the Celtic equivalent of Yin and Yang. It's early June and the end of one of the longest hardest seasons he's had, and it's time for him to look back and evaluate his year, analyse it. The year he tracked down Steve Davis.

He's still on the road of course. The bookings will tail off a bit over the summer and in August he'll go on holiday to Florida with Dennis Taylor and Doug Mountjoy and all their families, but there are still days ahead when he'll be away from home. He's just been at home for almost a week after spending the week before with Annette and the kids at Pontins, and he knows Annette took it a bit rough when he had to leave yesterday teatime. She didn't want him to go away. 'Though it's only for three days it's hurt her now,' he says. 'She can't accept now that I'm going away. In the season you accept it more because it's happening all the time. She was all right when I phoned her after I'd gone, but before I went I could see it. She was just moping about the place.

"Are you all right?"

"Aye, aye."

'But I knew what it was. The thing is I didn't want to go away yesterday either. I'd enjoyed my time at home and at camp. But really we've managed very well over the years, considering the way we both are. We've held our marriage together, which is an achievement in itself in this kind of life. Our marriage has got stronger and stronger, maybe partly because I'm away sometimes, if you look at it truthfully. If I was home all the time perhaps it wouldn't be so strong, I don't know. But it is because we miss each other all the time when I'm away.

Then when you get home it's nice. But snooker is a great strain on married life. You've got to accept it. If you want the life you've got to accept all those bloody hard things.' The thought occurs that if Annette Griffiths knew how constantly she is in her husband's thoughts she might find his absences easier to bear.

Terry Griffiths himself has a fatalistic attitude to things. He believes that he is meant to play snooker. He believes that often one particular player is fated to win or lose, though his instincts have been proved wrong before on that count. 'I never wanted to be a professional snooker player,' he says. 'I never had ambitions. The only thing I thought about when I was young was, what am I going to be like when I'm twenty-five? What am I going to look like? Am I going to be married? Will I have children? I never wanted to be this or be that. But for some reason I went into snooker.

'Why you choose it I don't know. That's fated to happen. It must be. Everybody could be successful at something. They've got talent at something. The lucky people are the ones that choose it right. I don't know what it is but there's got to be something else that makes it all happen. It helps you a lot if you believe that because winning and losing in snooker are part of the life. If you win the other guy loses. You've got to be part of one or the other all the time, because you're not going to lose all the time and you're not going to win all the time.'

It is interesting to hear a sportsman ascribe success and failure to destiny — most competitive people believe that they alone have total control and many are even affronted at the idea that their opponent could have a say too. That is why some of the best are unwilling to recognise that when they fail it is not necessarily because of their bad play — their opponent may simply have played better. Jimmy Connors was once observed jeering at Bjorn Borg's play and asking his friends, did that look like the greatest player in the world? He couldn't accept that when he lost it was because there was a greater player, and there are many sportsmen like him, looking back and seeing where they went wrong and from there making the illogical leap — if I'd done that right I'd have won. It would have been a different match but the result would not necessarily have been any different.

Terry Griffiths' belief in destiny, though, has had the effect of making him try all the harder. While most of the other players on the circuit have been demoralised by Steve Davis, Terry has seen it almost as a divine mission to try and undermine the Davis dominance of the game. In the 1981 World Championship he had recovered his form after the nightmare of his championship year, and felt an inner certainty that he would beat Steve Davis in the championship. 'I didn't think I was going to win the championship,' he says, 'but I *was* going to beat Steve. All the signs were there for me to win. Steve was the favourite and he'd knocked *me* out the previous year when I was favourite. He was starting to dominate the game and I knew it would come right that I'd stop him dominating — that things would make me stop him, not just me. I knew I was going to have all the luck because it wasn't right that one player should dominate. That was what I felt. I believe in those things. I felt the time was right. I'm perfectly right mentally, I've practised, I'm playing very well. Everything's set up for me to beat the fellow.

'I didn't think I was too good or anything like that. What I thought was we were fated to meet and all the circumstances of that match were in my favour. I thought, no matter what happens, if I have one or two bad games or all close games, all the luck will go my way and I'll win. Because it was wrong for him to win. He was starting to dominate the game and I knew it would be no good for the sport. I thought, I'm put there now to stop him.

'And I lost. I knew when he beat me that day he was going to win the championships. There was no way the boy's going to lose when I lost. Everything that should have gone against him didn't. I knew he was fated to win the championship that year.'

If destiny had let Terry Griffiths down he felt his game hadn't. He felt that he was playing well again and that he had the composure, the right mental attitude to win should fate allow him the opportunity. His awareness that it was not just he who would dictate what happened sustained him in what appeared to be one of his worst ever defeats, his three-sixteen loss to Steve in the 1982 Coral UK. 'He demoralised me,' admits Terry. 'He just played too good. He did not give me the chances. That was Steve's peak there. That was his best. But while it was a bad defeat for me he just did not give me enough chances to win, so it wasn't such a disappointment. The time I lost nine-nil to him, in the 1980 Coral UK, there was no way I could have won. I could have won three or four frames maybe but there was no way I could have won the match. Then it's hard to accept because you know you can't perform as you should. It hurts a bit then. This time I knew that if I'd had the chances I could have won. I had the game and the mental attitude.'

It may seem that in saying such a thing Terry Griffiths is just the same as all the rest, not admitting how good his opponent is. That is not the case, merely that while recognising Steve Davis's excellence he does not forget his own. He is one of the few players on the circuit to see that Steve's outstanding talents do not take anything away from his, that he is as good as ever he was.

In fact, recognising how good Steve Davis is has actually helped Terry Griffiths improve his own game, has indeed been a crucial part of that process. After the Coral UK this season, in spite of the crushing nature of the defeat he had just suffered, he went on TV to be interviewed by David Vine. 'How good is this Steve Davis?' asked David. The moment has stayed with Terry Griffiths. 'At the time he'd gone so far ahead of everybody else, he'd won everything. He didn't just win everything. He was demolishing everybody as well. When David asked me the question I'd decided what I was going to say. It was the first time I'd said this in public and none of the professionals had ever said it, especially the top ones — I'm talking about the three or four that could possibly beat him. I said, "He's just too good for us. We've all got to improve our game." I knew that anyway but now I was saying it in public, on the television. I said, "I've just got to improve. I'm not good enough now to beat him. And when David Vine said, "How good do you think he is?" I said, "I think he's the best that's ever played the game."

'After saying that, opening myself up on the television, I let something go inside. It's hard to explain really. You'd sort of admitted something to the world. It all went away from me then. The next time I played him I beat him.

'The trouble is you're among the other players all the time and they say things like, Well he's not going to keep on playing like that, or, The luck the guy has is unbelievable. He has all the flukes, all the kisses. And I'm thinking, Well he does have the run of the balls but he's knocking all the pots in. They'd never turn round and say, He's just too good. But that is the truth — he was just too good for everybody else. He raised the standard of the game up. Instead of admitting that you tend to say other things. When he came along first of all and he beat me nine-nil in the UK, he was playing superb then. He played brilliant. I thought to myself, All right I can do all that. He's not doing anything special.

'But he *was* dong something special, and you've got to recognise it. Until you recognise it you haven't got a bloody hope.'

He has orange juice and cereal then tea and toast for his belated breakfast as he ponders the world of modern snooker. He won't eat again till much later in the day as he has to drive down to Kent this afternoon. Snooker, he says, is like a jungle. People are jealous of the ones who have success because everybody's after the same things. He gets jealous too, but just slightly, not a lot, not like the others. It hurts them bad. It affects their game. He much prefers the amateur game. The people are much nicer. In the professional game they all hate Steve because he's been beating them so much. If it were the amateur game they'd just say, Oh he's a good player, isn't he?

He shrugs. It's better than working anyway. Snooker's not a hard life. He says he was chatting about that to John Virgo at Pontins. He's a born loser, John is. Lots of natural talent but the world's always against him. He says he likes John a lot. He's one of the few players you can have a good talk with.

Well, John said that the people don't realise what it's really like, the pressure. They all think it's bloody easy. They don't realise what the players have got to go through. Now Terry has thought a lot about this. Everybody does. He tells John that's the biggest load of rubbish he's heard in his life.

John's worked a bit, not much, but Terry's been all sorts of things — a bus conductor, a postman, a taxi driver. He was with Pearl Assurance for seven years. He remembers vividly one time he'd to go to Derby and didn't want to go. He comes out of the house and it's pissing down with rain. It's Friday morning which was his collection day with the Pearl. Hard going, getting money out of people. He'd be rushing around all day till eight o'clock at night, pick the kids up, rush back out and collect, miss ten people, go back round to them all, oh Christ. And here he is driving through the bit where he used to collect and he's warm and dry in his car while it's teeming down outside. If he had been collecting he'd have his mac on, his bag would be soaking wet, his biro'd be running everywhere. And here he is now getting X number of pounds just for driving up to Derby, playing snooker and going back home. 'All right then John,' he says to John Virgo. 'Go back to work then. You're getting paid for the pressure,' he says. 'That's why you get so much money. That's why you don't have to get up at six o'clock and work through till ten at night, and work overtime, and be looking for money all the time to pay your bills. You don't have to do that now because you're a professional snooker player.'

This pressure that they're paid so highly for, it's the easy explanation for almost every success and failure in modern sport, though it's far from the whole story. A cerebral player like Steve Davis, who uses his brain to control the pattern of the game, would hardly care to think that it was. It can't be denied though that his own formidable coolness and intelligence have created added pressure on other players in the past. Terry Griffiths has been the first one to exert consistent pressure on Steve Davis in his turn. It's hard to think of Steve Davis as anyone's prey but Terry Griffiths has tracked him down with the hard cold courage of the big game hunter. 'It had got to the stage where he believed he could do anything,' recalls Terry. 'He *was* more or less doing anything. Good players were saying, We can't beat this one because he's just way out there. It had just gone out of proportion, and he knew that nobody could beat him. He knew it you see. His confidence was so high. He'd had so much bloody success — and all of a sudden somebody was nipping away at him. And it was hard for him to accept.

'In sport nobody likes a tryer. If they know somebody's a hard hard tryer and doesn't give up people don't like that. It's like somebody grabbing you by the throat and you know they're not going to let you go. You know they're not going to go away. That's what I've done to Steve. He kept beating me and beating me, beating me heavy as well, but I kept coming back at him and back at him and back at him. And he knew it. He knew I was going to be there the next day and the next. He knew I was going to keep coming at him all the time.

'I really knocked him out of the World Championships. Because I'd knocked his confidence back. When he came into the championship I'd dented him. It has definitely stopped him from dominating the game. I don't think he will dominate now. He'll still be very successful, still win events, probably more than anyone else. But he will not dominate as he has done. It was all right for eighteen months but if it had gone on like that it would have killed the game. Bound to have harmed the game. People won't come and pay to watch one winner. In anything.

'What I've really done with Steve, I've brought his game down a bit. His confidence is down and that brings his game down a bit. Now he's nearer to the rest.'

The long war of attrition that Terry Griffiths has waged against Steve Davis all season has not prevented him joining the enemy camp. Terry, the man who up till now has arranged all his own bookings, answered all his own letters, even booked into hotels himself, has joined snooker's money man, Barry Hearn. Terry's not a money man.

182

He's got his nice house and his Mercedes and the Jag, and the Fiat Annette drives around at home. He can splash out on his kids too, buy them the things he never had as a child. He's got used to having money. But he could live on the dole if he had to. He says that when he and Annette spent a few days in London they booked a theatre taxi to take them to *The Sound of Music*. It was only a short hop down the road but the driver charged them £11.50 and they thought it was a real rip-off. Terry says he paid up but he never admitted to Annette that he'd given the driver a tip as well. When they took the kids to the Marble Arch Holiday Inn for a few days she wouldn't even let them have breakfast there because it would have cost £4 each. It was wasted on the kids anyway. All they wanted to do was swim in the hotel pool. They have to remind themselves sometimes that they've got money.

No he's not a money man, Terry. But Barry is. Even though he's a wealthy man he still has this drive to make money. Barry thinks he's a genius at it. He'll tell you that. He started off from nothing and now he's a very rich man. He and Terry are just complete opposites. 'All the snooker people told me it was a mistake,' says Terry. 'All of them. There wasn't one of them who turned round and said, I think it'll be good for you. I listened to all of them. I respect everybody's advice, but at the end of the day it's my decision.'

Now he's looking forward to working less and making more money. Barry's not generally noted for helping people work less — he has this compulsion to fill up their days with money-making activities. But Terry Griffiths is very much his own man and he and Barry have come to a compromise. It was a hard decision for someone as independent as Terry, but he's happy now he's done it. 'Really Barry has taken part of my mind. That's what he's done. He's taken part of my mind away, Barry has, and now he's going to work that side of my mind.'

It is not the side of his mind that plays snooker. He heads out towards the big gold Mercedes that is his home from home. Its tinted windows open at the touch of a button, the doors lock automatically, the sun roof rolls smoothly open — except that it's been raining in the night, sending water cascading over the plush sheepskin seats and he has to close it hurriedly. Money isn't everything. 'I've told Barry that it won't change anything,' says Terry. 'I'll still be after Steve next season.'

The Party to End Them All

They're famed for their parties in Romford, have had a great big victory bash after every one of Steve Davis's major championship wins. They know how to do the business there. 'Doing the business' is a Londoners' expression referring to excellence in any field of activity — Steve Davis does the business on the snooker table, Barry Hearn does the business in money-making. It's also a synonym for one particularly excellent form of activity — love-making. Snooker, sex and money. What more could you ask of life, or Romford?

It's a hot, sticky June night as Romford throws its first losing party. Barry Hearn is thirty-four today and that seems as good a day as any to bring an era to an end. The match room, which has seen so many titanic challenge matches between the top players, is going to become the Match Room Club. Barry Hearn says it will be a singularly . . . average sort of club, which only means it'll get a new coat of paint, someone suggests. Mizzle is mournful that there isn't going to be any snooker up here and says it's only going to be a casino. There'll be card games and lots of gambling. Lots of money up here, he says miserably.

The match room is cool after the crush downstairs where the snooker has been preceded by polite chit-chat over drinks and little canapes of smoked salmon and liver pate with olives. There will be a disc jockey along later from one of the smart clubs up town — the Valbonne. Barry has told the guy that there will be a big mix of people here, so although he can bring some of his freaky black music, he's to bring some white man's music as well. He also tells him it'll probably go on till six o'clock in the morning. The DJ rolls his eyes. 'It's going to be one of those nights,' he says.

The guests settle themselves down on the match room red leather banquettes. There are lots of young women in mother-of-the-bride type dresses, men with smart suits and pinky rings. Terry Griffiths is here with Annette, and there's Willie Thorne, Tony Meo, Ray

Edmonds as well as Romford's Stevie and his mum and dad. A couple of the London snooker writers have come and lots of snooker's business people — some of the Corals staff and little old Joe Coral himself, sitting under the big red banner saying 'Better Bet Corals'.

Barry Hearn introduces the people who have made the short seven-and-a-half year history of the match room so memorable — Geoff Foulds, the first Lucania champion in 1975; Terry Griffiths, who did extremely well at Romford and followed it up by doing all right in a few other tournaments, like the World Championships; Vic Harris, the All England Amateur Champion, probably more responsible than anyone else for bringing top class snooker here; Tony Meo, the Italian Stallion, who brings a touch of flash to the proceedings in his navy blazer and white trousers. He starts his exhibition frame against the Essex senior champion, Tony Puttnam, by breaking open the pack of reds. 'This game's getting too serious,' he says. 'Hurricane Meo,' murmurs one of the journalists. Hurricane Meo wins on the last black.

In the interval Charlie Smithers of the Water Rats tells a series of terrible Irish, Mafia and Jewish jokes. Some of the people have trooped downstairs for air but Steve Davis sits to one side, lounging on one of the banquettes. 'Don't sit there on your own Stevie,' says the comedian. 'Don't worry. You lost it but you'll get it back. You can always sell the car that you won for the 147.'

Downstairs the people are wall to wall in Barry Hearn's huge offices. Prawns on crushed ice are being served in plastic cups and there's a huge bowl of a suspiciously slimy mess that looks like sheeps' eyes but turns out to be that delightful London delicacy, jellied eels.

When the snooker starts up again Barry Hearn tells everybody not to hold back on the verbals because they'll regret it for the next twenty-five years. His wife Susan smiles briefly and puts on a pair of prim tortoiseshell glasses that are curiously at odds with the rest of her appearance. She is dark and sinuous, an almost beautiful woman with wide-set eyes and Cleopatra-cut hair and a heart-shaped face with a kittenishly pointed little chin. Her dress is sensational, a clinging black one-shouldered sheath slashed down the side with red sequins and with a jaunty black spangled bow on the shoulder. She didn't get it in Romford High Street.

Finally her husband introduces Steve Davis, the man who's changed the face of world snooker — and Romford and Plumstead. 'He had a bad result at the World Championships this year. You may have heard.' Steve is going to play the last game in the match room against a player he introduces as the only classy player he knows who's no good. This player, he says, is a fifty break man, though the audience crack up at the hilarious idea of Barry Hearn ever making a fifty break. The referee for this momentous match could be none other than Mizzle, the man whose name is defined in the dictionary as meaning 'to confuse'. He raises his hand portentously for silence. 'A bit of decorum please,' he orders. 'There's one great player here.'

Neither of the players has chalk but Barry seems to think it doesn't matter. He and Steve are dressed alike in grey baggy suits of the style that Graham Miles has so ably pioneered — the gardening suit. Just before they start Robbo brings Barry a drink on a silver tray. Barry says, well Steve gets away with it every day. 'Not on a silver tray,' is the retort. 'But you're not Barry Hearn,' says Barry Hearn. 'You're only Steve Davis.'

Only Steve Davis gets down to play his first shot. Barry contemplates the table. 'Now how would Tony Knowles play this?' Barry plays snooker as he does everything else, with an exuberant doggish enthusiasm that contains more effort than elegance and contrasts with Steve's catlike self-containment. Barry says if he tries any harder he's going to have a nosebleed, and is jubilant as he pots his first ball. 'For years I've watched rubbish play on this table,' he says. As he lines up his next shot, blue into the side pocket, someone in the audience heckles him. 'You're going to miss that.' Barry is indignant. 'Want to put some money on it?' he asks. He gets the shot. Maybe just the mention of money is enough to concentrate his mind.

Barry's enthusiasm for the role of snooker player extends to lengthy consideration of the position of the balls on the table, which arouses Steve Davis's acerbity. 'How much posing are we going to do here?' he chivvies his manager but Barry's determined to make the most of it. He says this is the longest time he's ever spent on the table. Unfortunately he misses his shot but he's in good company as Steve misses his too. 'Hands up all those who remember when he used to get those?' says Barry, but Steve just grins and says the last time he used those tactics was against Mizzle. 'You lost,' snaps Mizzle immediately.

Barry is receiving a seventy start and has now reached the spectacular total of seventy-six. 'Count the reds,' says Steve. 'Oh,' says Barry. 'He's getting ratty. I know I'm a mug. What's his excuse?' It's definitely a match that's more comic than classy, though Mizzle injects a touch of the big time into it by flinging his arms wide and saying in his firmest referee's voice, 'No camera shots please. With the greatest of respect.

186

Steve Davis and his girlfriend . . .

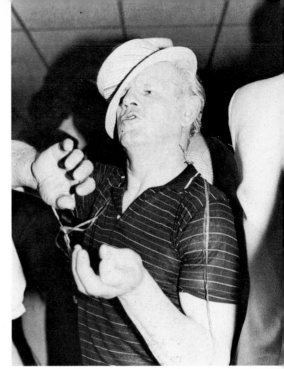

Mizzle . . .

Barry Hearn . . .

and Tony Meo at the Loser's Party

End of conversation.' Which last just about finishes the audience.

He and Robbo are in their smartest gear, Mizzle in his evening suit and Robbo, steelwool hair flattened into a mat on top of his head, in cream trousers and a maroon blazer. He's the current wellie champion of Romford, having spent this afternoon vanquishing the might of even Barry Hearn — fifty quid he took off him, and took money off all the others — at wellie throwing, where you throw old wellies at rubber tyres in a muddy field. Robbo doesn't explain why.

The match has now reached the exciting stage of eighty-nine to Barry Hearn and eighty-four to Steve Davis, with one black to go. Steve resists the temptation to pot it and is promptly told, 'It was nearer before you hit it, ginger,' by Barry. But just as Barry is about to take a shot at it, three men in bowler hats and aprons, flourishing Groucho Marx moustaches and gleaming tools, come in and start dismantling the table. It's a moment of pure Romford razzamatazz, with Barry the showman reading out the roll call of honour to the clinks and thuds of the table being taken apart. 'I've gone. Pass the Kleenex,' he says as he re-introduces Vic Harris, the greatest amateur ever, and if you hadn't known before that Vic Harris is one of the most loved people in Romford you'd know now by the warmth of the applause that greets him. 'Romford's Greatest Supporter,' calls out Barry and Mizzle comes out and bows. There are cries of 'speech' from those desirous of a rambling Romford discourse, but Barry says that would take two days. NO.

Then they all sing 'Auld Lang Syne', and Barry says the club's going to be open in three months and they've all to come down and see it. It's going to be very special. The table is still in bits on the floor as the people move gradually out of the match room for the last time.

Downstairs the hot June night hits you as soon as you move out of the cold stone walls of the staircase. There is a stampede for the food, chicken portions, crispy salads, little rolls and sandwiches, grapes, pate, melon, wedges of Stilton and Cheddar, huge bowls full of strawberries and cream. If strawberries are not in season they'll fly them in from California, says Robbo. A big cake shaped like a snooker table has pride of place. There are icing sugar cues and snooker balls round the edge and 'Best wishes Barry', scrawled across its virulent green top.

Some of the people start to drift home around midnight. Terry Griffiths almost forgets to take his cue with him when he goes. But the real Romford people stay on and on, dancing through the night. 'Let's have a party,' shouts Mizzle, but somebody else must have made the suggestion before him because people are dancing and singing and Barry Hearn is wandering round in his stocking feet with a bottle of champagne in his hand. Stevie's in his jeans now, coaxing girlfriend Helen Grogan out of a sulk, and Mizzle and Robbo have changed into short-sleeved shirts because it's up to them to keep the pace of the dancing going this hot sticky night.

Somewhere in the early hours of the morning party hats are given out, not just ordinary party hats but gorgeous extravagant gay creations, straw boaters with great big raffia flowers, green and white striped toppers, black matador hats with red cockades on the side and bowlers, bedecked with flowers and ribbons. There's a net on the ceiling holding dozens of coloured balloons. Barry cuts it at the corners and the balloons just keep falling and falling and people are blowing whistles with silver streamers on the end and they're all glittery in the pink and green disco lights, and it's hard to think of this as a losers' party as the dancers form a moving laughing chain around the room. There's a feeling here of gaiety, new beginnings. Wherever the Hurricane is tonight, or the senior Welshman, or even young Jimmy White, it's hard to imagine the World title next year straying far from Romford and this room, fizzing with energy and exuberance like the champagne Barry Hearn is spraying over the dancers.

Later, in a quiet moment, Mizzle says Barry was the one who put Romford on the map but there won't be snooker up there any more. He's very sad. The big stars won't come to Romford now. There won't be any reason. He says he was stood next to Eddie Charlton out in that very doorway when he first came here and he turned to Eddie and said, 'Eddie, welcome to Romford.' Mizzle flings sticky arms out in the gesture he must have used that day and says he felt overwhelmed that Eddie had come all the way from Australia and here he was in Romford. Ray Reardon and Alex Higgins have both played in the match room too. Mizzle says solemnly he was proud to meet such great stars and wipes a bead of perspiration from his face.

In the inner office where the dancing's going on, suddenly everybody's singing along with the record. It's Chas and Dave, the cockney singing stars,

Now everything I ever done was only done for you
But now you
Can go and do
Just what you wanna do.

I'm telling you.
Cos I ain't going to be made to look a fool no more.
You done it once too often,
What do you take me for?
Oh darlin', there ain't no pleasin' you

and the East End voices are punching the words out with the gusto of a football crowd. And maybe it's because they're Londoners or maybe they've *all* suffered at the hands of hard-hearted women, but something in the song's independence and male swagger appeals to the people here. Barry Hearn is bawling the words out, still clutching his champagne and thrusting the bottle periodically in the air at the bits that appeal to him.

And somewhere around four o'clock in the morning a young boy comes in and triumphantly tells his girlfriend he's 'got the business', as he proceeds to share the last tub of jellied eels with her.

There are pale pink streaks in the sky but not the twitter of a bird as dawn comes to Romford High Street. Two policemen look up from their inspection of the empty street and locked shops as the partygoers straggle down the High Street. They laugh at the crazy hats and general air of gaiety and want to know where everybody's been. Barry Hearn's party, says a girl in a pink ra-ra skirt and gold boots, her striped boater clinging at a perilously rakish angle to her head. One of the policemen shrugs. 'Never heard of him,' he says. The other looks appalled. 'You can tell how long *he's* been in Romford,' he says.

Index

191